"David, I don't want this."

"Don't you?"

She turned away from him. "If you persist, I'll have to return to New York and send someone else to complete your tour."

He was a man who gambled, not with money, but with something more valuable—his feelings. Sometimes he lost. Most often, he won. And sometimes there were delays along the way.

He wanted Augusta Lyon. Pursuing her wasn't the smartest thing he could do right now. Yet he could still feel the way her soft body had felt against his chest, could almost taste the lips that had trembled as he'd let his eyes linger on them.

Hands on her shoulders, he turned her around, then cupped her chin so she was forced to look up at him. He gave her a slow smile. "Denial is the first stage, Gussie."

He let go and walked to the door, closing it behind him.

Gussie clasped her hands tightly together to stop the trembling. She wished she didn't believe he was right.

Dear Reader,

Welcome to the Silhouette **Special Edition** experience! With your search for consistently satisfying reading in mind, every month the authors and editors of Silhouette **Special Edition** aim to offer you a stimulating blend of deep emotions and high romance.

The name Silhouette **Special Edition** and the distinctive arch on the cover represent a commitment—a commitment to bring you six sensitive, substantial novels each month. In the pages of a Silhouette **Special Edition**, compelling true-to-life characters face riveting emotional issues—and come out winners. Both celebrated authors and newcomers to the series strive for depth and dimension, vividness and warmth, in writing these stories of living and loving in today's world.

The result, we hope, is romance you can believe in. Deeply emotional, richly romantic, infinitely rewarding—that's the Silhouette **Special Edition** experience. Come share it with us—six times a month!

From all the authors and editors of Silhouette **Special Edition**,

Best wishes,

Leslie Kazanjian,
Senior Editor

PAT WARREN
The Lyon and the Lamb

𝒮ilhouette 𝒮pecial 𝒞dition

Published by Silhouette Books New York

America's Publisher of Contemporary Romance

To Alta Gregory, a class act,
with love and affection—
and the hope that one day
that gorgeous necklace from China
will be mine

SILHOUETTE BOOKS
300 East 42nd St., New York, N.Y. 10017

ISBN: 0-373-09582-1

First Silhouette Books printing February 1990

All the characters in this book are fictitious. Any
resemblance to actual persons, living or dead, is
purely coincidental.

®: Trademark used under license and
registered in the United States Patent and
Trademark Office and in other countries.

Printed in the U.S.A.

Books by Pat Warren

Silhouette Special Edition

With This Ring #375
Final Verdict #410
Look Homeward, Love #442
Summer Shadows #458
The Evolution of Adam #480
Build Me a Dream #514
The Long Road Home #548
The Lyon and the Lamb #582

Silhouette Romance

Season of the Heart #553

Silhouette Intimate Moments

Perfect Strangers #288

PAT WARREN,

the mother of four, lives in Arizona with her travel-agent husband and a lazy white cat. She's a former newspaper columnist whose lifetime dream has been to be a novelist. A strong romantic streak, a sense of humor and a keen interest in developing relationships led her to try romance novels, with which she feels very much at home.

D·A·V·I·D ◇ L·A·M·B

The San Francisco Caper

A BEAU KENDALL MYSTERY

LYON
BOOKS

"Riveting suspense in this classy mystery set in the City by the Bay. Lamb's Beau Kendall is a hard-boiled detective as well as a man of honor. And this time, folks, he even gets the girl. Another winner in this popular series."
RATING: ★ ★ ★ —*CHICAGO STAR*

Chapter One

Her name was Augusta, and she'd always hated it. Her friends called her Gussie, which was only slightly better, and she'd finally resigned herself to that. Augusta Jane Lyon. It made her sound formidable. Today Gussie wished it were so.

"Why is it that Fridays are always such bears around here?" she wondered aloud as she placed another folder atop an already-precarious stack on the corner of her desk.

Molly Judd caught the pile and straightened the folders before they hit the floor, then seated herself across from Gussie. "Probably because most of us live outside Manhattan. We're always anxious to catch an early train and get out of the city for the weekend."

"Mmm, guess you're right." Gussie frowned as she glanced at her watch. Only three o'clock. "I don't think this day's ever going to end." They'd had the usual editorial meeting that morning, which had seemed to last forever, leaving her barely enough time to make her luncheon appointment with a California literary agent who was in town for only the day. After that, she'd met with one of the illustrators who'd designed the book jackets for a new science fiction series, soothed the ruffled feathers of an author who'd been upset with editorial changes in her galleys and worked on some contractual problems on pending acquisitions with Molly. An ordinary day at Lyon Publishing.

Now, as she removed her oversize glasses and rubbed at the beginnings of a headache above her left eye, Gussie looked across at her editorial assistant. "I suppose if I weren't going on this ridiculous trip on Monday, I wouldn't feel as though I have a thousand things to do before I can call it a day."

Molly's blue eyes were sympathetic. "I had a feeling that's what's been bothering you." In her mid-thirties, Molly Judd had spent ten years working at Lyon, holding many positions from gofer to assistant. Divorced some time ago, after years of supporting a husband who'd been content to let her, Molly now had an active social life, the details of which she often confided to her good friend Gussie. Molly was bright, well-read and enormously personable. And she knew when to speak up and when to keep her mouth shut, making her the perfect assistant, which was just one reason Gussie valued their conversations.

Molly crossed her long legs. "There's no way Jared's going to back down on this one, I take it?"

Wearily Gussie shook her head as she dipped her hand into her ever-present bowl of M & M's. She could use a sugar jolt.

"You could rebel, I suppose," Molly suggested without much conviction. "Refuse to go and have him send someone else."

The day that pigs fly, Gussie thought, crunching the candy with satisfaction. "You'd better hope I don't, unless you want to hear the Lyon really roar." Everyone referred to her father behind his back as "the Lyon," a designation she was certain he'd caught wind of and enjoyed. It fit. Over the past thirty years, Jared Lyon had single-handedly built Lyon Publishing into one of the most respected houses in the business. Single-handedly if you didn't count her input over the past six years. Since a mild heart attack two years ago, he'd slowed down a bit, but he was still an imposing figure and very fond of control.

Jared Lyon didn't make requests, he gave out commands. And his latest one was making Gussie crazy.

Molly shook her head. "You know, Gussie, in all my years here, I've never once known an editor to go on a publicity tour with an author. And such an extensive one yet, from one coast to the other and back again!" She narrowed her eyes. "What do you suppose Jared has in mind? We all know he has a motive for everything he does."

Gussie leaned back in her chair, raising her hand to fuss with the pins in her French twist. "I don't know. We have publicity people on staff, including Arnie Walker, who's not my favorite individual, but the man knows his job. Yet I couldn't budge my father."

She could still picture Jared's dark brown eyes, very much like her own, studying her earlier in the week when he'd explained his latest plan and what he wanted her to do.

"As you know, Paul Raymond's retiring the end of the month. Damn fine editor. Been with me twenty years. I want you to take on Paul's best-selling author, David Lamb."

Before she was able to respond, to explain that she already had a heavy workload, Jared had held up his hand.

"Now, Lady Jane, just hear me out."

He had her smiling at that. Jared had never been fond of the "Augusta" her mother had insisted on naming her and often called her "Lady Jane," especially when he wanted to charm her.

"I don't have to tell you," Jared went on, "what a victory it was for us to coax David over last year from Columbia Press. The man came to us with eight books already in print and he's given us three more in just twelve months. He's the hottest thing to come along in mysteries since John D. MacDonald cranked out about a hundred for a career total. And this guy's only in his thirties. I spent some time with him at his home in California recently. Hell of a nice fellow. Men line up to buy his stuff, and women love him. You will, too."

She sat tight-lipped and unconvinced. Jared gave her one of his winning smiles, but she wasn't buying. She could easily see why he got people to bend to his will, especially women. Just a shade under six feet, he had wide shoulders, a flat stomach and a perpetual tan. He always wore white shirts, discreetly monogrammed on each cuff, and was very vain about his hair, claiming at sixty-two that he had yet to find his first white strand. Only his barber knew for sure, Gussie was certain. Few would have dared dispute him.

Jared Lyon was a killer in the boardroom, a fact that many an opponent could verify. There were those who hinted he was a killer in the bedroom, too, a persistent rumor that Gussie had chosen to ignore over the years, as had her mother. His temper was as legendary as his frequent acts of kindness. She would have walked over cut glass for him, yet she wished she understood him.

Sensing victory, her father shifted one of his beloved cigars that his doctor had told him not to smoke to the other corner of his mouth and went on. "David Lamb's a veritable gold mine, a writer whose work just gets better. We owe him the best editor we've got available, and that's you. Be-sides, he's asked for you specifically.''

Jared wasn't generous with his compliments. Unless it suited his purpose. *''Why is it I feel more wary than flat-tered?''* she asked him.

The old fox cleared his throat and laid the big one on her. He'd signed David to a brand-new multibook contract that included a ten-city, cross-country publicity tour to take place over several weeks. And Jared had promised his superstar that his new editor would accompany him every step of the way.

Gussie's mouth dropped open. *''I can't believe what I'm hearing.''*

''Sure you can. You spend too much time behind a desk, Gus. You need to get out in the field, meet some of our people around the countryside. It'll give you a different perspective.''

"He said the tour would give me a different perspec-tive," Gussie repeated to Molly.

"It might at that," Molly answered with a smile that re-vealed a large dimple. "Have you met David Lamb? I wouldn't mind spending a couple of weeks with him, I can tell you." When Gussie shot her a look of disbelief, she laughed. "If I weren't currently involved myself, that is."

"You're always 'currently involved.' And frankly, I wish you *could* take my place."

"When is the man of the hour arriving?"

"Jared phoned him that we were starting out Monday, so I imagine he'll fly from California Sunday sometime. No doubt my father's arranged a suite of rooms for him at some plush hotel. Nothing's too good for Lyon authors."

Molly nodded in agreement. "Have you seen his file? I think you might be surprised. David Lamb is—"

"Is probably thinking we're going to be so impressed with him that we'll fall all over ourselves seeing to his every whim. Champagne, caviar and curtsies." Gussie frowned as she searched through the maze of papers on her desk, looking for the Lamb file. "I hate to disappoint a superstar, but I'm not real good at bowing and scraping. And I *don't* impress easily."

"He doesn't seem like he'd be real full of himself. I mean, his books are very good. His people are down-to-earth and..."

Gussie stopped her search to glance up. "You've read his books?"

Molly nodded enthusiastically. "I was a fan of David Lamb's before he moved over to us. I love mysteries, and Beau Kendall is so likable."

"Who is Beau Kendall?"

"This continuing character David uses. He's a detective, but not your usual sort. No trench coat or cigars and no womanizing. He's sensitive and..."

Gussie held up a hand. "Before you start gushing, why don't you just go find me a copy or two of his books? I'll take them home and read them over the weekend. I knew I should have gotten around to this earlier. Maybe they'll give me some insight into his character."

Molly stood. "I think you're going to be pleasantly surprised." Leaving, she closed the door behind her.

Gussie sighed. She could use a pleasant surprise about now.

Rolling back her desk chair, she stood to remove her pale yellow suit coat, draping it over the chair back. As she walked across the thick gray carpeting to the bank of windows, she massaged her tense shoulder muscles through her silk blouse. Sixteen floors below, the late-afternoon traffic crawled along Fifth Avenue like so many tiny toy cars. If the windows had been open, Gussie was sure she would have heard the impatient honking of the New York cabbies as they maneuvered around buses and delivery vans. A typical May afternoon in the Big Apple.

She swung her gaze to the left toward East Fifty-eighth Street, only four rather short blocks away, and saw the tip of her apartment building stretching toward the clear blue sky. Uncharacteristically, Gussie wished she were there right now, curled up on her ivory sofa, sipping tea and reading one of the manuscripts she carried home nearly every night. It wasn't like her to want to leave her office much before six or seven. In fact, if she gave in, her early departure would undoubtedly shock much of her staff.

And should she leave, before she stepped off the elevator in the lobby, someone would have paused by Jared Lyon's office, reporting on her unexpected behavior. By the time she slipped her key in her apartment door, the phone would be ringing and her father would want to know if she was ill. It wasn't necessarily that he was overly concerned about her health. After all, she was twenty-eight. It was more that Jared Lyon prided himself on knowing everything that went on at Lyon Publishing, from large to very small. He wanted to be in on things. And what Jared wanted, Jared got.

She'd go on this damn tour her father had arranged, Gussie thought, because it was just another part of the job she would then have mastered. Just as she'd mastered a stint in nonfiction, how-to books, anthologies and now popular fiction, so that when the day came that Jared stepped down as head of Lyon Publishing, no one, including the great man himself, could say she didn't know every single facet of the business. She'd cater to her father's new wunderkind, making him look good coast to coast. She'd be editor, publicist and mother confessor if that's what it took to keep David

Lamb happy. She'd do it and do it well. But she didn't have to like it.

Gussie sat back down at her desk, wishing she had thought to ask Molly to bring in some fresh coffee. As her glance drifted over the desktop, she spotted David's file folder. Aligning it in front of her, she opened to find his picture stapled to the left cover.

She noticed the eyes first. Though it was a black-and-white shot, she was certain his eyes were blue. But it was the expression that caught her attention. Self-assured, challenging, intense. She'd worked with enough writers to know that some were glamorous, confident, perfect celebrity material. There were, of course, other authors who looked like your Uncle Henry or the man who pumped gas at the corner service station. She'd hoped for the latter, but gotten the former. In spades.

His hair looked to be blond, and the cut seemed careless, as if he hadn't wanted to sit still long enough for a barber to really style it. So it fell casually, this way and that, curling here and there, looking more rumpled than windblown. His nose had an odd tilt, as if perhaps it had been broken once, or maybe just rearranged a bit. His mouth was full and slightly open, but not quite smiling.

He was staring directly at the camera with a hint of amusement. Gussie was not amused. David Lamb had the look of a man used to having his way, a man difficult to ignore. Women, she felt certain, rarely took him lightly. Small wonder he got along so well with Jared. They'd obviously popped out of the same mold.

There was no question in Gussie's mind. It was going to be a very long tour.

The door opened as she closed the file, and Molly came in carrying steaming mugs of coffee. Two books were tucked under her arm. She set down the cups and held the books out to Gussie. Gussie took a sip from her cup, grateful that her assistant seemed able to read her mind.

"The top one's my favorite, though I like them all."

Gussie took the books, examining the first one as she sipped her coffee. "*The Equinox Assembly.* What's the title mean?"

Molly pulled her chair closer. "It has to do with a mysterious meeting that's supposed to take place during the equinox. A group of wealthy men are to congregate at a certain location and a specific time, each with a need to locate a very valuable missing book. Only they start dying one by one, and it's up to Beau Kendall to find out who's killing them and why, and where they were to assemble, and even exactly when. Because the equinox varies from year to year, it's really clever how Beau figures it all out, especially the when."

"And, of course, he saves the day."

Molly smiled. "Certainly. But he goes through a lot first. It's really a very imaginative mystery."

"Mmm," Gussie murmured noncommittally. She moved the books aside and opened the folder again. "I suppose we should go over this itinerary once more so we can make sure all the arrangements are in order."

"I've got a duplicate copy listing all the hotels where you'll be staying, the luncheons, the interviews and all appointments. Will you be checking in with the office, or do you want me to call you daily?"

Running a finger down the list of cities, Gussie all but moaned aloud at the lengthy tour. "I think it'd be best if I called you sometime during each day. Providing I have the energy to dial."

Molly laughed. "It does sound a little grueling. Has David Lamb ever done one of these publicity tours before?"

"As a matter of fact, he has," came the deep-voiced answer from the direction of the door that had been left ajar.

Molly swung about in her chair as Gussie looked up. Oh, no. She recognized the face she'd been studying just moments ago. If it wasn't her superstar author in the flesh, and two days early. Just what she needed on a busy Friday, she thought as he stepped inside.

"I just finished a late lunch with Jared. He had to rush to another appointment, but he told me to be sure to stop in and say hello." David Lamb kept his expression bland as the blonde rose to welcome him while the woman behind the desk was struggling to hide a frown. "I hope I'm not interrupting anything important."

"Mr. Lamb, it's good to meet you," Molly said, extending her hand. "I'm Molly Judd."

He reached to shake her hand, giving her a warm smile. "Paul Raymond spoke highly of you. I'm glad you'll be assisting on my books."

Molly beamed. "Thank you. It'll be my pleasure."

Watching them, Gussie took the moment to study her new author. He was a visual delight in green slacks, yellow shirt, a plaid jacket and a tie that had definitely seen better days. His clothing choices didn't seem to fit the hard, lean look of him or the rangy, purposeful stride. His hair was as unkempt as his picture had indicated, his eyes a deeper blue than she'd imagined. And they still held that hint of amusement as he turned to her.

She hadn't moved from behind her desk, preferring to have him come to her. David Lamb may have surprised her, but she'd learned long ago from Jared that it was best to quickly establish just who was in charge in business dealings. With the ease of long practice, Gussie hid her feelings, put on a smile and held out her hand. "We weren't expecting you until early Monday."

"I think the unexpected keeps life interesting, don't you?" David asked, shaking her hand and giving her fingers a small squeeze. Her hand was small, the skin soft, but there was strength in her grip. He'd unnerved her, but her eyes on his were steady. Often one could learn a good deal about someone if one caught them off balance, he'd realized some time ago. Jared had given him a glowing report of her editorial accomplishments without revealing much personal data except that she was single, stubborn by nature and somewhat opinionated. None of that worried him. He was curious, however, to discover the woman behind the mask.

And David felt certain she was wearing one. He wasn't a man who left much to chance, though his casual attitude belied his cautious nature. He'd carefully researched both Lyon Publishing and all its editors before changing houses. He'd learned that Augusta Lyon was a creative editor, knowledgeable and very professional. Beyond that, he'd uncovered very little, the publishing world being a close-knit community that guarded its secrets. Mysteries had always intrigued him, and the woman before him was no exception.

Removing her hand from his, Gussie wished she could tell him that she found unexpected arrivals of an author on a Friday afternoon when she had a thousand things to do a real pain in the posterior. Instead she motioned him to take the chair next to Molly, who was looking at him with something bordering on awe. David Lamb was just a man who happened to write books. She'd have to remind her assistant of that before she drooled on his sleeve, she concluded as she put her glasses back on.

"We were just going over the itinerary," Gussie began. "I presume you've been sent a copy?"

He nodded, crossing his long legs. "Tell me, what do I call you?"

Gussie's eyes snapped up from the paper she'd been glancing over. "I beg your pardon?"

David gave her an innocent smile. "The inscription on the door reads Senior Editor. Your desk nameplate reads Augusta J. Lyon. Jared calls you 'Gus.' I was just wondering, what do your authors call you?"

Clearing her throat, Molly stood. "I'll get some fresh coffee." Quickly she scooted out the door.

A man who spoke his mind. Or was he baiting her? Gussie folded her hands over his file and leaned forward. "We're fairly informal around here. What did you call Paul Raymond?"

"By his first name. But 'Augusta'?" He shook his head in dismissal. "I had you pictured as leaning toward stout, with horn-rimmed glasses and orthopedic shoes. No offense, but you're much too lovely for that name, and much younger than I expected."

She didn't know whether to be annoyed or pleased. She did know that this first meeting had somehow gotten off the track. She'd read that David Lamb was a charismatic charmer. But she didn't care to be charmed. Perhaps it was time she made that clear. "I suppose you'll have to take the choice of my name up with my parents. Most people call me 'Gussie.' Think you can live with that?"

He'd seen a spark flare in her eyes for a split second before she'd returned to her professional demeanor. He'd also seen the faintest touch of a blush. So she wasn't used to compliments, especially on the work scene. And she had a quick temper, but had learned to control it. She was not in the least impressed by his celebrity. That alone appealed to him. But there was more.

"I'll work on it. And you can call me 'David.'"

"Thank you." She hoped he didn't catch the sarcasm she'd tried to keep to a minimum. Gussie again picked up the itinerary. "If you'd like to go over this..."

"Did you decorate this office yourself?" he asked, leaning back in the chair, looking around the comfortable room. An antique bookcase, framed needlepoint on the wall opposite the bank of windows and a curved oak desk with African violets in hand-painted pots on two corners. Feminine yet functional. He wondered if it represented her personality or some decorator's.

Gussie picked up her pen and toyed with it impatiently. How was she going to get this man to two dozen appointments if she couldn't keep his attention for two minutes at a stretch? "As a matter of fact, I did. Do you approve?"

"Oh, I don't think you're a lady who needs a man's approval, are you, Gussie?" He rose and walked over to study the needlepoint. "Did you do this?"

He was definitely getting on her nerves. Gussie stood and shrugged into her jacket. Somehow she seemed to need the comfort of more propriety. "No, my mother made it." Settling again in her chair, she closed the folder and decided to ignore his first question. "Since you don't want to talk about the tour, I can only assume you're satisfied with it. If you'll tell me where you're staying, I'll pick you up Monday morning and..."

"Actually, I do have one small change. I'd like to squeeze in a stop in Sioux City, Iowa." David sat back down and regarded his new editor. She'd put on her jacket as if needing its protection. Since her silk blouse was cut almost austerely, he wondered why.

She was undoubtedly a lady who prided herself on being in control and one who became nervous when she lost it. It was something to keep in mind. Most women he'd met in the business world looked the part, but Gussie went to extremes.

Her thick, dark hair was wound around in some sort of twist that would have had her looking very mannish if she didn't have the most striking high cheekbones. She wore minimal makeup, but her fresh complexion hardly needed any. Even her large glasses couldn't hide eyes that were huge, velvety and intelligent. Just now they held a look of long-suffering patience.

"Sioux City, Iowa," Gussie repeated. "Not exactly a booksellers' hub. May I ask why you wish to include that city on our already-strenuous tour?"

"I owe a friend a favor." He gave her his best boyish smile. "You don't mind, I hope?"

Cornfields and katydids. Mind? Why should she? "I suppose not. Anything else?"

"Can't think of a thing." He watched as she bent to make a notation on the file. She had a beautiful mouth, full, almost too wide. Too bad she was stingy with her smiles.

Rising, David eased a hip onto the edge of her desk. Spotting one of his books next to a bowl of candy, he tapped the cover. "What did you think of this one?"

Gussie shifted in her chair. "Sorry. I haven't read it yet. I plan to get to it this weekend."

A little behind in her reading, but that was understandable. She handled a lot of authors. David let his gaze skim the room again. "Sammy said I'd like it at Lyon Publishing, and it seems he was right."

Only her eyes moved up to seek his. "Sammy?"

"Yeah. Sammy Levitz. He's the nephew of an old friend from college. He works here and told me I should switch."

Gussie frowned. "Sammy Levitz. The name doesn't ring a bell."

"Probably not. He's with the cleaning crew, working his way through college with a night job. Sammy runs into quite a few editors who stay late. That impressed him, so I thought I'd give Lyon a try." He could see the disbelief on her face. Actually, he'd told the truth, as far as it went. Sammy had rattled on about the people at Lyon Publishing, prompting him to investigate further. He'd met Jared Lyon several years ago, had admired his ability to spot new talent and his style. Yes, the man had a recognizable style. It would seem his only daughter had her own.

Gussie leaned back and removed her glasses. "Are you saying you switched from Columbia Press to Lyon on the word of a teenage cleaning person?"

He watched the merriment dance in her eyes, changing her whole face. "Yeah. Sammy's a good kid. Anything wrong with that?"

She had to look away. Wouldn't her father have apoplexy if he knew this best-selling author had changed publishing houses on the advice of a college kid who pushed a broom? "No. Nothing at all." Gussie choked back an uncharacteristic giggle. "We may get along after all, David Lamb."

David leaned closer across the desk toward her. "We'd get along a lot better if you'd let loose with a smile. Editors intimidate the hell out of me. All of you with your big blue pencils."

She gave him the smile he'd asked for. "I seriously doubt if *anyone* intimidates you."

"You'd be surprised."

Her eyes landed on his tie. There was no question in her mind. It had to go. "Where did you get that tie? It's... different."

He'd forgotten he had it on. He ran his fingers down the length of it. "It was a gift."

"Mmm. From a fan?"

"Not exactly. The maître d' at this highbrow restaurant your father took me to for lunch wouldn't let me in without a tie. When I told him I didn't own any, he dug this up from somewhere." He glanced down at it. "You don't like it?"

She studied the assortment of red dogs on a blue background. Dug it up was right. "It's awful."

"I thought everyone liked man's best friend."

Gussie rose. "Did you? Perhaps we'll pick up a tie or two on our travels. I'll call for you at your hotel in the company limo bright and early Monday morning. Maybe you want to rest up for your busy tour until then."

"No, no," said a high-pitched voice from the doorway. "No rest for the wicked." Chuckling at his own joke, Arnie Walker strolled toward them, his hand outstretched to David. "Hey, buddy. Arnie Walker from Publicity. Good to see you." He grabbed David's hand for a hearty shake. "I heard you were in town early. Good, good. Drinks and dinner tonight, the whole nine yards on good old Arnie. We get acquainted and go over the tour. You have any questions, any problems, you save them for old Arn. You can come, too, boss lady."

This Friday was definitely out of control, Gussie thought as she sat back down. First David's arrival and now Arnie, a man who knew a hundred ways to annoy her, including never using her name. Gussie tried not to grind her teeth. "I think I'll pass, thanks all the same. I'm sure you two have much to discuss."

Arnie, who was a couple of inches shorter than her own five-foot-seven even in his elevator shoes, looked all the shorter next to David, who had to be over six feet. Running his thick fingers over his thinning red hair, the officious little PR man nodded, acknowledging her refusal.

"I'm afraid I can't make it if Miss Lyon won't be joining us," David told him smoothly. "It's in my contract. Where I go, she goes. I feel strongly about the author-editor relationship."

Arnie's thick brows shot up. "You don't say? Okay, boss lady. Ball's in your court. Say you'll come. We got lots to discuss, eh?"

Heaving a deep sigh, Gussie wished she could pop them both. Seeing her fantasy of an early evening and a long soothing bath rapidly disappearing, she gave it one more shot. "David, you really don't *need* me tonight and . . ."

He turned those challenging blue eyes on her. " 'Need' is a relative term."

Gussie knew when to fold. She wasn't going to debate that one. "I'll pick you up at seven."

Slowly David Lamb shook his head. "We don't officially start till Monday. *I'll* pick *you* up. What's your address?"

While Arnie snickered, she clenched her teeth, wrote down her address and held the note out to him.

"Thank you." David took the paper, then slipped his fingers around hers. He held on, caressing the inside of her wrist with his thumb, feeling the softness, the suddenly erratic pulse.

His eyes, bold on hers, were hot, hungry, for just an instant. Oddly breathless, Gussie struggled with a flash of heat, a flush of desire. In any given business week, she brushed hands with people a dozen times. Why, suddenly, would this one man's touch so unnerve her? Regaining her composure, she pulled back and gave in to a frown. "Now if you'll both excuse me, I have a lot to do."

"Certainly." David pushed back his cuff and glanced at his watch. He saw her eyes widen as she noticed his timepiece. "See you in two and a half hours."

"Yeah, boss lady, see you later."

Gussie stared after them as she reached into her candy dish.

Molly returned, her expression openly curious. "I thought I'd stay out of the way. So what do you think of David Lamb?"

Swallowing, Gussie sighed. "He wears a Mickey Mouse watch and mismatched clothes. His one borrowed tie is circa 1950. He wants to make an unscheduled stop in Sioux City, Iowa. Molly, what am I going to do?"

Molly smiled openly. "Fasten your seat belt. It's going to be a bumpy ride."

There were many forms of intimidation, Gussie knew, and she'd run across most of them. But intimidation by charm she'd not seen in such megadoses before David Lamb had walked into her life this afternoon. She turned off the hair dryer and picked up her brush. Was his charisma practiced or totally natural? Perhaps she'd find out tonight.

Reaching for her pins, she wound her hair into the French twist she wore during working hours. Though it was evening, the dinner was still a business meeting as far as Gussie was concerned. She'd been only twenty-two when she'd started at Lyon fresh out of college and the boss's daughter to boot. A young-looking twenty-two, despite all she'd gone through. It had been hard enough gaining the respect of her coworkers as Jared's daughter without looking like a teenager.

So she'd taken to wearing quiet, tailored suits, her long hair coiled up in a sophisticated style, and even oversize glasses, though she needed only a minor correction. Perhaps she hadn't fooled anyone, but she'd *felt* older. As she pushed in the final pin, Gussie thought that now, six years later, she'd gained the respect of most everyone at Lyon and probably no longer needed the props. But the look had become such a part of her facade that she hesitated to abandon it. There was comfort in the familiar.

Moving to her closet, she stared inside for a long moment, trying to decide. On the right, neatly aligned, were her many business suits and blouses, in subdued colors and simple styles. No one in her workaday world had ever seen her in the outfits on the left side. There hung her comfortable slacks and sweaters for the at-home evenings when she let her hair down and kicked off her heels. There were casual outfits and several cocktail dresses for occasional outings with a few carefully chosen friends. And there were her faded jeans and sweatshirts that she wore at her ranch in Cold Spring, in upstate New York, on the getaway weekends that refreshed and renewed her. The many sides of Augusta Lyon, Gussie thought as she reached for her blue suit.

The rich blue was nearly the same shade as David Lamb's eyes, she noted. Eyes that could be challenging one minute and filled with humor the next. For a minimum of two weeks, she'd be in his company constantly. It was a long time to be with a veritable stranger. She remembered the heat brought on by only the lingering touch of his hand on hers, the flash of hunger in his eyes. A long time to be on guard.

Fastening her watch, she saw that it was nearly seven. He'd be prompt most probably. She wasn't used to being picked up. She usually called for the client. But David Lamb was a man who liked to take over. They would butt heads regularly on the upcoming tour, she was certain.

Grabbing her handbag, she walked to the living room just as the doorbell sounded. She stopped a moment to glance at her image in the foyer mirror. The woman in the glass looked professional and in control, except maybe for a hint of vulnerability about the eyes. She'd have to work on that. Taking a deep breath, Gussie swung open the door.

He stood there, wearing a silly smile and holding a big red balloon. The message on it read I love the Big Apple, and the Big Apple loves me.

Since when, Gussie wondered as she felt a smile form, had she become susceptible to schmaltz?

Chapter Two

A little lady with blue hair was selling these on the corner," David said as he stepped in. "I thought you might like one." He held the balloon out to her.

She might have guessed candy and flowers would be too ordinary for David Lamb. "Thank you." Gussie took the balloon from him, carefully avoiding touching his hand. "Balloons remind me of the circus."

He caught a suggestion of nostalgia in her voice as she turned and thrust the balloon's stick into a huge philodendron in the corner of the tiled foyer. "Do you like the circus?" He could more easily picture her at the ballet or the symphony.

Gussie stood back, still smiling at the balloon. "I haven't been in years. I think I was ten the last time Aaron and I went together." She shook her head. "A long time ago."

"Aaron was your brother, the one who died?" David saw the smile leave her face.

"Yes." Gussie shook off the mood. "I'll just get my jacket, and we can go."

David watched her walk down the hallway, then swung his gaze to the large room two steps down from the marble foyer, separated by a polished wood railing. It was beautifully decorated, as he'd known it would be. Gussie Lyon had money and taste. Peaceful pastel colors set off by a magnificent wall of floor-to-ceiling windows looking out on Manhattan at twilight. He shoved his hands into his pants pockets and stepped down, walking over to take in the view. Yes, most impressive.

Though San Francisco was his town, he liked New York, liked the hustle and bustle, the anything-goes feeling, the excitement that hummed in the air. He wondered if Gussie really enjoyed living here or if she stayed in Manhattan because of Lyon Publishing. He wondered, too, if she was happy working for her father. The time he'd spent with Jared recently had shown him that he wouldn't be an easy man to work for or to live with.

David watched the scene below as lights blinked on while the sky darkened. His research had uncovered the rumor that Jared had been grooming his only son to take over his publishing empire, though the man himself had never mentioned Aaron. Had her brother's untimely death made Gussie decide to work for Lyon, or had she been planning to all along? His writer's mind was always questioning, always wondering about the people he met, an occupational hazard that David had gotten used to. In fact, he found it a good tool in getting a handle on people. And he wanted a handle on Gussie Lyon. Curiosity, that's all that it was.

Yet he remembered how warm her hand had felt in his this afternoon, how her dark eyes had softened at his touch, while her pulse had pounded against his thumb. Something there, David thought, something to think about. He was not a man to ignore the obvious. Hearing her returning, he swung about.

She'd slipped on her glasses and carried her jacket draped over one arm. He walked up to her, wondering if the glasses were necessary. She was fussing with her handbag, not meeting his eyes. It occurred to him that she was nervous, and he wondered why.

"You have a wonderful view," he told her.

"Yes, isn't it?"

"I'll bet you sometimes turn off all the lights and just sit on the couch and watch the lights of the city."

Gussie glanced toward the window. She had done that a few times when she'd first moved in, but not in a long while. There was always so much to read, papers to go over, evening functions to attend with or for Jared. "Unfortunately, we get caught up in work and sometimes don't take the time to enjoy the simple things." She turned to face him. "I imagine you do, too, always dealing with deadlines."

"I learned a long time ago to take time out to play. It's healthier."

She tucked her keys into her bag as she cocked her head at him. He didn't look like a man terribly concerned with his health. Or with his wardrobe. He'd changed to a tweed jacket worn over an open-collared shirt and blue jeans. She wondered if that antique tie was stuffed in his pocket. "Do you take vitamins daily and get eight hours' sleep each night?"

"I do take vitamins, but I don't sleep conventional hours. Sometimes when the writing's going well, I lose track of time."

She started toward the door. "Forget to eat, forget to go to bed?"

David took her jacket and held it for her. "Do all your authors tell you the same thing?" His fingers touched her nape as she shoved her arms into the sleeves. He didn't miss her quick shiver of response. Fleetingly he wished she'd worn her hair loose and free, falling softly around her oval face.

Gussie stepped away from his nearness. "Some forget to eat, some tell me they eat while they type. Others have insomnia, and a few can make do on two hours a night when the pressure's on. And some treat writing like a job and are fairly well adjusted."

He moved to within inches of her as she put her hand on the doorknob. "Are you well adjusted, Gussie?"

His eyes seemed to look right into her. She tried to put a dash of amusement in her own. "I suppose I am, for a harried editor. What category do you fall into?"

He shrugged. "Probably neurotic as hell. Everyone in any form of the arts is, I think. We seek approval, applause and attention."

Gussie opened the door, shoved in the lock button and stepped out into the hallway. "Well, for the next couple of weeks, I guess it's my job to see that you get a healthy dose of each from your adoring public."

With a hand at her elbow, David guided her to the elevators and pushed the button. "I wonder if we aren't looking more for personal approval from a special someone rather than mob attention. You know, like Whistler painting to gain his mother's approval."

His moods were mercurial, from silly to serious in the space of minutes. She wouldn't have guessed that of him this afternoon. "Now you sound like Beau."

He raised a brow. "I thought you hadn't read any of my books?"

The elevator doors opened, and she stepped into the empty car. "I read a couple of chapters in my bath tonight."

He smiled at the picture that formed in his mind. "And?" He followed her in and the doors wheezed shut.

"And what?"

"Did you like him?"

"Not bad."

" 'Not bad'! I demand a new editor."

Gussie laughed. Amazing, she thought. The man had millions of books in print and one lukewarm opinion had him sputtering. "Please do get a new editor. And have him take you on your tour."

The doors opened, and she stepped out into the lobby. She started toward the double doors, but David stopped her and turned her to face him.

"Are you really telling me you don't like Beau?"

"Are you really telling me it matters to you?"

"Certainly it matters. The author to editor relationship is very important. Like client to attorney, or patient to doctor. Sometimes like confessor to priest. Special, almost sacrosanct. Tell me you don't mean it."

If Gussie hadn't seen his lips twitching and the laughter in his eyes, she'd have begun to think he was taking himself a shade too seriously. Six years in the business, and she still marveled at the insecurities of writers, even the successful ones.

"All right," she said finally. "Beau is different." As is his creator, she silently amended. "He's not your usual detective. He's intelligent, warm and funny. And I like the fact that he's got a woman in his life, one who is his equal."

"Well, now, that wasn't so hard, was it?" Taking her arm, he maneuvered them outside. "So Mandy got to you, did she?"

She wasn't mistaken. There was definite relief in his voice. "Yes. She's very well drawn." She watched his face as he indicated to the doorman that they needed a cab. "Is she patterned after someone you know?" Now where had that come from?

David smiled down at her. "No. She's patterned after someone I'd *like* to know. We all have our little fantasies." A cab pulled up within inches of where they stood. While Gussie scooted in, David slid a bill into the doorman's hand and followed after her. "The Four Seasons, please, driver."

Gussie settled back. The Four Seasons with its stark beauty, an extravagant menu and impeccable service—it would seem that Arnie Walker had been instructed to pull out all the stops for David. Yet he seemed less interested in where they were eating than in the somewhat inane conversation they were having.

"And what are yours?" David asked as he angled his body toward her.

"What do you mean?"

"Fantasies. Do you have any?"

Didn't everyone? Only some weren't foolish enough to reveal them. Slowly Gussie crossed her legs, then found herself all but hurled against David as the cab spun around a corner. Straightening, fighting down her surprisingly quick reaction to his nearness, she shook her head. "I gave up fantasies a long time ago. I find facing reality enough of a challenge."

David reached over and took her hand into his, examining the smooth skin, the lightly buffed, unpolished nails, then the palm. "I think not." With one finger, he traced a crease that circled her thumb. "See this line here? This is your dream line. And it's long and solid." He shifted so that he could look into her eyes. "You have fantasies, all right, Augusta. You're just not about to share them, are you?"

He had the kind of eyes a woman could easily lose herself in. Too large, too deep a blue, with lashes too thick for a man. Yes, a woman could get mesmerized just staring into his eyes while his fingers caressed her hand. Certain women, that is. Fortunately Gussie wasn't one of them. She pulled back her hand and dropped her gaze. This much touching had not been part of the bargain. Letting herself soften had gotten her into a peck of trouble once before. She wasn't about to let it happen again.

Moving over on the seat, Gussie peered out the window, and saw that they were pulling up in front of the restaurant. None too soon either. "Arnie's out front pacing. I guess we're a little late."

The cab had barely stopped, when Gussie pushed open the door and stepped out. Hurrying to Arnie, she gave him a big smile, surprising him as much as herself. She was anxious to get this evening over with, to have the weekend alone.

Monday morning would be here all too soon.

At precisely six o'clock on Monday morning, Gussie stood under the awning outside her apartment building as the company limo pulled up. While the doorman loaded her luggage, she dodged the raindrops and ducked inside. Adjusting her raincoat, she smiled at the driver. "Looks like it's going to pour all day, Simon."

"Yes, ma'am. Hope you're heading for a sunny spot."

"Washington, D.C., but I think they've got rain, too."

"Probably so. There's hot coffee in the pot already made."

"Mmm, thanks." Gussie gave him the address of David's hotel while she poured herself a steaming cup. Taking a bracing sip, she leaned back and went over her mental checklist one more time as Simon eased out into traffic.

Though she'd never personally been responsible for such an extensive tour herself, she was an experienced traveler who believed in making lists.

She set down her cup and slipped her clipboard out of the side pocket of her briefcase. A quick perusal told her she was as ready as she'd ever be. She had no idea what David had spent the weekend doing, but she'd certainly kept busy. Getting her clothes ready, packing, writing last-minute notes to Molly. And going to bed early, a luxury she'd have to do without for a while, she was certain.

She sipped more coffee as she remembered Friday night's dinner. The maître d' had raised a haughty brow, then taken David aside for a chat about his missing tie. As Gussie had predicted, David had pulled the ratty thing from his pocket and proceeded to string it around his neck. The pained look on the maître d's face had been priceless as he'd tried to choke back his disapproval.

Arnie had managed to monopolize the conversation through the endless courses that he'd preordered, accompanied by assorted wines that she'd barely tasted. She'd had trouble stifling yawns, but David had been polite and gracious to the effusive PR man, who'd actually brought out a book for him to autograph.

Gussie had been out with writers before, but none with David's large following and familiar face. She'd been unprepared when two women recognized him from his book jackets and had rushed over requesting autographs on slips of paper. While she'd listened, they'd gushed on about the wonders of Beau Kendall, a man who was evidently very real to them. She'd been intrigued mostly because the women were well dressed, attractive, professional looking, not the groupie type she'd always thought hounded celebrities for autographs.

David hadn't seemed to mind the interruption, taking it all in his easy stride, charming them effortlessly. As they'd left with a smile and a sigh, Gussie couldn't help wondering if this was something that happened to him frequently. Personally, it would cause her to lose her appetite.

When Arnie had ordered a nightcap all-around, she'd decided enough was enough and had begged off. David had insisted on going outside with her and seeing her safely into a cab. As he'd helped her in, he'd squeezed her hand, then stood on the curb, watching the car pull away.

This touching business would have to stop, Gussie told herself as she gazed out the window of the limo. She would somehow have to make David see that it was most unprofessional. Besides, she was beginning to enjoy the feel of his hand in hers a shade too much.

He was waiting outside his hotel, bareheaded and seemingly oblivious to the rain. When Simon dashed out to open the trunk, David tossed his bag inside and greeted him before climbing in beside her.

"Isn't it a beautiful day?" he said as he shook the moisture from his hair.

"I suppose so, if you're a duck," she answered. "Want some coffee?" She might have guessed he'd be one of those annoyingly cheerful morning people.

"Thanks." David settled back and examined the plush interior with its small bar, TV and even a shoe buffer. "I'm impressed. Tell me, do all Lyon authors get this royal treatment?"

"I doubt it."

He took his time examining her while she poured. In the soft light, her complexion was rosy, her scent light and morning fresh. Under her raincoat, she had on another conservative suit. He was beginning to think she owned nothing else. "How do you decide?"

Gussie handed him his coffee and refilled her cup. "I don't. I leave that to my father." She took a sip. "I imagine it has something to do with sales. Didn't they wine and dine you when you were with Columbia Press?"

"I didn't give them much chance. I'd usually come into town unannounced and pop up to the offices."

She should have known. "I'll bet that thrilled them."

He shrugged. "Maybe not, but you can learn a lot with surprise visits." She was all business this morning, clip-board beside her, notes at the ready. His hands itched to take the pins from her hair, to see just how long it was, to feel the silky strands. Would loosening her hair loosen the uptight lady? he wondered.

"I have something for you," Gussie said as she removed a box from her briefcase. She watched as he set down his cup and took the package with a smile. Susceptible to gifts, was he? Something to file away.

The box was long and thin and difficult to disguise. David drew out a striped tie and another in a muted paisley print. His lips twitched as he pretended to examine them thoroughly. "Not as tasteful as my relic, but I do thank you."

"Perhaps while we're in Washington, you can donate yours to the Smithsonian," she suggested.

"You wound me." David leaned closer to her, drawn by her scent. "How do you do it?" he asked.

"Do what?"

"In this somewhat smelly city in the midst of a down-pour with bus and car fumes clogging the air, you smell like—like spring. Whatever is it you're wearing, don't stop."

She tried not to look pleased, to dismiss his words as part of a practiced spiel. "I think the fog is clouding your brain."

"I don't think so. Do you like rain?"

Yes, the weather. Much safer. "Not especially. It's usually inconvenient."

"I suppose it is, in the city." He shifted his gaze out the window, watching the drops slither down the glass. "My house is south of San Francisco, on the ocean, and my office looks right out to sea. When there's a storm, the waves get so high that they roll in and cover my dock. And when the thunder rumbles and the lightning splits the sky, I stand at the window and look out, and it feels like the world is coming to an end. It's fascinating." He turned to her, surprised to find her listening intently. "I guess you think I'm crazy."

"No. You make it sound like something I'd like to see."

The simple statement shouldn't have pleased him so much. "Then I'll show it to you sometime."

Gussie turned to stare out at the rain. It was the writer in him, able to effortlessly snare her imagination with words. Yet she, too, had stood looking out at a storm from her apartment window and found the fury outside mesmerizing. Who'd have thought that a man who wrote detective stories would have the soul of a poet?

Simon lowered the window between them. "What airline, Miss Lyon?"

Gussie gave him the information as she reached into her briefcase for the tickets. "Simon will see to our luggage, and I'll go to the counter and check us in," she told David.

He put his hand out for the tickets. "I'll check us in."

Somehow she'd known they'd have this discussion. "Look, I know you're more used to leading than following, but let's get this settled now. You take care of the interviews, the autographs, the mingling with the fans. I get us where we have to be, on time and with a minimum of fuss. Agreed?"

"Wouldn't it be simpler if we did things together?"

"No. You do your job, and I'll do mine." She saw the frown skitter across his forehead, then disappear. She had the feeling he'd let her win too easily.

The limo pulled smoothly to the curb. Simon scarcely had the door open before she was out and heading for the terminal entrance. At the counter, she glanced over her shoulder and saw David sauntering along, hands in his pockets, his face studying each passerby. He wasn't fooling her. Despite her smooth exit, the discussion was far from closed. Gussie could spot a man who never gave up from a hundred yards. She'd spent her formative years living with one.

Gussie had insisted on first class, and without hesitation, Jared had agreed. The sky, it would seem, literally was the limit when it came to their newest superstar. She'd finished two of his books over the weekend and understood why. As a writer, David Lamb was a born storyteller, imaginative and original, even to jaded editorial eyes such as hers. As a man, he was unrelenting, exasperating and too damn appealing.

Sitting back in her window seat, she watched as the blond flight attendant made a little ceremony out of checking that David's seat belt was buckled. He obviously was aware that he was attractive to women, she thought as he gave the blonde a warm smile. Why that annoyed her, Gussie wasn't quite certain. Would she rather spend several weeks dragging an overweight, bulbous-nosed, cigar-smoking writer all over the countryside? Not really. But he didn't have to exude such—such sexuality.

Gussie sighed and closed her eyes. That was it then, the thing that had been bothering her about David Lamb. Each time they were together, he reminded her almost hourly that she was a woman. A dangerous reminder and one she had no time for.

They were taxiing down the runaway just before lift-off, when she felt David grab her hand and clutch it in his. Her eyes flew open as she turned to him. "What is it?"

"I hate flying," he said. He drew her closer, pulling her arm across the console between them. "Just let me hold on to you for a few minutes and I'll be fine."

She tried not to be suspicious, to believe he was sincere, as he intertwined their arms. He bent his head toward her, closing his eyes, while his fingers caressed her hand. She hated her skeptical nature, but the whole thing smacked of a practiced ploy. He looked perfectly fine. Would he really go through this charade at eight in the morning?

They were leveling off, and she could stand it no more. "How did you manage to fly from California to New York with this . . . this affliction?"

He sighed deeply and opened his eyes. "If I don't have someone to hold on to, I drink. Two, sometimes three quick shots of bourbon. I thought if I did that with you at this hour, you'd think me a little odd."

Gussie already thought him odd, and not just a little. Odd or a very good actor. She frowned as he moved their laced hands firmly into his lap. "How long have you had this . . . problem?"

"A long time. It makes life a living hell." He looked away, but not before she caught the laughter in his eyes. He barely managed to swerve out of the way as she pulled free and punched his arm a good one.

"You are certifiable." She shook her head and sat back in her seat. "Bourbon or hand-holding. You have no shame."

David laughed in agreement. He waited until they'd both been served coffee before leaning closer again. "I have to do something to keep this boring tour interesting."

"The first day and you're bored? I thought this tour was your idea?"

"No, my agent's. She's a firm believer that a cross-country tour like this is necessary now and then."

"You could have said no." And we could both have stayed home, Gussie thought.

"Have you met Nellie Brewster, my agent? Mean lady. Weighs close to three hundred. No one argues with Nellie."

"Mmm, I'm sure." She turned to look at him. "Why *are* you doing it? Is it money? Do you like the attention? Neither one's a crime, you know."

David set aside his coffee thoughtfully. "Attention? Sometimes. But for the most part, I have to be real careful not to become reclusive in my house by the sea. I like money, or rather the things it can buy, but I'm not obsessive."

"Then why?"

David had a feeling that she wouldn't like knowing Jared had suggested the tour. She'd like even less knowing her father had wanted Gussie to accompany him, had all but insisted. At the time, he hadn't cared much whom they sent along. Since meeting Gussie, his interest had been piqued.

He shrugged as he searched for an answer to give her. "It's part of the job. Writing's a very competitive field. I'm well aware that I'm not writing Pulitzer stuff here. There are a lot of talented mystery writers out there knocking at the door. I feel that the guys who are visible last longer. The public likes to break bread with you, for some reason, to talk with you, to get to know you. I did one of these things a couple of years ago at Columbia with Francine, my editor there. In just three months, my sales increased thirty percent. You can't argue with figures."

Gussie had seen similar statistics at Lyon, though she didn't think such exposure would work in every case. Some writers got tongue-tied in front of more than three people.

Others couldn't resist defending their work when questioned, and a few actually antagonized newspaper reviewers.

"Besides, being on my good behavior for a couple of weeks is a challenge, and I like challenges. Do you?" He watched her hand toy with the paper napkin as she considered that.

"Sometimes."

"Why do you work so hard, Gussie? You don't need the money."

She'd heard this one before, many times. "There are a lot of reasons to work other than money. A sense of independence, personal satisfaction . . ."

He reached for her hand again, effectively cutting off her thoughts. "The chance to meet handsome and charming men such as the one seated next to you."

Gussie watched him fold her hand inside his, then raised her eyes. "I can't decide whether you have a really high opinion of yourself or whether, for some obscure reason, you only want me to think you do."

His smile was slow and somewhat cocky. "Let me know when you decide." He lowered his head and placed a lingering kiss in the palm of her hand.

Gussie's pulse, rapid and jerky under his thumb, revealed far more than she'd intended, he was sure. In her eyes, he saw confusion and something more. A quick flash of awareness before she lowered her gaze and removed her hand from his.

This was not at all the way she'd thought their tour would go, Gussie acknowledged with a pounding heart. And this was only the first day.

Determined to regain control, she reached for her lists. "As you know, our first stop is at the television studio for the taping with Charley Farrell. Then we have the hotel luncheon where you're scheduled to speak about ten minutes. After that, there's a book signing arranged for three o'clock and..."

Closing his eyes, David listened to her drone on. His ability to tune someone out yet nod in the right places was something he'd developed years ago in college. It left his mind free to roam where it would. And right now, his mind preferred to dwell on just how long it would take him to get Gussie Lyon to take down that gorgeous hair, literally and figuratively.

Two of David's books had been set in Washington, so Gussie had been fairly certain they'd get a good reception. The packed auditorium for the morning video taping with local veteran talk show host Charley Farrell verified her assumption. Charley himself took them to the side of the stage and parted the curtain for a peek.

"That's something, young man," Charley acknowledged in his southern drawl. "I usually do pretty well with most of my guests, but just look out there. They're standing in the back and even along the sides." He shook his head. "Looks like you got yourself a bushel basket of charisma." Chuckling, Charley led them backstage.

Gussie walked along with Charley's fatherly hand at the small of her back guiding her. The very thought of taping live in front of that vast group of whispering men and women had dampened her palms. Yet David looked as calm as if he were to entertain old friends in his own living room. It took a special breed to love the limelight, she decided as Charley swung open a door.

"Now, little lady," Charley went on, "this here's what we call the greenroom, even though it's painted a sickly yellow. You can wait in here while the boy genius and I get pretty. Come on, David. Those folks in makeup get real cross if we don't let them throw a little powder around."

"Not for me, Charley," David said. "Thanks anyhow."

Charley squinted up at David. "You sure? Those TV lights are damn hot, and when you sweat, you look all shiny. Those ladies out in the audience want you looking cool as a cucumber."

"I'll be cool. Don't worry." He nudged Gussie into the room. "Just let me know when you're ready for me."

"Right you are."

The greenroom. Did every television studio have one, or the equivalent? Gussie wondered as she walked toward one of two striped couches. A large TV monitor hung from brackets on the far wall, and a plastic ficus stretched its dusty leaves toward the only other person in the room, a blond woman trying to look younger than she was in a tight red dress and impossibly high red heels.

"Hi," she said, giving David a big smile as he seated himself next to Gussie. "I'm Aileen Ames. The singer on the *Ted Broderick Show*, you know."

"Hi, Aileen," David answered as he stretched his arm along the back of the couch.

"I've been on *Donahue*, and my agent thinks he can get me on *Geraldo*. Do you watch the Broderick show? We're syndicated, you know." She continued to ignore Gussie and address her remarks to David as she toyed with a huge, chunky bracelet on her wrist.

"Can't say I do," David answered, amused at her.

The girl frowned as if thinking hurt her forehead. "Say, are you someone important?"

David felt his lips twitch. "Not very. I'm a writer. David Lamb. Mysteries."

"Oh. I don't read much."

Somehow that didn't surprise Gussie. She glanced toward the door, wishing Charley would hurry.

"And this is Gussie Lyon," David said by way of introduction.

"Gussie?" Aileen giggled. "My grandfather's name is Gus. He's real nice."

"How sweet," Gussie murmured through clenched teeth.

David shifted in his seat as the door swung open. An energetic golden retriever scurried in, followed by a tall, thin man holding his long chain. Nodding all around, the man backed into the only chair while the dog sniffed the perimeters of the room.

"Hello. I'm Lloyd and this is Lancelot." He grinned proudly. "I trained him."

"Really?" Aileen smiled. "What's he do?"

"Lots of things. He plays dead, and he counts. But his best trick is this here." Lloyd pulled a long instrument from his pocket. "He plays the harmonica."

Aileen's eyes widened. "No kidding?" Lancelot sauntered over and began nuzzling her. Daintily she ran her red-tipped nails along his back. "He's just adorable."

"Isn't he, though?" Gussie muttered under her breath.

David leaned close to her ear. "You really don't like dogs, do you?"

"I love dogs. I dislike thirty-five-year-old ingenues."

David coughed to hide his laugh.

"He's just the cutest thing I've *ever* seen," Aileen gushed as the dog licked her hands. "How old is he?"

"He's just a pup, really," Lloyd explained. "Only eight months old and—whoa! Lancelot!" He jumped up. "Stop that. Oh, miss, I'm mighty sorry."

Gussie watched the dog's raised leg quiver while Aileen tried to escape from the flooding. She was grateful the woman's squeals drowned out her laughter. Apologizing profusely, Lloyd dragged the animal out the door, following a tearful singer with soaking feet.

"Well, that's show biz," David commented with a smile.

"Couldn't happen to a sweeter girl," Gussie said as the door opened again.

Charley Farrell's assistant poked his head inside. "Mr. Lamb, you're on next. Miss, you can stand in the wings and watch if you like."

Relieved to get going, Gussie hurried out the door. Walking alongside David, she wondered if he was as nervous as she was for him.

The man had nerves of steel, Gussie decided.

She'd been standing on the sidelines for over twenty minutes, watching and listening. Charley Farrell was down-home friendly and common as an old shoe, which was one reason his show was so popular. He was like a favorite uncle invited into viewers' homes for a chat, one who introduced people and let them do their thing. He'd been at it for twelve years, and he'd mastered the technique.

But it was David she found amazing. He hadn't been at it for twelve years, and yet he was relaxed, affable, charming, sexy, intelligent—and she'd run out of adjectives. How did he do it? She hadn't a clue.

The live audience laughed in the right places and, even more important, listened when he spoke. A gift. It surely had to be a gift. During commercial breaks, he'd chatted with Charley as if he'd met him years before instead of less than an hour ago. If the rest of the tour went this way, she'd die a happy woman, Gussie thought.

There was a camera monitor near where she stood, and she moved nearer to study David Lamb during a close shot. He had a nice, solid face. His eyes were such an unusual shade of blue. Odd but she hadn't noticed that tiny dimple at the right corner of his mouth. Or was it the left? Did camera angles reverse things, she wondered, like mirrors, and . . . stop!

Gussie deliberately looked away, gazing out at the audience, instead. So he was good at this part of his job and he was attractive. So what? It did make her work easier, but that was all. With some effort, she switched her mind to the phone call she'd make later to Molly, checking on details for the next day.

She was halfway through her list, when she heard the applause begin, then raise in volume. Looking up, she saw David strolling toward her, his cocky grin firmly in place.

"How'd I do, coach?"

She struggled to keep her expression pleased, but not unduly so. "It was a good first showing," she said calmly.

His eyes told her she wasn't fooling him. "Be careful. You're going to turn my head with that lavish praise."

As the audience continued to applaud, she heard Charley's drawl calling David back onstage. With a wink, he walked back on for a bow.

"Well, I'll be damned," Gussie muttered as she clutched her clipboard to her chest. First a superstar writer and now a TV personality. How the hell was she going to cope with both?

Chapter Three

There was absolutely nothing that helped her relax and unwind more than a long, luxurious bubble bath, Gussie decided as she sank into the hot water. Spring had arrived in Washington, heralded by a light but chilling rain. Reason enough to rush to her room and run a hot bath, if not so much for the warmth as for the wonderful way lying back in a tub of water encouraged her mind to float free.

Already four o'clock, and yet she had two more events to get through. First she was to meet David in his suite at six for his interview with Beverly Knox, the book reviewer for the local paper. Gussie had read several of Beverly's columns and had found her to be fair-minded and honest. She was also a hard-hitting journalist who asked some extremely pointed questions, and Gussie couldn't help wondering how Beau Kendall would fare under Beverly's scrutiny. His creator would undoubtedly charm her, she thought with a sigh, as he had nearly everyone within the city limits.

Gussie reached for the fragrant moisturizing soap she always took on her travels and began to work up a lather. Though she wore conservative clothes and no frills to work, underneath she preferred her special scent and silk underthings. It was a contradiction no one knew about and few would have suspected.

After the meeting with Beverly, they were to attend a booksellers' dinner in the hotel ballroom, where David was to be the guest of honor. Undoubtedly it would last until the wee hours, and they were scheduled to fly on to Dallas first thing tomorrow. If today was any example, David thrived on the hectic schedule. She, on the other hand, was already wishing she could skip the evening and climb into bed, with or without a good book.

The day's events, she had to admit, had run smoothly, for the most part. The luncheon had been well attended and a huge success. The book signing had been a minor disaster narrowly averted. It hadn't been anyone's fault that the order for David's books had somehow gotten delayed or misrouted so that when she and David had arrived there'd been no books to sign.

While Gussie had searched her notes, looking for a name to call, David had taken over with his casual charm. He'd joked with the fans and had wound up autographing paper bags carrying the bookstore's logo, which pleased the owner, who'd happily passed out rainchecks. The giddy readers had left extolling David's virtues to one another. Again the boy wonder had come through.

When she'd checked them in at the front desk an hour ago and handed him his key, he'd seemed as fresh as he had when she'd picked him up in the morning. Not Gussie. She had tired feet and a fuzzy brain. Sinking lower into the bubbles, she decided both were improving.

She'd also changed her mind somewhat about David Lamb. He was a star who expected no star treatment, a definite plus in her book. It was lucky for him, too, for she'd have been hard put to dish it out. Yet there were many she'd seen today who would have gladly volunteered for the job.

He was a man who caused a woman to pause, to fantasize, to daydream a little, even as practical woman as Gussie had schooled herself to be. Despite all his good points, he was a man to stay away from, a man definitely not for her.

There'd been only one man in her life she'd allowed herself to fall for, and she could scarcely remember his face. It had happened a long time ago, but the effects lingered still. She had men friends now, men she knew through her family or through business connections, undemanding men she was comfortable with. Maybe one day, when she was more firmly in control both personally and professionally, she'd relax and devote the time and energy to build a lasting relationship. Maybe.

Gussie ducked under the water, rinsing the suds from her limbs. And if she chose to get involved with another man, it would be a man vastly different from the charismatic Mr. Lamb. A man more serious, less frivolous. A man more predictable, less flamboyant. Someone who would attract less attention and fit in with her preference for a quiet lifestyle.

Rising from her bath, Gussie reached for a towel. Truth be known, she neither wanted nor needed a man right now. She had work that challenged her, an apartment she'd carefully decorated, family, friends and money in the bank. What more was there? Drying off, she resolutely ignored the niggling voice at the back of her brain that insisted on reminding her of moonlight and roses, of romance and a touch that could heat the blood in moments. Reaching for her robe, she told herself that that little voice had led her down a painful, crooked path once before, and that she'd do best to ignore it now.

She was towel-drying her hair, when she heard the knock at the door. What now? Gussie thought as she left the chain in place and opened the door a crack.

He stood there with one hand behind his back, his hair windblown and damp. Holding the towel in front of her robe for added protection, she looked at him questioningly.

"I have something for you, a remembrance in appreciation for the ties."

"It isn't necessary."

"It is to me. May I come in?"

"I've just come out of my bath. I'm not dressed."

"You're covered. I'll only stay a minute."

How could she refuse? Reluctantly she slid the chain back and stepped away from the door, opening it wider. Her hand went to her throat, very aware that she wore nothing under the satin of her short robe. She took another step back.

"Your hair—it's not up." He sounded almost shocked.

"No. I was just going to fix it." Self-consciously she ran her hand over the wet strands.

David cleared his throat. He hadn't meant to say it out loud, but her thick hair falling just to her shoulders gave her a softer, more approachable look. "It makes you look so different."

He couldn't seem to take his eyes from her. Feeling a bit exposed, she countered by raising her chin a fraction. "You have something for me?"

He'd almost forgotten. "Yes." He brought his hand forward and held out the small, deep purple African violet snuggled in a terra cotta pot. "I noticed you had these at your apartment and on your desk. I thought this would make you feel at home."

Gussie let out a breath slowly as she touched one of the velvety leaves. How had he known just what would get to her? That he'd even noticed she had them at home and at work surprised her. That he'd bothered to dash around in the rain to find her one astounded her. "It's lovely. Thank you." Her hands were a little unsteady as she took the pot and put it on the small table by the door. Unexpected gifts were an uncommon thing in her life.

David looked around at the small sitting room, the archway leading in to an even smaller bedroom, and frowned. "Why are you in this inadequate room when I have a huge, two-bedroom suite? Get your things. You're moving in with me." He held up his hand. "No arguments."

He was doing it again, trying to take charge. She touched his arm. "David, no. This room is fine. I can't stay with you for several reasons. Think how it would look, for one."

"I don't care how it would look. It's silly for me to rattle around in all that wasted space while you . . ."

"Please. I'm hardly roughing it."

He leaned toward her. "Maybe I want you near me, for midnight consultations."

She saw that his eyes were dark blue and waiting. Perhaps she should try a lighter approach. She put on an amused expression. "Are you trying to flatter me?"

"Are you trying to test me?"

It wasn't working. She stepped back. "Certainly not. David, we're both business people. We've just spent a lot of hours together under stressful conditions and . . ."

He shook his head. "That was professional. That was David Lamb, the writer, and Augusta Lyon, the editor." He took a step closer. "I'm talking about the personal part. The man to woman thing between us."

She could smell the rain on his hair, see the light stubble of blond beard on his strong chin. Dear God, this would never do. "There is no personal part, no man to woman thing between us." She turned to pace, something she did when she was nervous. It occurred to her she might look slightly less than authoritative with her hair still dripping, her bare feet stomping on thick carpeting and her body clad in a thin robe that didn't quite come to her knees, but she couldn't stop now. "What gave you the idea there was?"

In two quick strides he was beside her, then close up against her. "What gave you the idea there wasn't?" He reached up and slowly touched her cheek with just his fingertips. Her eyes darkened in response as she sucked in a deep breath.

What would it hurt to let herself go, to give in to that powerful pull vaguely remembered? Gussie asked herself. This man could take her places she'd only visited in her dreams, she'd wager. She could feel herself softening around the edges, could feel the warmth spreading. His mouth was so close she could feel his breath on her own lips. No! She pulled free of him. "David, I don't want this."

"Don't you?"

She turned from him. "If you continue, I'll have to return to New York and send someone else to complete your tour."

He was a man who gambled, not with money but with something more valuable. He dared reach out his feelings toward someone, though he might get slapped down from time to time. Sometimes he lost. Most often he won. And sometimes there were delays along the way.

He hadn't consciously decided he wanted Augusta Lyon. Yet the knowledge was there, inside him, already a part of him. Pursuing her wasn't the smartest thing he could do right now. There was Jared and the implied trust he'd placed in him. There was the unprofessionalism, for another. Yet he could still feel the way her soft body had felt close up against his chest, could almost taste the lips that had trembled as he'd let his eyes linger on them.

But a smart man knew when to press his advantage and when to back off and wait for the right moment.

Hands on her shoulders, he turned her, then cupped her chin so she was forced to look up at him. He saw no fear in her eyes, but rather an honest hesitancy. He'd respect that. He was a patient man. He gave her a slow smile. "Denial is the first stage, Gussie." He let go and walked to the door, closing it behind him.

Gussie clasped her hands tightly together to stop the trembling. Denial. She wished she didn't believe he was right.

He was wearing pink socks. Gray slacks, a white shirt and pink socks. Gussie took a deep, steadying breath as she entered David's suite. She wondered if he dressed offbeat purposely or if he simply didn't give a damn. He closed the door behind her and led her to the sitting area alongside the bay window. A slender redhead wearing a smart green suit rose as David introduced them.

"It's good to meet you, Miss Knox," Gussie said as she ignored David's attempt to guide her to the two-seater and took the lone chair. "I admire your work."

Beverly Knox glanced at David. "And I envy yours."

Another conquest, Gussie thought. Captivated before they'd barely begun. She settled back, crossing her legs. "It has its moments."

"I'm sure." She poised a gold pen over a small notepad and smiled at David. "As I was saying, could we start with your background, David, when you began writing, why you settled on mysteries, things like that?"

David braced an ankle on his knee and began talking, looking as at ease as ever. Gussie half listened as he recited his early beginnings, sticking close to the information she'd read in his file. He threw in an occasional anecdote, winning the expected smile from Beverly Knox. Obviously his wardrobe peculiarities didn't matter a whit to this reporter.

"There've been a goodly number of detectives in fiction," Beverly went on, "continuing characters that captured a large readership for their creators. Comparisons naturally come to mind. I wonder if you'd care to comment on some of them. For instance, John D. MacDonald's Travis McGee series featured a slightly eccentric hero who lived on a houseboat in Florida."

David nodded. "I like old Travis. There's a caring quality to him, despite his having a new female interest in every book."

Beverly took notes as she talked. "Probably the most famous is James Bond. How do you feel about 007?"

"Ian Fleming was highly imaginative. The special effects in the books, even more spectacularly depicted in the movies, stood out more than the characters. James Bond could be predictable, kind of like a modern-day Batman with all his futuristic devices."

"And he was quite a womanizer."

David shrugged. "That's what the fans of those books were looking for, the hard-living, hard-loving playboy detective."

Crossing her legs, Beverly leaned forward. "Television's also given us countless detectives, from Philip Marlowe to Columbo to Spenser, many originating in book form. Which would you say most closely resembles Beau Kendall?"

Thoughtfully David shook his head. "I've never consciously compared them. I like to think Beau is different, unique, and stands on his own." He ran a hand along his chin. "If I had to choose, I'd say he comes closest to Robert

Parker's Spenser. He's a man of the eighties, in tune with today's thinking, not hard-nosed, not macho, just a real person."

"I see." Beverly shifted green eyes to Gussie. "Miss Lyon, as David's new editor, I'm sure you're very aware how popular his books are, with male and female readers. What do you think is the basis for Beau's appeal?"

Gussie wasn't pleased to be drawn into the interview, but saw no way short of rudeness to not answer. "Beau's very human. He makes mistakes and learns from them, which I think appeals to the average man weary of superheroes. And he's sensitive as well as faithful to one woman in one relationship, which certainly appeals to women readers. He's an all-around nice guy who happens to be a detective."

Beverly folded her notebook with a small smile. "And now that you've spent several days touring with David Lamb, do you feel that Beau Kendall is patterned after his creator?"

Why, the sly fox! Did she think she was going to trap her into that kind of admission? Gussie returned her smile. "Well, so far, I haven't seen David round up any bad guys in black hats, but perhaps he's saving the big scene for our tour finale."

Nodding at Gussie's careful answer, the reporter turned back to David. "There is one other thing. I'm not really an exposé writer, yet if there's one thing I've learned through the years it's that readers love knowing about writer's lives. Not just how and why they write, but how and where they live, their likes and dislikes, something about their personal lives that makes them feel they know that person. So far you've kept a low profile, never revealing the location of your home, details about your family, if there's someone important in your life. Does this tour mean you're going to share more of yourself with your fans?"

Gussie saw the warm congeniality leave David's face for the first time and hoped he wouldn't say anything too damaging.

He rarely gave in to his temper, unless it was serious. This frequently asked question was more annoying than angering. "No, it doesn't. Beverly, I know you're just doing your job, but I hope you'll understand. I put out a product, a product of my imagination and research, a damn good one, I think. And I hope the public will like and accept it. But *I'm* not that product—my books are. I'll go around the countryside, talk with the readers who show up, autograph books and eat dinner with all who are interested enough to join us. But other than to reveal that I live near San Francisco where Beau Kendall lives, I won't talk about my home. My family and anyone who's significant to me deserves the same privacy I freely give to my fans." He stood, giving her a crooked smile. "We don't delve into the personal lives of our butcher or our druggist. I don't see why writers should be exempt from that courtesy."

Slipping her pad and pen into her purse, Beverly rose. "There are those who feel that people in the public eye are fair game."

"Do you agree with that thinking?" he asked.

"No. I believe we're all entitled to our privacy." Her glance drifted to Gussie and back to David. "And to protecting our relationships." She held out her hand. "David, it's been a pleasure."

"Thank you for your time." He moved to the door.

Beverly flashed a quick smile at Gussie as she stood. "Anytime you want to trade jobs, let me know."

David closed the door after her and shook his head before turning to find Gussie gazing out the window. Walking over, he thrust his hands in his pockets. "Think she'll nail me to the wall?"

"No, I think she agrees with you but she felt she had to ask the question in case you'd suddenly turned publicity mad and would now kiss and tell."

He stood behind her, watching the rays of the setting sun dance in her hair. She was wearing another of her androgynous little suits, this one black, with a high-necked blouse. Her scent wrapped itself around him, and he found his hands moving to rest on her shoulders.

"I'm not one to tell, but I do like kissing. Do you?"

Since his visit to her room earlier, she'd known they'd have to have a talk, to set the record straight. They had a long tour to work through and this...this touching was making her edgy. She shrugged off his hands and turned to face him. "David, you need to know something about me. I didn't think it necessary to bring it up before, but I see now that it is."

"You're involved with someone?" Fleetingly he wondered if even knowing that he'd be prepared to back off. The thought took him by surprise.

"No, I'm not, and that's the point. I don't wish to be, not with you or anyone else."

"Why is that?"

"I have my reasons. I want us to have a good working relationship. Please don't spoil it by trying to change it into something I have no interest in." A good speech, Gussie thought. She'd been rehearsing it for over an hour. She wondered how convincing she sounded.

He reached to touch her hair, just a stray curl at her ear, and felt a small shiver take her. No interest, eh? "I told you the first stage was denial."

She moved out of reach. "You see what I mean? This touching is highly...annoying. Why can't you look on me simply as your editor? Pretend I'm a man and..."

His laugh rang out, full and throaty. "Right. And I'm the Easter Bunny." He ran his hand down the lapel of her jacket. "I must say your clothes aren't styled to make a man's heart pound."

Why did his statement hurt, even though she'd chosen her business wardrobe with that very thought in mind? "They aren't meant to." Moving from the window, she reached into her pocket for the roll of antacids that she'd picked up this afternoon to replace the M & M's she loved. Stomach churning, she popped one into her mouth and chewed as she paced.

"And you should talk about clothes. Often as not, you're a walking rainbow. Look at you tonight. We're going to a formal dinner, and you're wearing pink socks, for heaven's sake." She rounded the bend, swallowing the soothing mint, hoping it would do its job quickly. "Pink socks! There's your reason. Somehow I can't see myself getting involved with a man who wears pink socks."

David bent to pull up a pant leg, as if surprised. "They're pink?"

She stopped in front of him. "Can't you see that they are?"

"I can see, but I can't tell. I'm color-blind."

Gussie cocked her head, wondering if this wasn't another trick, like his fear of flying. Yet he looked as if he were telling the truth. Color-blind. That explained a great deal. A smile tugged at the corners of her mouth. "Why didn't you tell me sooner? I thought you were . . . well, never mind what I thought."

"I can tell dark from light, and some bright colors, like red. But pastels blend together, and blue, gray, tan—they all look alike to me. When I was a kid, my mother used to hang the blue shirts with the blue pants and so on so my classmates wouldn't laugh at me. At home, I don't pay attention, but traveling, I sometimes still screw up." He glanced down at his shirt and pants. "How's the rest of me?"

Gussie truly wished he didn't remind her of a little boy. "Fine. If you had a pink tie, we could just let people think you planned it that way. The eccentric writer."

He slipped on his suit coat. "If you moved in here with me, you could check my wardrobe every morning and make sure I don't embarrass myself."

"And you could stick a flower in my teeth to make sure I didn't look too mannish."

So his comment had bothered her, had it? Good. He wanted her to feel something, and that was a start. He moved closer. "Did I say that?"

She tried to look nonchalant. "Not in so many words." His hand was cupping her chin before she'd realized he'd reached to her, his thumb slowly caressing her lower lip. Gussie felt the floor tilt just a bit as her eyes raised to meet his.

"No one with a mouth as beautiful as yours could ever be mistaken for a man."

She'd always thought her mouth too wide. And beautiful? She knew she wasn't, not in any conventional way. Her eyes weren't bad, but her face was too thin, her cheekbones too prominent. And besides, there was the irrefutable fact that no one—no man, woman or child—had ever labelled her *beautiful*. If she were, surely someone would have mentioned it by now.

She knew she wasn't ugly, either, just average looking. She'd grown used to that thought and could live with it. And she wished David Lamb hadn't come along to make her question and doubt. He was just a charmer, she reminded herself, a man who enjoyed women and thought they needed a generous dose of compliments daily. Well, not Gussie

Lyon, thank you very much. She moved away from his touch and made a little show out of checking her watch.

"We've got to go. It wouldn't do for the guest of honor to be late." Picking up her purse, she marched to the door.

"Wait." David went behind the bar and bent to retrieve a box from the small refrigerator. With a smile, he held it out to her.

Through the white plastic cover, she could see the corsage nestled in green paper, could smell the fragrant gardenia. Why was he doing this? She groped for an amusing remark so he wouldn't see just how defenseless gifts made her feel. "Does this come under the heading of bribery, so I'll misplace my blue pencil when you mail in your next manuscript?"

"Perhaps." David removed the delicate flower and poised it over her left shoulder, wondering where she wanted to wear it.

Still disconcerted, she reached for a quick retort, hoping to keep him from returning to the dangerous touching she was by now enjoying too much. "Or is the flower to feminize my severe little suit?"

He waited until he'd pinned the corsage in place, then sought her eyes. It was then that he saw the hurt. Unknowingly, he'd hit a sore spot, though hurting had never been his intention. Could it be that she didn't know how lovely, how desirable she was? Perhaps he could show her.

"A writer believes in words, Gussie, but there are times when actions speak much louder." He closed his mouth over hers before she had a chance to speak or protest.

The kiss had been meant as an apology, an explanation, a reassurance. But it quickly got out of hand. He dragged her against him, tasting her at last the way he'd wanted to since he'd seen her seated so imperially behind her big curved desk. But even he hadn't guessed how fast his system could move from lukewarm to hot, from curiosity to need, from exploration to possession.

Though he'd surprised her, he'd discovered a few surprises himself. The cool, controlled businesswoman was giving as good as she was getting, her mouth opening in invitation, the struggles he'd predicted nonexistent. Amazement at her responsiveness gave way to passion as his hands moved into her hair.

The kiss was an explosion. Suddenly Gussie's blood was racing and her heart soaring. Her arms went around him, the need to be nearer becoming an ache. This couldn't be Gussie. Not conservative, contained, rational Gussie Lyon.

He nibbled on her lip, and she heard a soft moan, only hazily realizing it came from her. It was frightening to know that he could liquefy her so effortlessly—frightening and exhilarating. His mouth returned to claim hers, and she was waiting and anxious for more of his taste, for the rippling pleasure. To be wanted this badly, this wildly... How long had the dream lain dormant inside her, to be wanted like this? A lifetime, maybe longer.

David ran his hands down her slim frame, felt her shudder, then press closer. In their time together, he'd seen curiosity in her eyes and an occasional hint of awareness at his touch, but he'd not dreamed she'd kiss like this, holding nothing back. He'd not known she could make his pulse pound like this, turn his knees to water, bring him to the edge so quickly. He decided he needed a little space and a lot of time.

A bit breathless, he moved back and saw that she was breathless, too. Hands still on her shoulders, he watched her lashes flutter open. Her eyes were filled with arousal and a residue of shock. Her beautiful mouth swollen from his kisses beckoned him, and he returned for a lingering kiss, surprised again that she met his lips willingly. He felt weak and drained and took a deep breath as she leaned against the door.

He was amazed that his hands weren't quite steady. Amazed and annoyed. He needed to say something, the right something.

"I wanted you to know that I didn't mean you dressed wrong or that you weren't feminine and very appealing. I thought a kiss would show you better than I could tell you. So I . . . no, dammit!" He ran a hand through his hair and saw she was watching him intently. "To hell with reasons and explanations. *I wanted to kiss you.* No excuses. So I did."

He looked sincere and a little shocked and suddenly worried. Well, he needn't be. Gussie pushed away from the door, her hands raising to repair her hair. She searched her bag for her lip gloss. "I'll be ready to go downstairs in a moment."

His eyes dark and angry, David whirled her around to face him. "Is that all you're going to say?"

"What do you want me to say? You've already said it all. You wanted to kiss me, so you did. I . . . I obviously wanted the same thing. I shouldn't have. It won't happen again."

"Just like that."

"Yes, just like that." She pulled free of him, growing angry herself. She was in no mood to rationally discuss a kiss that had altered her world, while her heartbeat was still not under control and her lips still trembled from his. "Look, David, chalk it up to jet lag or fatigue or tour inexperience. That shouldn't have happened. You're a professional and so am I. We have a *working* relationship that I believe we both value. Let's not mess it up by losing control again."

His eyes narrowed as he watched her turn to the mirror to fix her makeup. "You're a cool one, aren't you? Augusta

Lyon, always in control." Grabbing her shoulders, he whipped her around, fingers of steel clutching her upper arms. "I don't know who you think you're fooling, honey, but I've kissed a lot of women, and I sure as hell know when one is kissing me back because she *wants* me, not because she lost her head for a moment. You can pin your hair back up and put on your professional face, but it's too damn late. I've seen you now, I've tasted you, and I know. You can lie to yourself all you want, but it won't change a thing. You want me every bit as much as I want you."

She couldn't back down, not now. "If I did, for a moment there, I'll get over it. I have before."

He stared her down, wondering what he was seeing. Had someone hurt her? Was that why she'd propped the shield into place the moment she could? Her father hadn't even hinted at her personal life. Something was there and David wasn't about to let it go. He'd told her the truth, that he'd kissed many women. But not one had made him feel quite the way Gussie Lyon had a few minutes ago. Something to explore.

He eased back, deliberately softening. "Tough lady, are you?"

"When I have to be.'

"You don't have to be, with me."

She clicked her bag closed. "That's a matter of opinion. It's getting late. Let's go down and see if we can find you a suitable tie."

But David was too keyed up to let things lie unresolved. He pulled her close up against him, his hands more gentle now, but still insistent. "This isn't over between us. You can't go backward in a relationship, and we've already moved way past the usual editor to author friendship."

She was not a woman given to temper, but he was sorely testing her patience. If only she'd thought to stop that first kiss. But she hadn't, and now she had to make sure he behaved, even if it meant mouthing words she didn't quite believe. She wasn't sure she could handle another onslaught and walk away unhurt.

"Look, I know you're a bright fellow, so listen up. It's over, finished. We shared a moment together and now we move along. The earth is still spinning, and life goes on. Blame me, if it makes you feel better. I will finish this interminable tour with you because it's part of my job. I will get you to all your appointments, make sure the press loves you, hold your hand in airplanes, if necessary, and even match up your clothes so you don't look like you dressed in the dark. But I have not before, nor will I again, kiss one of my authors, nor go to bed with him. And I will not, understand *not*, get involved with you, David Lamb. Do I make myself perfectly clear?"

"Perfectly. Just one thing." He watched her roll her eyes heavenward. It was all he could do not to applaud her performance. "What about me? What if *I* want to kiss you again?"

She let out a huff of air. "You will take up morning jogging, cold showers or vigorous sets of tennis. Your choice. But you will *not* touch me again."

He reached his hand out and she glared at him.

"I just wanted to straighten your corsage. It got a little crushed."

Gussie adjusted the flower. "Small wonder it's not in shreds."

"Yeah, that was quite a kiss." Silently she walked to the door. It wasn't in him to let it go. "Didn't you think so?"

She moved out into the hallway. "Having a little ego problem, are you? Never been rejected before?"

He locked the door and moved beside her. "That wasn't a rejection we just went through in there, Gussie. It was only a postponement.'' Taking her arm, he led her to the elevators.

The gushing was getting to her. Gussie stifled a yawn and tried to pay attention as the woman seated on her right went raving on about the wonders of David Lamb's books, his looks, his magnetism. She silently agreed that most of it was true, but this was the fourth or fifth dinner guest who felt it necessary to share her feelings about David with her, and she was getting understandably tired. And incredibly bored.

They had found David a pink-and-gray tie in the lobby shop, and he'd strolled into the ballroom foyer, which had already been set up for the cocktail party, looking surprisingly well put together. He'd immediately been surrounded and had scarcely been without two or more hovering females as well as many interested males alongside him since. How did he stand it? Gussie wondered.

The dinner had been passable, what she remembered of it, the speeches never ending and the music now playing at least three decibels too loud. She truly wasn't meant for the touring life, Gussie decided as she stole a glance at her watch. If they had too many more of these evenings, by tour's end she'd be ready for a rubber room.

And David wasn't faring much better for a change, she noticed, though he hid his discomfort more politely. The man seated on his left at their large round table had decided to entertain him with the plot of a book he was working on that he just knew would fascinate David, and he hadn't stopped talking for the past half an hour.

As the band moved into a quiet number, her conscience nagged at her. She could rescue him. He did look pitiful and long-suffering, his eyes a little glassy, his smile painted on. All right, but if he made one false move . . .

With no small effort, she excused herself from her dinner companion and walked over to tap on David's shoulder. She almost laughed at the relieved expression on his face as he quickly hopped to his feet.

Gussie gave the balding man an apologetic smile. "I hope you don't mind if I borrow David for a few minutes. He promised me a dance, and I have to leave soon."

The novice writer looked a little disappointed, but nodded his consent. David nearly knocked over his chair following her to the dance floor.

"Lord, what took you so long? That man is rewriting *War and Peace*, the unabridged version."

"I hope he doesn't discover I'm an editor. He just might slip the manuscript under my door."

"Fat chance. It undoubtedly weighs fifty pounds." He smiled as he swung her around the circular dance floor. "Do you like to dance?"

Her hammering heart told her she liked dancing with him. "I don't do much of it, but yes, I do."

"It's positively the most socially accepted form for holding a woman close in your arms in front of a roomful of people."

Gussie glanced up at him in mock disapproval. "Are you by any chance a pervert?"

"Not by chance, by design." David laughed and moved her a fraction closer.

When the number ended, she was oddly disappointed. "Well, that's it for me. I've wined and dined and chatted and listened until I'm worn out. We leave for Dallas fairly early. You go continue to be charming to your adoring public. I'm slipping between the sheets before I fall on my face."

David didn't bother to hide a yawn. "I've had it, too. Come with me to say good-night to the folks in charge, and I'll walk you to your room."

What she didn't need was him walking her to her room. But she couldn't come up with a polite refusal, so she did as he asked. The leave-taking took another twenty minutes before they were able to make their way out of the ballroom. Gussie stepped off the elevator and paused.

His room was to the left and hers to the right. She gave him a good-night smile. "I'll leave a wake-up call for six and see you downstairs for coffee at seven, okay?"

Ignoring her intentions, he took her arm and moved her toward her room. "Fine."

She swallowed down a quick surge of temper. The man absolutely *had* to have it his way. She reached for the safety of business conversation. "Our first function in Dallas is a luncheon put on by a chain of bookstores. I believe I mentioned it to you already. After that, there's an interview set up with CNN that I have to verify when we arrive, a local TV spot at four and..."

They'd arrived at her door. David took her key, inserted it and swung open the door. She was still rattling on.

"Dinner, thank heavens, is on our own. But there's an evening autographing scheduled at this shopping mall and..."

He backed her up close to the doorframe and leaned into her with a hand on either side of her head, not touching her. Frowning he studied her suddenly still face. Her eyes were a little sleepy, he noticed, and a little unprotected. "Don't you ever quit working?"

"I was just going over tomorrow's schedule."

"We've got plenty of time tomorrow for tomorrow's schedule. We haven't finished today yet." Slowly he moved his head toward her.

"Yes, we have." She pushed against his chest. "I told you, it's over."

"I was only going to blow a speck of dust from your cheek."

"My, my, David Lamb. You must think I fell off the turnip truck only last week." She saw him smile that slow, heart-stopping smile that won them over from California to Connecticut, and Gussie knew she had to get inside quickly.

He straightened then, studying her cheek. "No, really." He reached with one finger to brush at her cheek. Then he dipped his head to brush his lips across hers ever so quickly, ever so lightly, before she could move. Stepping back, he grinned. "Just wanted you to know, Miss Lyon, that it ain't over till it's over."

Whistling, he walked toward the elevators, his hands stuck in his pockets.

Shaking her head, Gussie went inside and leaned against the closed door. Involuntarily her hand touched her lips, still feeling his warm breath, remembering his taste. No, it wasn't over. Did she really want it to be?

Chapter Four

Dallas had drained him. Two days of nonstop sessions had him sagging with relief to be leaving. David pulled out the footrest of the first-class seat and stretched his weary legs. Outside the plane window, the evening sky was streaked with filmy purple clouds as they flew westward toward San Diego. After serving an elaborate dinner, the flight attendant had dimmed the overhead lights, leaving the cabin in a cozy twilight. Next to him, Gussie had her eyes closed

She looked fragile in sleep, tilted back on her side, her face turned toward him. It surprised him to realize it. She was so capable awake, so efficient, her clipboard always handy. When she wasn't talking to hotel personnel or luncheon caterers or booksellers attending to a dozen small details, she was on the phone, checking ahead to their next function, their next stop on the tour. She went head to head with reporters, public-relations people, hotel managers, bookstore owners, even talk-show hosts if they didn't perform according to plan. She rescued him from overzealous fans, insistent would-be writers and hangers-on. Plain and simply, she was a marvel. And she'd never been on tour before.

Shifting to face her, David noticed faint shadows of fatigue where her dark lashes rested on her cheeks. He'd been unable to convince her to wear her hair down—yet. He remembered how soft, how silky it had felt the evening he'd kissed her and his hands had wandered up. Her mouth was free of makeup, making her look younger, gentler. He remembered all too well and much too frequently how avid and responsive her lips could be.

He'd behaved with admirable restraint the past couple of days, mostly because she'd kept him too busy to leave much free time. Except for taking her arm crossing streets or brushing her fingers as she handed him something, he'd hardly touched her. Never before had he deliberately kept such arm's distance from a woman he wanted. But, then, never had he had to pursue a woman who also wanted him, but somehow found it necessary to deny that fact to herself.

He hadn't managed to discover yet why Gussie seemed determined to have nothing to do with him outside of business. He'd decided it probably wasn't him, but rather any man. Why would a beautiful, intelligent, passionate woman swear off men if not because she'd been burned before, burned badly? Yes, David thought studying her as she dozed restlessly. That had to be it.

He'd almost asked Jared yesterday when he'd called David in his suite. The call itself had surprised him, catching him in the late afternoon as he was changing for dinner. Seemingly Jared had just phoned to ask how the tour was going, how they were getting along. David knew that Gussie spoke daily to her assistant at Lyon, and Molly could have updated Jared easily. Yet the Lyon had chosen to inquire himself. Had it been a warning, to make sure David wasn't coming on to his daughter? Or had it been quite the opposite, an attempt at matchmaking? Interesting.

Certainly a father shouldn't have to hover over a daughter who was nearly thirty to make sure a man wouldn't seduce her. If there would be a seduction between them, it surely would be by mutual consent. Was Gussie much less experienced than her assured manner indicated? Remembering the way she'd returned his kisses, he doubted that. Yet she'd seemed almost surprised at her own reaction, then refused to admit she'd had one. Of one thing David was certain: no woman kissed a man like that unless she felt something. Something scary, perhaps, and unexpected, but something powerful, too. Gussie Lyon was a bit of an enigma, he decided.

He watched as she sighed, then settled back into sleep, and he wished he could rip out the console between them and hold her, just hold her. He knew she liked to be thought of as a cool, controlled executive, but yesterday, he'd discovered she had her soft side, as well. After a luncheon given by a local mystery writers' group, he'd been standing talking with their president, when Gussie had excused herself to make a couple of calls. As he so often found himself doing, he'd watched her wend her way through the tables toward the phone. Before she'd gotten to the door, a young man had stopped her.

Whatever he'd had to say had evidently interested Gussie, for she'd dropped her impatient look and was soon listening to him intently. David had kept her in his line of vision for at least ten minutes while the well-dressed man had talked on. Finally he saw Gussie accept a large manila envelope from him, shake his hand and leave the room. Later, when he'd mentioned the incident, she'd somewhat sheepishly admitted that she, who had strict rules about such things, had taken his manuscript and promised him she'd read it.

Since he'd seen her politely but firmly turn down several other such requests, he'd had to ask why this particular writer had gotten to her. "Because I liked his eyes," she'd explained. He'd looked skeptical, but she'd refused to say more. He could see, on her lap along with her glasses, the manuscript she'd been reading before fatigue and a bit of wine had caught up with her. Reading it as she'd promised the young man. Yes, an enigma, David thought, smiling down at her.

He reached over to brush a strand of hair from her cheek, and her eyes opened instantly. Stifling a yawn, Gussie stretched lazily.

"Why aren't you resting?" she asked. "I thought you told me you were tired."

"Tired is different from sleepy. Besides it's—" David checked his watch "—nearly eight in the evening, and you haven't gone over tomorrow's schedule yet. Are you feeling all right?"

"Mmm, I'm too drowsy to pull out the schedule. I remember the morning and afternoon are pretty hectic. Then there's nothing until after noon in L.A. the next day, a television taping. And that evening's the big party at our West Coast publicist's home for a whole group of Lyon authors. I understand his house is pretty lavish. Arnie Walker's flying in for the gala." She gave in to the yawn. "Personally I can hardly wait."

"Sounds like it. You don't care much for Arnie, do you?"

She shrugged, wiggling around in her seat to get more comfortable. "He's good at his job and the editors respect him. He's just a little pushy for my taste."

"And what is your taste?"

"In men?"

"No, in cabbages. Of course in men."

She sensed a trap here, even in her sluggish state. "Well, personally I prefer very short men with weak chins, pot bellies and webbed feet. But they're hard to find."

"Cute, A.J."

Gussie raised her head. "What did you call me?"

"A.J. Augusta Jane, isn't it? 'Augusta' sounds like a dowager aunt, and 'Gussie' reminds me of a truck driver. Will it bother you if I call you 'A.J.'?"

She was quiet a moment. "It's what my brother used to call me. Aaron hated all our names. He had this book where he looked up the meanings of names, and he'd go on and on about them."

He wondered if she was aware her face had softened and saddened. It was the first time she'd willingly spoken of her brother. He wasn't about to let the moment slide. "And what did he tell you?"

"Augusta means *majestic* and he used to laugh because I was always so small, especially compared to him. By fourteen, he was over six feet, with these massive shoulders. So he called me 'A.J.' because nothing else fit and letters were neutral, Aaron decided." Her voice held a trace of melancholy. "I tried so hard to compete with that man, and I never even came close."

There were times David was content to be an only child. "What does Aaron mean?"

"Aaron means *enlightened*, and I think he tried to be, although somewhere along the line, he lost interest. Mother's name is Dolores, and that means *sorrowful*, which Aaron thought suited her. But it was the meaning of my father's name that really got him. Jared means *one who rules*. That certainly hits it on the old nail head."

She'd said it without bitterness. "Did Aaron try to compete with your father, to be brighter and more innovative, so one day he could run Lyon Publishing?"

Gussie sighed, wondering if she really wanted to walk down memory lane. She shouldn't have had that glass of wine, she decided belatedly. Alcohol always loosened her tongue. "At first he did. I don't know why, because my father was already grooming him to take over. As you may have guessed, Jared's a great taskmaster, not given to compliments, a man who expects a great deal from everyone. After trying for some years, Aaron decided he couldn't do it. So he gave up and became a playboy."

"I think I read where he died in a plane crash."

"Yes, he was flying his own plane. But if it hadn't been the plane, sooner or later, it would have been his speedboat or his sports car. Aaron grew fond of the fast lane."

"His death must have devastated Jared."

"It did, but I think that discovering that Aaron no longer was interested in following in his footsteps was almost a greater disappointment. Poor Dad. Those weren't good years for him. Both his children disappointed him terribly."

"Both? I can't believe you would."

She turned to look at him. "Less than a week and you know me so well?" She shook her head. "Don't be too sure. I nearly broke his heart. If I hadn't been so headstrong, maybe he wouldn't have thrown himself into his work and later had that heart attack. We'll never know, I guess."

"Come now, you must know that Jared loves you. It's pretty obvious to me, and I don't even know him well."

Sitting up, Gussie raised a hand to check the pins in her hair. "Oh, sure. But I'll bet not a day goes by that he doesn't wish that Aaron was back working alongside him." Squinting, she looked toward the front of the cabin. "Could you signal a flight attendant? I'd like something cold to drink."

While they were served, David thought over what she'd said, trying to put together how all that had affected Gussie. He needed more pieces to the puzzle. He waited until she'd settled back with her soft drink before he probed a little further. "Did you go straight from college to work at Lyon?"

"Yes." She was telling him too much, a man she would only have occasional brushes with after this tour. What was there about him that caused her to blabber on? He was too good a listener.

"Were you just dying to get in there, to learn it all, to become an editor?"

Sipping, she shook her head. "No, I wanted to go into fashion design." She smiled at his surprised look. "You'd never have guessed that having seen my wardrobe, would you?"

"Oh, A.J., I know you've got a couple of soft, feminine things tucked away in your closet at home. I even understand why you play down your looks at the office. Makes you feel more in control, right?"

"Play down my looks? This is the way I look, nonspectacular, everyday average."

David leaned across the console until he was almost nose to nose with her. "Do you really believe that?" he asked. "Can't you see that you have gorgeous hair, rich and thick and so vibrant even a color-blind guy can appreciate it? But you wind and twist and hide it like some small-town librarian, why I can't imagine. Your eyes are so full of life. They snap and crackle when you're breathing fire and grow dark and smoky when you become aware there's a man watching you, a man who desires you. And your mouth—the memory of the taste and feel of your mouth has me wrestling the sheets every night since I kissed you. I haven't seen your body, but I've touched it, felt it, imagined it. Do you want me to go on?''

Gussie swallowed hard, wondering if the entire plane-load of people could hear her heart pounding. She had only enough energy to give a quick shake to her head. To her enormous relief, he settled back in his own seat.

He'd stunned her. Good. It was time. "So what do you think of that?''

She took a fortifying sip of her drink. "I think I'll take a another look in the mirror tonight. I've obviously missed a few things.''

"You do that. Now, you were saying, you'd planned to go into fashion design?''

"Yes. I knew my father would never choose me over Aaron to head Lyon Publishing, so I thought I'd go in an-other direction. I enjoyed fashion, as most young women do, but I took some business courses, as well, because I wanted my own company eventually. But my plans were changed when Aaron died just before I was graduated. My father was so broken up that I went to work at Lyon, plan-ning to stay just until his grief eased. Then something hap-pened. I discovered I loved the publishing world and that I was good at it. Needless to say, Jared was pleased. I was second choice, but I was the only Lyon left. So I stayed.''

Second choice. So that's how she thought of herself. He didn't like the sound of that. "First choices are sometimes made with the emotions. Second choices are made with the intellect and usually turn out to be wiser ones.''

She turned to him, feeling almost as warm at his words as she had by his nearness. "What a nice thing to say. Thank you.''

He took her hand, lacing her fingers with him. "I'm a heck of a nice guy, didn't you know?''

"Actually, you are. If you just weren't so much into touchy, touchy, I could really like you."

"Let's be brutally frank, A.J. Can you honestly say you don't like my touching you?"

She studied him a long moment, then dropped her gaze. "No, I can't. The problem is, I like it too much."

"Then enjoy. And let me enjoy."

Reluctantly she took her hand from his. "I just can't, David. I can't go into it, but I won't let myself get involved again. It took me too long to get over my last mistake."

So he'd been right. "You're so certain we'd be a mistake?"

"I can't risk it." She drained her glass just as the announcement came that they were starting their descent into the San Diego area. In the nick of time, Gussie thought as she fastened her seat belt.

"So, Mr. Lamb, tell us, where do you get your ideas?" The blond talk-show hostess leaned forward over her desk and gave him a toothy smile while she waited for his answer.

Seated in the front row of the television audience, Gussie watched David sit back in the deep leather chair and cross his long legs, looking as if this were the first time he'd had to answer that question instead of at least the hundredth. This was the last appointment of the day, and she had reason to be glad. They'd been at it since leaving their hotel at six that morning.

"Same place everyone does, I guess," David began. "From life experiences, from observations of people and from my imagination."

"Oh, I think you're being too modest. I know my imagination could never create the assortment of people you've paraded through your books. And they're all so real, so different. How do you manage to keep them straight?''

David had been thinking that Polly MacGiver was highly imaginative to have thought that a gauzy, nearly transparent blouse and a short, leather skirt would look right on a body that had to be forty and holding, but he kept his smile in place. "We all know lots of people—friends, neighbors, coworkers, relatives. Fifty, seventy, a hundred people easily. Some we know well, some not so well. But we manage to keep all of them straight, right? It's the same with characters in a book.''

"I see. Let's explore Beau Kendall a bit. He's a decent guy in his personal life, one who has a monogamous relationship with this woman attorney, Mandy, and even hints of marriage now and then. Yet you're single, and your picture's appeared in the paper occasionally over the past four or five years, each time with a different woman. How do you explain the inconsistency?''

David frowned, annoyed at the line of questioning. "I don't see an inconsistency. I'm not Beau Kendall.''

"But there is much of your thinking, perhaps even your ethics, that goes into his creation.''

"That's inevitable to some extent with every writer. The fact that I date a variety of women does not mean I'm against a monogamous relationship.''

"Yet you're thirty-four, very good-looking, and you've never married. Why is that?''

Like a dog with a bone. David felt his eyes grow cool. "I would imagine that my readers are far more interested in my books than they are in my personal life, wouldn't you, Polly?''

Polly gave him a pouty smile. "On the contrary. I'll bet your *female* readers out there in TV land would love to know why you're not married.''

Gussie nearly groaned out loud. Why did they let this bubble brain of a woman host a talk show? She saw David shift in his chair and wondered how soon they'd be breaking for a commercial.

"I consider marriage a very serious step, especially in view of the divorce rate today. I would never take it lightly. When my own Mandy comes along, I'll know."

"How sweet!" Polly cooed. Catching the eye of the assistant producer, she saw that he was signaling for a break. Swinging her heavily lashed eyes to the camera, she smiled broadly. "Don't you go away. We'll be right back with more questions for David Lamb."

Amen, Gussie thought as she watched the red light blink off. She wondered whether she should try slipping a note to Polly, requesting a return to the format they'd discussed before the show, or just let things slide along. As she watched the stage, David covered his microphone and leaned close to Polly, whispering something. The woman's eyes widened briefly before she dropped her gaze and nodded.

When the red light came back on, Polly looked into the camera, but her smile was a little off center. Glancing down at a sheet of prepared questions, she picked up the pace. Only now she stuck to the subject of David's books, drawing him out, involving the audience. Gussie decided she'd give a week's pay to know what David had told the overblown blonde who'd made the mistake of trying to boost her ratings at his expense. After another ten minutes, she slipped from her seat and headed backstage. This should be priceless, she thought.

"I told her the next personal thing she asked me," David explained as he settled back in the cab, "I'd turn the tables and start in on her love life, inviting questions from the audience, as well. Since little Polly's deeply involved with a very married local politician, I didn't think she'd want that."

The shock made Gussie sit up taller. "Blackmail? You wouldn't have?"

"Probably not, but Polly doesn't know that, so she behaved."

"How do you know she's having an affair with a married man?"

"Honey, all of California's like a small town. Gossip, gossip."

"What if your information wasn't correct and she went on poking and delving?"

"I'd have gotten up and walked off at the next personal question."

She wasn't sure if that didn't shock her more. "Not a very professional thing to do."

"What would you have me do, confess to a television audience that I sleep in the nude, prefer satin sheets and get turned on by candlelight in the bedroom?"

She sent him a patient look. "Now, David, she wasn't getting *that* personal."

"She would have. She's a small-town personality who thinks she's invincible. I thought it was time she learned she wasn't." He stretched his arm across the back of the seat as he angled to face her. "Enough about Polly. Where would you like to go for dinner? Do you remember that I mentioned my friends, the Slades, are coming by the hotel for a drink later? I'd like you to meet them. Jerry's written over a hundred detective stories for magazines, as well as a novel that might interest you, and Kelly runs a boutique. You'll like them."

"I'm sorry, but it'll have to be some other time. I've had a change in plans. I'll drop you off at the hotel, and then

I'm flying on to L.A. I've arranged to have my bag sent ahead. Arnie phoned this afternoon, and there're some details he needs my help with for the party tomorrow night. You enjoy your friends, and I'll see you around noon.''

"Why didn't you tell me earlier? I'll go with you."

"Don't be silly. I'm going to be busy. Why should you give up an evening with your friends?" She saw that the cab was pulling up in front of their hotel. "I've already signed the bill. All you have to do is check out in the morning and bring me the receipt. Would you mind?"

He was damn annoyed and damn tired of having her call all the shots. She hadn't seemed terribly anxious to meet with the Slades when he'd suggested it earlier today, but he hadn't thought she'd duck out. "Yes, Mother, I think I can handle getting your receipt." He leaned forward to the driver. "To the airport, please." He turned to Gussie. "I'll see you off, then."

Gussie looked exasperated. "That's not necessary."

"Look, when we're attending a tour function, you're in charge. When we're on free time, I do as I please. Right now, it pleases me to accompany you to the airport. Say 'thank you, David.'"

She tried not to grind her teeth. "Thank you, David." Folding her arms across her chest, she sat back and glared out the window. Why did he make everything so difficult? Just like her father, wanting, *needing* to be in charge.

Actually, she didn't have that much to do in L.A. except tie up a few loose ends and check on Arnie's arrangements. But tonight she felt the need for a little alone time, time to regroup, time to think.

She needed a little time and distance from David Lamb and the feelings he was arousing in her.

The cab pulled up in front of the terminal, and Gussie turned to say goodbye to David. But he'd already jumped out and was paying the driver. Scowling, she scrambled out and onto the curb.

"No, don't. Take this cab back into town. I'll be fine from here." She shifted her briefcase only to have him take it from her and start propelling her toward the double doors.

"I'll just check you in. Give me your ticket."

Gussie couldn't think of a time in recent memory when she'd been so furious. But, then, few people could anger her so completely and so quickly as David Lamb. She also knew she wasn't about to start a shouting match in an airport terminal. With a frustrated sigh, she thrust her ticket toward him.

Damn stubborn woman, David thought as the ticket agent did his thing. As a child, she'd probably climbed on her two-wheeler and ridden off alone first try rather than let someone assist her. What were a few scraped knees compared to a loss of independence? She couldn't, she simply *couldn't*, accept help for fear she'd lose a tiny scrap of control over her life. He had the overpowering urge to make her lose control in the most basic way, and soon.

Thanking the agent, he found Gussie pacing impatiently at the end of the concourse. Without preamble, he took her arm and marched her toward security clearance. He'd never even been tempted to be rough with a woman before. It seemed Gussie was destined to lead him into many firsts.

At the gate, most of the seats were taken, but he found a small island of privacy by a window. He angled her into it and checked his watch. "Ten minutes before boarding. You have any more instructions for me before you go? Don't you want to tell me what to wear tomorrow, remind me to brush my teeth tonight? Aren't you concerned that I'll miss my morning flight without you to check me in and buckle my seat belt?"

The angrier he'd gotten during their near run down the corridor, the cooler she'd become. Perhaps she *had* hovered a bit too much. "If I've been a little too bossy..."

His dark eyes glared into hers. "If? *If?*"

"All right. I apologize. Is that what you wanted to hear?"

"I don't know what I wanted to hear." He shifted his gaze out the window at the late-afternoon sun bouncing off the tarmac. "Damn, but you sure raise my dander. Do you know, in some circles, I'm considered a mild-mannered man? Would you believe that?"

"I've seen occasional flashes of it," she admitted.

Not a woman to back down. But, then, he'd known that from the first. He had the insane urge to rip the pins from her hair and bury his fingers in the thick locks, to throw her onto one of the black vinyl couches and show her what losing control was all about. Obviously he couldn't do that. But he could leave her with something to remember him by. He took a step closer. "Not one to give much, are you?"

"Not really."

"I guess the only solution then is to take." Before she had a chance to guess his intentions, he clamped his mouth over hers and took.

A jetway door opened nearby, sending in the soft whine of a plane's arrival. The announcement of the pre boarding of Flight 457 to Los Angeles boomed over the loudspeaker. And alongside them, a toddler cried out as his father caught him trying to run away. Peripherally, David heard it all, but as if from a great distance as desire whipped through him.

He knew he was a patient man, a precise thinker who painstakingly mapped out a story from first shred of an idea to its conclusion, slowly and methodically. Now all patience fled as he lost himself in the delight of having Gussie exactly where he wanted her. Straining against him, clutching him, wanting him. She could deny, she could talk, she could turn away from her thoughts. But not from this.

This was passion, pure and primitive. His mouth molded to hers, already familiar, achingly so. Her taste flowed through him, recognizable, alluring, captivating him. Her body fit against his so well, as if made for him, as if it were the other half of him. Without a plane, he had taken off on the wings of desire. The first kiss he'd chalked off as a fluke. But there was no mistaking this. And it shocked the hell out of him.

What had happened to denial? Gussie wondered as her arms dropped all pretense and moved to enfold him to her. What had happened to resistance, to indifference, to the aloof response she'd always been able to bring about? Gone, all of it gone, replaced by the wild seduction of his mouth on hers, the mind-shattering feel of his hard limbs wrapped around hers, the magic of his breath mingling with hers.

Foolish. She'd been foolish to deny that this was what she'd been wanting. She curled her fingers into his jacket and pulled him closer, needs she hadn't acknowledged in years springing alive inside her. He was hot, demanding, insistent, and Gussie discovered that that was exactly what she wanted.

He deepened the kiss, and she moved from lost to drowning. She was drowning in the depths of feelings never felt before, hardly imagined, barely dreamed. He was both hard and tender, real and unreal, sending her senses humming, blocking out all reality. She who had taught herself iron-clad control now gave it up willingly, joyously, if only he would never stop holding her.

He should pull back, he should let go, David knew, for the lesson he'd intended to teach by now had surely been learned. But suddenly the teacher was the pupil, learning how fragile was his hold on his own control where she was concerned. He wanted to fly away with her to a place, any place they could be alone. He wanted to be the hero she'd fantasized about in books, the man who would walk through flames for her, the one who would hand her dreams to her. He wanted . . . he wanted Augusta Jane Lyon.

Finally he let go, and Gussie came off her tiptoes to once more rest on solid ground. She was returning to reality slowly, eyes dazed, mouth trembling a little. She'd steeled her heart, guarded it religiously, forced it into submission. Yet in one breathless moment, he'd made her question everything. And she dare not let him know.

Shakily reaching for the briefcase she'd propped against the wall, she became dimly aware of people moving past them to board the plane. She hadn't the faintest idea how long the kiss had lasted. She only knew it could never have been long enough.

"You see, Evelyn," a robust man with a beard was saying, "if you kissed me goodbye like that, I'd sure as hell hurry back." Two men standing nearby joined in a laugh of agreement.

The buzzing in her brain eased as Gussie felt her face flush. She'd never *ever* been a part of such a public display. The fact that she'd participated in the kiss as wholeheartedly as David had was not the point. Without him starting it, there would have been no kiss. Embarrassment led to fury as she shifted her briefcase and raised blazing eyes to his face.

The fact that he was grinning didn't help her frame of mind.

"How could you embarrass me like this?" she asked through clenched teeth.

"Lighten up, A.J. Life's too short to keep popping a gasket at every little thing." David was enjoying her anger. She was something to behold when, as his mother used to say, she got a bee in her bonnet. One strand of hair dangled across a flushed cheek, and her eyes were spitting fire, her chest heaving as she fought for control. Life with Augusta Jane would never be boring, he decided, if someone could cure her of this silly notion of trying to harness all of her honest emotions.

"This was *not* a little thing in my book." Gussie tightened her grip on her briefcase. "I'm going to finish making the arrangements in L.A., then I'm flying back to New York. I'll have my replacement phone you." She turned on her heel and marched toward the gate.

He caught up with her in three easy strides. "Running from the truth is the second stage, A.J. You may be a little uptight, but I didn't think of you as a quitter." Affecting nonchalance, he strode through the waiting room, taking it deliberately slow.

Belted into her seat, Gussie sat trying to compose herself as the plane took off. The man was infuriating, obstinate and maddeningly persistent. He overruled her decisions constantly, took matters into his own hands regularly and pushed her to her limits daily. She'd check in at her hotel and call Jared at home and tell him she'd had it with his superstar.

Reaching into her pocket, she found an antacid and shoved it into her mouth. He was also ruining her health. She couldn't remember having a burning stomach in years, not since...well, there was no point in recalling all that. Her father would have to understand. She was an editor, not a baby-sitter. This was a job for someone who was willing to check Mr. Wonderful's clothes, hold his hand crossing streets and tuck him into bed each night. There was a limit how much she'd do, even to keep Jared happy.

Her father would be disappointed in her. The thought floated to the forefront of her mind and lodged there. So disappointed. He'd listen as she would explain the situation, nod and agree to replace her, if she fought hard enough. But she'd be able to hear the disappointment in his voice across the three thousand miles that separated them. Damn!

Another thought intruded. She'd promised her mother after Jared's recovery that she'd try to lighten his burdens, not add to them, to not make waves whenever possible, for his health's sake. Returning with her tail between her legs, admitting she couldn't handle one difficult but important writer, would not please either parent. Double damn!

Stuck. She was again stuck, as she had been before and probably would be again. The very thought of being even partially responsible for another heart attack her father might suffer was more than she could comfortably live with. Gussie swallowed the mint and tasted surrender. So she'd handle David Lamb and a dozen more like him if she had to. She had good reasons for walking away from him, ones he wouldn't imagine.

Gussie accepted a glass of wine from the flight attendant with a distracted smile. He'd accused her of running from the truth. Was she? she asked herself. The truth was she couldn't afford to disappoint her father again. She took a sip of the tart wine, letting the cool liquid calm her. The truth also was that, after only a week in David Lamb's company, she wanted him. More truth. Getting involved with him would be detrimental to her well-being and counterproductive to all her plans. So perhaps, in a sense, she was running.

Could she run far enough, fast enough?

Whatever had come over her, kissing him like that? Each time he'd touched his lips to hers, she'd turned into someone she scarcely recognized. Under his magic spell, she'd begun to dream of a quiet place where they could be alone and see just how far this incredible passion could take them. She'd begun to dream of answering that burning need, begun to entertain thoughts of... of love.

Ridiculous! Gussie took another healthy swallow. A woman didn't fall in love because a man had wonderful eyes, an appealing sense of humor and knew how to kiss like there was no tomorrow. Hell, anybody, everybody, knew how to kiss.

Not like that! David hadn't just kissed her. He'd taken possession, crawled inside, branded her. And for the life of her, she simply didn't know if she had the strength to resist his magnetic pull.

Now that she'd decided to ride out the rest of the tour, would he be able to wear her down even more? She'd have to be on guard, watchful, careful. She'd have to keep in mind what had happened once before when she'd let awakening desire rule her head. And she'd have to remember that, even if she were in the market for a man, David Lamb was too much like Jared Lyon to be a viable candidate. She would be jumping from the frying pan directly into the fire.

Gussie drained her glass and set it down. She could do it. Years of discipline simply couldn't fly out the window because of one man. And that's all he was, she reminded herself. Merely a man. Gazing out the window at the cloudy sky, she wondered why her reassurance to herself had a hollow ring somehow.

David watched Kelly Slade maneuver her way toward the rest room and turned back to his friend Jerry. "She looks good, even with that rotund little belly," he commented as they moved together to the archway of the hotel restaurant off the lobby. The dinner they'd shared had been filled with reminiscences and with catching up. Their friendship went back to their mutual college days and had remained solid despite the fact that they seldom visited each other.

"Yeah, she feels good," Jerry said, "but she's getting awfully anxious for the baby to arrive. She's tired of all the potty stops and being uncomfortable in bed."

David shook his head. "Three children. When we were rooming together at Stanford, I never thought I'd see the day when you'd be so domesticated." Jerry had been wild in his youth.

Jerry shook back his sandy hair and grinned. Lean and athletic, he still looked as if he belonged in college. "Neither did I, pal. But Kelly's a wonderful mother, and, frankly, I enjoy the kids as much as she does. Working from home, I spend as much time as she does with them. She's cut down to four hours a day at the boutique. I think this'll be the last one, though. Kids take a gigantic commitment."

As David recalled, commitment had been the farthest thing from his friend's mind when he'd met Kelly. But he'd fallen like the proverbial ton of bricks, and suddenly marriage was all he'd talked about. David had wondered if that bright flame would endure with the test of time, but here it was ten years later and they'd sat at the dinner table holding hands.

David nodded in agreement, wondering if he could ever commit to one person forever, to say nothing of children and all they entailed. Unbidden, Gussie's face swam into focus in his mind, taking him by surprise. She had no interest in marriage, commitment and children, he was certain. But, then, neither did he.

"Hey, buddy," Jerry said, putting his hand on David's shoulder, "you holding out on me? You seem a little preoccupied tonight."

Shaking his head, perhaps to clear it, David set aside his vagrant thoughts. "Nah, it's just this tour. It's pretty tiring and not even half over."

"I'll bet it's tough. Women drooling over you, pushing and shoving to buy your books, slipping you room keys." He saw David's smile begin. "Or is it this new female editor who's got you so distracted, the one who didn't stick around to meet us?"

"No, I've got a new book on my mind. You know how it is when your brain's busy putting together a plot. Even when you're with people, sometimes you drift off. And I told you, Augusta had some things to take care of in L.A."

"Uh-huh. That's quite a name, Augusta Jane Lyon. What's she like?"

Exasperating, exhilarating, unnerving. Beautiful, exciting, passionate. David cleared his throat, aware that his friend was watching him carefully. "I think she's a damn fine editor. Here comes Kelly." And not a moment too soon. Old friends had a way of looking through you.

"Well, David," Kelly said, sliding an arm about his waist as they strolled to the door, "it was great seeing you again. When are you coming for a real visit, one where you can stay with us for at least a couple of days?"

He smiled down into her pixie face. "Invite me for the christening. I'll be there."

"Terrific," Kelly said, reaching up to kiss his cheek.

"I'll hold you to that," Jerry said, giving him a bear hug. "And bring your editor friend. Hailing from New York, she might enjoy a stay at a beach house."

"I'll keep that in mind." David watched them go through the revolving door to the street, then turned and walked toward the elevators.

A day at the beach. Why hadn't he thought of that? She just might enjoy it. He'd make the arrangements tomorrow morning. Their schedule was light enough to handle it. That's what they needed, some time away together without appointments scheduled every hour or two. Then maybe they could explore these brand new feelings that were making them both jumpy and irritable.

David stepped into the elevator and punched the button for his floor. What if she didn't show, if she really went back to New York? No, she was too much of a professional to quit in the middle of a commitment.

Humming, he stepped off on his floor, his mind jumping ahead to the calls he would make. It was about time somebody knocked little A.J.'s socks off, and he was just the man who could do it.

Chapter Five

"You mean Arnie's not there yet?" Molly asked, her voice crackling over the phone wire.

Standing in the wings backstage at the television studio, Gussie frowned as she gazed toward the stage where they were setting up. "The flight he was scheduled to be on arrived last night, but he hasn't checked in at the hotel." Gussie tucked the receiver under her chin and held it in place with a raised shoulder as she glanced at her watch. "And it's half an hour to air time, and David hasn't shown for this television taping. The producer's getting a little testy."

"I can imagine. Well, I talked with Arnie yesterday morning and he assured me everything was in order for the party at Sid Brown's tonight. I'm sure he'll be there momentarily."

Gussie crunched down on an antacid, wishing she felt as confident as her assistant sounded. "I certainly hope you're right." She turned and looked toward the stage door. Where was David? She never should have left him.

"You still chewing on those M & M's?" Molly chuckled. "I'd be as broad as a barn if I ate as much candy as you."

She was tempted to explain she'd graduated from chocolate to the hard stuff, medicinal mints. Grimacing at the chalky taste as she swallowed, she decided a change of subject would ease her nerves. "You been behaving without me? How's that new man you were seeing, Brad or Rad or whatever?" She'd actually missed hearing about her assistant's colorful love life the past week. With what her ex had put her through, Molly deserved some good times.

"Chad." Molly laughed. "A thing of the past. Easy come, easy go. But I met someone else. His name's Elliot and he's *so* good-looking. A psychiatrist."

As she made the appropriate noises into the phone, Gussie wondered if she was living vicariously, listening to Molly's adventures instead of having her own. Quickly she dismissed the thought. "I don't know where you get the energy." Or the patience, she added silently. "How are the reporters on the tour shaping up?"

"Terrific. You're getting good press, wonderful feedback and selling bundles of books. I spoke with Jared this morning, and he's very pleased."

Not pleased enough to call her, though. At least he could find nothing to criticize. "How's he look, Molly? Tired? Is he overdoing?"

"Stop worrying. He looks fine. He went golfing yesterday and got a little sun." After working with Gussie for years, Molly could seemingly pick up on every little nuance in her voice, even over the telephone. She paused a long moment, then plunged in. "How is it working with David Lamb?"

Gussie let out a deep breath. Molly was her one confidante, but her feelings were too ambivalent to mention even to her. "He's more popular than I'd thought, interviews well, and he's a very entertaining speaker. My father was right. He's a gold mine."

Molly wasn't fooled. "Honey, you sound tired. Is anything bothering you?"

She should have remembered that Molly was often *too* perceptive. "Perhaps I'm not used to touring. I'd feel a lot better if these two clowns would show up and..." She heard the stage door close and looked up. Well, it was about damn time. "Our boy wonder just strolled in, Molly, so I've got to run. Check with you later."

"Want me to make some calls and try tracking Arnie down?"

"No, forget it. I'm sure we'll muddle through even if he doesn't show. I'll call you tomorrow, if I'm still in one piece after this gala party."

"Stay out of the headlines," Molly warned with a laugh.

"I'll try." Gussie hung up the phone as David walked up to her.

He was wearing a bright cream-colored sport shirt, open at the throat, kelly-green golfing pants and boat shoes with no socks. His hair was windblown, his cheeks ruddy, and he offered her a smile that held more challenge than apology. Gussie thrust her hands into her jacket's pockets so he wouldn't see that she had them balled into fists.

"Are you aware that you're on in ten minutes?"

"Yup."

Yup? "Are you aware that this is not a local show but a national one, broadcast from coast to coast? That Todd Sherman is an important man with a viewing audience in the millions?"

"Yup."

"You don't have time to change clothes or go into makeup or..."

"Are *you* aware that when I left you yesterday at the airport you were sputtering and fuming, and I arrive today and you're still at it?" David shook his head disapprovingly. "You'd better learn to worry less and smile more, A.J. You're a perfect candidate for an ulcer."

That was pretty funny coming from the man who might very well be giving her one. "Your plane landed hours ago. Where have you been?"

"I didn't take the plane. I rented a car and drove up the coast. Beautiful drive. Too bad you couldn't have enjoyed it with me."

Turning, he spotted Todd Sherman coming toward him, wearing a big smile. David had appeared on his show several times and liked the man, liked his upbeat manner. Todd sat in a comfortable chair and chatted with his guests without pressure or embarrassment. He'd been tops in the ratings for years.

"Hey, David, good to see you," Todd shook hands warmly. "Getting any tennis in, or are you still tied to your typewriter?"

"Not lately, but I hope to soon. Todd, have you met my new editor from Lyon Publishing, Augusta Lyon? A.J., meet Todd Sherman."

Todd took her hand in his big one. "Good to meet you. I know your father. Hell of a nice man."

"Thank you, Mr. Sherman." So David knew Todd Sherman. Why hadn't he mentioned that small fact?

"Call me 'Todd.'" He turned as he heard a buzzer go off. "Guess they want us onstage. Come on, David. Time to go make a living."

"Will you be here?" David asked Gussie, noticing she'd gotten herself under control when she'd seen that no one was really upset because he'd arrived at the last minute.

"Of course."

He turned to follow Todd, then remembered something. Withdrawing a package from his back pocket, he held it to her. "I think you should stick to these."

Gussie watched him amble onto the stage. Walking closer to the curtains, she tore the tissue paper from the package. M & M's. She tried not to be pleased. The man was a writer, that's why he was so observant. No big deal. Slipping the package into her pocket, she kept her hand on the packet as she listened to David and Todd chat, like two friends on the back porch.

"You ever been to Madagascar?" Todd asked.

"No, but I've sure been to the library. Armchair research. Not as much fun as traveling to each location in person, but it serves the purpose."

"No one reading your last book would ever guess you hadn't been there in person."

"Then maybe I shouldn't have told you."

The live audience gave them the expected laugh. Leaning against the doorframe, she watched David's mouth form that slow smile. Despite her warnings to herself, she zeroed in on that mouth, remembered the feel and taste of it pressing against hers and fought the knowledge that she wanted to experience that loss of self again. With some effort, she made herself follow their dialogue.

"So tell me, David," Todd went on, "what are your future plans for Beau and Mandy? They going to get together and make it legal one day soon? Or are they going to live happily ever after?"

The audience, fully aware that Todd was in the midst of a turbulent divorce from his third wife, laughed in appreciation.

"Might cut down on some of their fun times," Todd added.

David shifted the angle of his chair ever so slightly and, in doing so, found his gaze drifting across the stage right into Gussie's eyes. "Then again, with some people, it might be when the fun begins."

"Didn't know you had such a sense of humor, David," Todd said.

Her hand tightening on the packet of candy, Gussie held his gaze and wondered if she wouldn't have been better off never having heard the name David Lamb.

"Hey, boss lady," a croaky voice at her elbow whispered. "Hear you been looking for me."

Gussie turned to see Arnie standing a few feet from her, resplendent in a striped double-breasted suit that seemed to accent his lack of height. She really didn't feel like dealing with him right now, but had little choice. "I thought you told me you'd be flying in last night so we could meet early this morning?"

"I did get in last night, but I stayed with friends. A certain friend, that is, if you get my meaning." He grinned, adjusting his tie.

Gussie remembered why she didn't particularly like Arnie Walker, and his bragging about his many conquests was just one reason. "I'm not impressed. Are you here to work or play?"

"No need to worry. Everything's under control. I just came from Sid's place and we're all set to roll tonight at seven." He reached into his pocket and handed her a folded sheet of paper. "Here's an updated list of all the invited guests."

Pushing back her distaste for the man, she took the list and studied it as Arnie turned to watch David and Todd on the stage. The list did seem to be fairly complete. The sooner this party was over and she could get away from Arnie, the better she'd feel. She'd have to be sure their contact tonight would be minimal before she gave in to temptation and told the little weasel exactly what she thought of him.

"That's some boyfriend you got there, boss lady," Arnie said as he faced her again.

She saw red. "David Lamb is *our client*, not *my* boyfriend. And don't you ever call me anything except 'Miss Lyon' from this moment on. Do I make myself clear?"

Obviously jolted, Arnie quickly nodded. "I didn't mean nothing, bo...Miss Lyon, honest. I kid around, you know. Most people, they don't mind."

"I'm one of them who does. Try to remember that."

"Yeah, sure." He dug out a cigar, then thought better of lighting it. "See you there tonight."

She watched him walk away, still angry. Boyfriend, indeed. She didn't have a boyfriend, male companion or significant other in her life. And she didn't want one, either.

Hearing the audience applaud for some moments, she turned and saw Todd shaking David's hand, indicating the end of the taping. Crossing her arms over her chest, she waited for him. She only hoped he would cooperate with the rest of today's schedule. She was in no mood to put up with another feisty individual, genius or not.

California casual was anything but, David thought as he stood on the terrace of Sid Brown's hillside home. The house itself rambled and spread out, conforming to the woodsy terrain, with wings and garages and cabanas attached to the main structure. The patio area was terraced, and overflowing flower beds surrounded clusters of wrought-iron furniture, redwood benches and deep-cushioned lounge chairs. Hanging baskets dotted the trellised overhang, and beyond the patio lay an enormous pool accented by subdued lighting. A sloping lawn disappeared into the thickness of trees that assured privacy for the seventy or so guests who roamed the grounds and sleekly decorated interior. Some digs, he decided, turning to study the cast of characters.

As Arnie had predicted to him in a call apparently meant to assure one and all that he wouldn't embarrass them, everyone was dressed to the nines. Evidently the word had gotten around about David's disregard for what he put on his back. Reluctantly he'd worn the rented tux Arnie had had sent up to his room, but he wasn't happy about it as he ran his finger along the tight collar line. Still, when in Rome...

The women wore anything from lavish gowns to outfits that looked to him like filmy pajamas, many of them laden with jewelry and smelling expensive. The men seemed to be divided into two groups: the writer types, their slightly shaggy, intellectual faces peering out over half glasses and the Hollywood types wearing iridescent dinner jackets and sporting pinkie rings. David had never been comfortable with either group, and tonight was no exception. Where the hell was A.J.? he wondered as he strolled inside.

Moving to the huge bar set up at the far end of a glassed in room, he wondered, also, if they had anything as mundane as beer. With a look of distaste, the white-jacketed bartender found one and poured it into a long-stemmed glass before David could tell him he preferred his beer straight out of a can. Taking the glass, he decided this was not going to be his night.

Sipping, he stood off to the side, trying to avoid people and still keep the doorway in his line of vision. He could cheerfully kick himself for letting A.J. talk him into going on ahead since she had to meet with several other Lyon editors and writers who were there for the party. The meeting must have broken up already, because he'd seen Arnie arrive some minutes ago, smiling around a big cigar, a six-foot blonde on his arm. Interesting man.

He was about to try to locate a phone, when he saw her standing in the large, open foyer, listening intently to an animated woman with a wild hairdo. For a long moment he just stared. She wore a simple dress, dark and probably black, high necked and long sleeved, but the surprise was that the back was bare, dipping low to her slender waist. And her hair was down, softly curled around her face and falling to just brush her shoulders. The sunset rays that drifted in through the open doors haloed her in a rich glow.

She laughed at something the woman said, a short musical sound, then looked up and saw him. Caught unprepared, her eyes warmed at first sight of him, before she assumed her usual guarded look. David hoped he didn't look stupid, standing there staring at her. Quite simply, she took his breath away, a first for him. Later, he'd have to think about that. Depositing his glass on a nearby table, he walked to her as her companion moved away.

"Nice party," he said, his eyes memorizing her face, feature by feature. "Wanna leave?"

She almost smiled. "I just got here."

"I know. I'll give you five minutes to circulate, then meet you at the cab stand on the corner."

So he was bored and unhappy. And gorgeous in a tux. So what? Gussie hated parties like this, too, and had to force herself to attend. But she wasn't about to let him know. She raised a brow. "I thought you were a social being, comfortable in any situation, and I was the uptight, small-town librarian?"

David sent his eyes on a journey of her from top to bottom. "It's possible I was wrong. I apologize. Let me make it up to you by taking you away from all this."

She smiled and took his hand, shaking her head. "We can't just yet. I think that might be considered rude. Come on and I'll introduce you around."

He was keenly aware that that was the first time she'd reached out to touch him willingly. Her hand snugly in his, he decided perhaps he could put on a pleasant face and behave for a short time. Very short. Stepping into the throng, he drew her closer. "Are you sure there are people here I want to meet?"

"Yes, now stop pouting." She spotted a man across the room waving to her. "There's Rod Gorney, one of my sci-fi authors. You might enjoy talking with him."

David doubted it. He wasn't feeling very friendly tonight, for some reason, but he allowed himself to be led over.

The evening dragged. Someone grabbed a wineglass from a tray and stuck it in his hand. He drank, though he didn't particularly want it. He smiled and nodded as A.J. drifted away at someone's insistence. He even made conversation, not only with Gorney but with several others Arnie brought over and a couple of people who simply came up to talk with him about his books. He ate from the sumptuous buffet and smiled some more as he tried to keep track of his editor.

Half a dozen or more of her Lyon authors were present and wanted a word with her. He watched her with this one and that, listening politely, laughing occasionally, seldom even glancing his way. And he was jealous.

There was no getting around the emotion, that's what it was. Not jealous as a lover might be, but jealous that someone else held her interest, captured her attention, was the object of that slow, warming smile. Draining another glass of wine, David set down the glass with irritation. Jealousy in any form wasn't a pleasant thing to experience. He decided to get over it.

Joining a lively group, he listened awhile and soon found himself talking and nodding. When they began to wander off, he found another cluster of people to join. Writers loved to talk almost as much as to write, so there was no lack of conversation, no lulls or boring silences. The problem was, no matter where he was standing or who was talking to him, his eyes roamed the room, keeping A.J. in sight. That was another first for him. An unpleasant first.

Finding a cup of strong, black coffee, he finally gave up his plan and stood off to the side watching A.J., Arnie and a big, handsome football-player type in a huddle by the bar. The coffee went down, hot and scalding, and David scarcely noticed. He was tired of talking with strangers and tired of trying to keep an eye on someone who hardly knew he was in the room. He could argue that it was her job to talk with the people here, but she didn't have to enjoy it so much, nor to ignore him in the process. He was acting like a petulant little boy, and he was tired of that, too.

Coming alongside A.J., David touched her arm and waited until she turned to him. "I'm leaving. You ready?"

Gussie searched his face briefly, decided he meant it. "Yes, I'm ready." She smiled at the big man and nodded to Arnie. "Nice meeting you, Nathan. Good night, Arnie."

David endured the handshakes with a smile. He could afford to be generous now that they were on their way out. It took a good ten minutes to work their way to the door as several people stopped to say their goodbyes. At last, they stood in the lilac-scented air of the circular drive and waited for the valet to bring them David's rental car.

When the Mercedes convertible drew up, he helped her in, tipped the boy and sped away with a juvenile squeal of tires.

A.J. didn't comment as he maneuvered down the canyon road. He was glad. He didn't feel much like talking, either. And he certainly didn't feel like smiling another minute.

They were stepping off the elevator and walking toward her room before Gussie decided he'd simmered down enough to talk rationally. For the life of her, she couldn't imagine what had gotten into David Lamb.

"For an amiable fellow, you certainly seem upset tonight. Is anything the matter?"

He took her key and inserted it. "Amiable. Is that how you think of me?" He swung open the door. When she didn't step inside, he took her arm and propelled her in, then followed.

Gussie snapped on the table lamp in the small sitting room and tossed her purse onto a chair. "It's how I *did* think of you. What happened?" His eyes were dark, his face like thunder. She wasn't afraid, just puzzled.

"May I remind you that this is *my* tour and that you're supposed to be with me?"

Of all the reactions, this was one she hadn't expected. Brushing a lock of hair from her cheek, she faced him. "I've practically been glued to your side for a week now. I should think you'd be glad for a short respite. Besides, may I remind you that I have a job to do and that it includes keeping more than one writer happy?"

He knew he was being unreasonable. What he didn't know was how to stop it. "Not on this trip. Right now, your job is to keep *me* happy."

Her eyes narrowed, but no other part of her moved. "I've done about all I'm going to do in that regard. If you're unhappy with me, I can be replaced in a moment. There's the phone. Call my father."

He moved closer. "Leave your father out of this. This is between you and me. I think it's about time we talked about this thing between us."

She tried to ignore the sudden pounding of her heart. From the corner of her eye, she'd watched him all evening and wondered why he looked like a man ready to explode. Perhaps she had her answer. With effort, she kept her voice steady. "I told you before, there is no *thing* between us."

"Is that a fact?" In one quick step, he was close up against her, one hand on the bare skin of her back, the other moving into the wild thickness of her hair. "Let's test that."

Gussie saw his mouth lowering to hers and knew she should turn her head, or break the embrace. But she stood frozen to the spot, waiting, steeped in confusion, in mounting desire. Then his lips touched hers, and her resistance slipped away with the residue of her anger.

He was right, and she was wrong. This was the third time he'd caught her like this. Three times and out. There *was* something between them, something so new to her realm of experience she had yet to put a name to it. Attraction, desire, addiction—whatever it was, it was frighteningly powerful. Yet she resisted the knowledge.

Fear leading the way, she tried to pull back, to step away. But his hand moved to cup the back of her neck, while his other arm circled to bring her hard up against his chest. Still she struggled, clamping her lips closed, angling her head, fighting to keep from going under. She couldn't, wouldn't let him control her.

Against his mouth, she spoke in a breathy whisper. "Let me go, please."

David dropped his arms, yet his mouth lingered on hers, barely touching, awaiting her reaction. When she didn't move away, he ran his tongue along her lips in a gentle, undemanding caress. His lips brushed across hers, feather soft, almost playful. At last he felt her give a little, open a fraction, her breath sweetly mingling with his. He could feel her denying herself a deeper response, but he gave her time, patiently stroking.

Perhaps it was the unthreatening nature of the kiss that had her slowly softening, Gussie thought as she let her eyelids drift shut. Perhaps it was that he let her lead the way, to experience and savor the kiss, instead of overwhelming her the way he had before. Or perhaps it was because she knew she could break away at any moment, could move at her own pace.

Her hands were suddenly on his chest, moving slowly, inside the open tuxedo jacket, feeling the warmth of his skin through his shirt. She felt him deepen the kiss and went with it, her tongue tangling with his, recognizing the special flavors that were his alone. She reached upward, her hands trailing along his hard neck and up into his hair. And her heated blood was racing, racing.

He could stand it no longer. With a moan, David's hands touched her back, then slid lower to press her to his hardness, wanting her, needing her. She stiffened, and he knew he'd gone too fast, been too anxious. She pressed her palms against his shoulders and pulled back. Instantly he loosened his hold on her.

He fought to get his breath as he saw the sudden fear leave her eyes when she realized he wouldn't push. Never had he been this confused, or received so many mixed signals from a woman. She wanted him, that was obvious, but she would go so far, then pull away as if frightened of the next step. He had to know what demons plagued her.

His hands rested lightly at her waist as he saw her breathing even out. "I'm sorry if I rushed you," he began. "A.J., are you a virgin? Is that why intimacy frightens you?"

She gave a short, bitter laugh and turned from him. "Far from it." Suddenly cold, Gussie wrapped her arms around herself and walked over to look out the window. The lights of Los Angeles blinked in a warm summer sky, yet she felt a chill.

David walked over to join her, searching for the right words. "Will you tell me what it is that stops you when I know you feel something?" She was silent so long that he thought she wasn't going to answer, but finally she turned. He was shocked to see how haunted her eyes looked.

"I can't deny that I feel something, David. But I can't give in to these feelings, and I can't go into all the reasons why. I never meant to lead you on, but suddenly, you touch me, and we're out of control. I can't have that. I can't go through all that again."

He saw the sudden moisture in her eyes and knew she was close to tears. "You must know that it's not just physical, that I care about you." There, he'd said it, put his feelings into words and knew he'd spoken the truth. "This kind of slipped up on me, too. I wasn't looking. It just happened."

She shook her head. "Oh, David, you've picked the wrong woman to care about. Go back to the party and find someone else. I don't want this. I'm not ready."

The party? What a laugh! "I think I'll wait you out."

"That may take a while."

"I can be patient." Gently he touched her cheek, then cupped her chin. "I'll give you time and lots of room. I just won't give you distance. Deal?"

She could promise him nothing. He would discover that in time. Lust she could have fought against, been strong and firm. But caring was another story. She didn't have much experience with caring. And could she even believe his declaration? Too tired to fight him, she nodded, hoping she wouldn't hurt him.

David hugged her to his side as he walked them to the door. "We have a little break coming, a couple of days before we're due in San Francisco, and we can both use the time." He turned to face her. "I want you to cancel the plane reservations, to drive with me up the coast. On the way, I'll show you my house on the sea. No sudden moves, I promise."

She searched his eyes and saw only gentleness and sincerity. Pushing back the wariness that was such a part of her, she agreed. With a light kiss on her forehead, he left, closing the door behind him.

Gussie went back to stare out the window. Holding out her hand, she saw it still trembled. It was worse than she'd thought, worse than she'd imagined. Wanting was one thing. For years, she'd denied herself things she'd wanted and had gotten fairly good at it. But caring was another. She hadn't allowed herself to care for a man in ten years. And now there was David.

How was she going to get past David?

Tilting her head back against the headrest, Gussie let the ocean breezes caress her face. She turned to see David smiling at her and felt a rush of pleasure. They'd set out at daybreak and now the powerful little car was chewing up the miles along the coastal highway.

Carefree. She felt carefree, a brand new feeling. Wouldn't Molly, who fluttered over her like a big sister, be surprised to hear her say it?

She'd called Molly this morning. Sitting packed and waiting for David, Gussie had felt a little nervous as she'd explained to her assistant that she'd had a change of plans. Instead of just holing up in a hotel room and catching up on rest and paperwork during this short break on their tour, she and David were driving to his house on the sea. The sudden silence at the other end of the line had spoken volumes. Molly was not one to miss that this was decidedly unlike Gussie.

"Then you're getting along well?" Molly asked.

"It's not what you think." Why did she feel defensive? Perhaps because Molly knew her history, knew how shattered she'd been the last time.

"Oh. And what am I thinking?"

"With your romantic nature, I know *exactly* what you're thinking." Gussie had laughed, wondering if that alone wasn't an enormous giveaway. Though apprehensive, she couldn't deny that she was also a little excited. Embarrassed at feeling that way at her age, she tried to cover it up. "We have some things to go over. You know, strategy for the rest of the tour, and so on. And it's nice and quiet at his house."

"Mmm-hmmm. Listen, Gussie, you don't have to explain to me. I'm all for nice, quiet times." She'd paused then, sounding as if she weren't certain she should say more. "Just be careful, will you? David Lamb seems kind of... experienced, you know?"

That made her bristle. "Oh, for heaven's sake, Molly. I'm not a child."

"Children aren't the only people who can get hurt. Shall I let Jared know about this change of plans?"

"I see no reason to."

"Right. Then you'll call me when you get to San Francisco?"

"Yes."

"All right. Have fun, Gussie."

She'd rung off then, feeling as though she were still in high school, calling home for permission to stay over. Then she'd heard David's knock on her door and she'd scrambled up, anxious to get underway.

From behind her sunglasses, she studied David's strong, capable hands on the wheel, his tan profile, his unruly hair whipping about. How had he known this was exactly what she'd needed, the fascination of controlled speed, the exhilaration of the mighty little sports car, the freedom of the open road? His thoughtfulness was something she could easily get used to.

"See that road cutting up that hillside?" David asked, interrupting her thoughts.

Gussie squinted up at the winding path disappearing into thick trees. "Yes. Looks pretty isolated."

"That's the road that leads to a house Jerry Slade and I rented right after college. It's way up there, just a shack, really, owned by some widow who's probably not made a repair on it since we moved out ten or eleven years ago. Valuable property, but a buyer would be better off tearing down the house and starting over. I always thought I'd like to buy it one day and do just that. Breathtaking view and even has beach access, though the stairs are rickety and pretty steep."

She looked at him. "Why? Does the house hold good memories?"

He shrugged. "Some. We were young, without much money, both trying to write the great American novel. On the side, so we could eat, I wrote magazine articles and whodunnit pulps and Jerry pumped out detective stories."

"And he's still writing them?"

"Yeah, but he's getting closer. His last novel's a winner, I'd bet. Think you might want to read it?"

"Is that why you asked me along to meet him the other night?"

The engine missed a beat as David sent her a frosty glance. "I don't use people, Gussie."

Whatever had made her ask? This casual, trusting camaraderie between a man and a woman was new to her. So was voluntary touching, but she placed her hand on his arm nonetheless. "I'm sorry. I wasn't thinking." She saw his hard jaw relax. "You helped him with the book, didn't you?"

"Not really. I read it, offered a few suggestions. It's his work, all the way."

"I'm sorry I missed meeting him. I'd be glad to read the book."

She sounded sincere. He decided to accept that at face value. The trouble was, she wasn't used to trusting. Maybe in time, she would learn. "Good. I've got a copy at the house."

"How long did you and Jerry live up there?"

"Only a year. Kelly had gone to college with us, and right from the start, Jerry was crazy about her. But after graduation, he didn't think he should ask her to marry him when he could barely support himself. After about a year apart, while she worked in L.A. and he lived up there trying to write, Kelly took matters into her own hands. She came after him, told him she *chose* to be with him, with or without money. So he gave in and married her. Now they're expecting their third child."

"Still, they must have had some rough times in the beginning."

David shot into the passing lane around a tour bus, then eased back over to the right. "Sure did. I don't suppose you can easily relate, with your background."

She leaned back, shifting her eyes to the sky. "People with money have rough times, too, David. You'd be surprised."

"I didn't mean that you've always had smooth sailing. No one does."

"No, they don't. Tell me about your childhood."

He liked her like this, interested, relaxed. Even her clothes were casual, a cotton blouse, linen slacks and sandals, her long hair caught with a gold clip at her nape. And she wanted to know more about him. It was a start.

"Uneventful about sums it up, but happy. Typical small-town family in the Midwest. My dad runs the local hardware store, coaches Little League baseball and plants a garden every summer. My mom keeps house, goes to Red Cross meetings every Wednesday night and makes the best blueberry pie in the county. Every year, they take a vacation in their Winnebago." He smiled over at her. "Exciting life, eh?"

"Don't knock it, David. It sounds like a good life, a comfortable life. Maybe excitement's the wrong goal."

"What's the right goal, A.J.?"

"Happiness, contentment and..." She couldn't say the word that came to mind, couldn't chance that he'd misinterpret it. "And mutual respect."

His eyes still on the road, he reached over for her hand. She couldn't know how conditioned he was as a writer to read between the lines. He'd promised her time, but not without ever touching her. He laced his fingers through hers, resting their twined hands on his thigh.

Turning to gaze off to the side, she blinked rapidly. He'd seen through her, Gussie realized. She couldn't remember a time when someone had been able to read her so well. Or had cared enough to try.

Chapter Six

The house was tucked into a rocky hillside, tan stucco with a cedar-shake roof, angled in such a way that you could easily miss it from the winding road that led in from the highway. Vegetation grew in wild disarray in the front, but was sparse in the rear so as not to detract from the magnificence of the sea.

Gussie stood on the edge of the sloping green lawn where it disappeared into the white sand leading to the ocean. She drew in a deep, salty breath. Yes, *magnificent* was the word. She looked up at David standing beside her. "How do you ever get anything done with this out here? It's mesmerizing."

"It is, isn't it?" It was foolish to be pleased because she found his view fascinating. Who wouldn't? Yet it pleased him nonetheless. He strolled to a huge old palm, its dark green fronds stretching into the late-afternoon sky, and braced a hand on its rough bark.

"I just love it here. I start off my day with a run down the beach, then work for four or five hours. Then I take a swim, have some lunch and go back to work. Evenings I often stroll along out there, working through my plot problems." He gazed far up the irregular shoreline. "There's not another house for half a dozen miles on either side. I'm a bit of a nut about privacy when it comes to my home."

"So am I." Gussie gazed longingly at the beach, wishing she could slip off her sandals and feel the warm sand oozing between her toes. Then she'd roll up her pant legs and run along the shoreline, feeling the foamy water wash over her feet. Wouldn't David think her a little odd if she did just that, the sophisticated New York editor with her prim clothes and proper ways? She sighed, wishing she could shed that image for just a few days. But David already had glimpsed more than she'd meant him to see. If she dropped her guard more, all her protective walls would come tumbling down, leaving her vulnerable, defenseless.

David turned to face her. "Do you like the sea?"

"Yes. Years ago, my folks used to have a cottage in Maine. It was often too cold for swimming, but there was this large rock formation down the beach. I used to go sit on it for hours, just watching the waves, the gulls diving for breakfast and small fishing boats coming in with their early-morning catch. A good place to sit and daydream." She glanced up at him, embarrassed at her fanciful meanderings. "I was very young," she added, trying to explain away her dreamer tendencies.

"Do you still go there?"

"No. After Aaron died, they sold the cottage."

A lot had changed after Aaron died, it would seem. Her face held such a wistful look as she stood staring out to sea. What was she seeing or remembering? David wondered.

Maybe she needed a little privacy. "Say, why don't you take a swim while I get dinner going?"

"Mmm, that sounds great. But I didn't pack a suit."

"I have one in the house, which would probably fit you."

She sent him a knowing look as they walked back. "And don't ask who left it here?"

He grinned down at her. "That's right."

Well, why not? The lure of the ocean was too much for Gussie to resist. Trying not to appear too eager, she followed him into the guest room, where he'd already placed her bag. He took out a plain black one-piece suit from a dresser drawer and held it out to her.

"This looks about right. As soon as I've got things organized, I'll join you."

"I feel guilty, not helping with dinner."

"Don't. You've been seeing to my needs for a week, now it's my turn."

Gussie bent to open her bag. "I could get used to this spoiling. Let's have a trade-off. I'm not much of a cook, but I'll make breakfast in the morning."

"It's a deal." He strolled out, leaving her alone.

Heaving a sigh, Gussie looked around the large, comfortable room with its queen-size bed covered with a beautiful, delicate quilt. Fingering it, she guessed his mother had probably made it. The sweet scent of oleander drifted in through the high, open window. From a distance, she could hear the ocean waves moving in their never-ending rhythm.

A very peaceful place, she thought as she unbuttoned her blouse. A place, like her ranch in Cold Spring, where a person could renew the spirit. She had so little time to spend up there. What must it be like to live and work in the place you loved most? Wonderful. David was lucky, but then he'd also worked hard to earn that privilege.

Passing through the kitchen on her way out back, she held a large towel draped around her neck, suddenly shy. But David's glance toward her as he sliced tomatoes was casual, almost brotherly, so she relaxed. "Don't be long," she said, opening the door.

"Okay." David raised his eyes to the window and watched her gingerly walk across the sand. She dropped the towel and kept going toward the rolling waves. He stopped slicing as he admired her long legs, the way the suit clung to her. She raised her arms for a long minute, tipping her face up to the sun, shaking her hair and letting it fall against her shoulders.

He moved to the side, still keeping her in view. He knew she felt alone out there and probably wouldn't want to be observed, but the sight of her relaxing by inches, opening a little more each hour today, drew him like a magnet. Suddenly she began to run, splashing into the frothy waves. She bowed her head, stretched forward her arms and dived in. In moments, he saw her head bob up as she moved out aways with long, sure strokes.

Finishing the tomatoes, he set them aside and began to wash the potatoes for baking. Living in New York, she probably rarely visited the sea anymore. Yet she seemed to love it. She'd put together this life for herself, working and living in Manhattan, with plenty of money to travel, yet she almost seemed to be trapped within a radius of one square mile. He couldn't help wondering if Aaron's death and her father's needs had put her there and now she couldn't find a way out without hurting her parents, or if she truly loved the life she was leading.

He put the potatoes in the oven and went back to the window. She'd come out of the water and was bending to examine something in the sand, probably a seashell. The beach was filled with them. Rising, she pulled back and threw her find into the water, then ran her hands through her wet hair. She shot a quick glance toward the house, then turned to jog down the beach.

David wondered how many of the people in her life had seen her like this. Had Jared or her mother? Who were her close friends? Had there been one special man in her life, only one?

He marinated the steaks automatically, his thoughts wandering. *Far from it,* she'd answered when he'd asked her if she was a virgin. Had she been different then, when she'd known that man, open and trusting? Had he hurt her, been the one to cause her lingering distrust? *I can't go through all that again,* she'd said. Setting the meat aside, he wondered if she'd ever bring herself to tell him of her obviously painful past. Time. It would take time.

Quickly he set the table, then changed into his suit so he could join her. Maybe tonight, in this peaceful place, with good food and a little wine, she'd open up to him. Go slowly, he warned himself. Beneath that cool exterior, he'd discovered that Gussie Lyon was far more fragile than he'd first imagined.

"I'm stuffed," Gussie said, leaning back in her chair. "David, that was delicious."

She'd finished her dinner, the first time he'd seen her do that all week. She was also on her second glass of wine. And he hadn't seen her chewing those chalky pills all day. He set down his own empty glass and smiled at her. "There's something about the sea air that enhances the appetite, don't you think?"

"I don't know if it's your cooking or the sea air, but if I stay much longer, I'll soon need a whole new wardrobe."

"Stay and I'll buy you one."

He couldn't know how tempting his offer was. Gussie couldn't remember a day she'd enjoyed as much, not in a very long while.

They'd played in the water like two children, splashing, swimming together, gathering shells. David had walked with her far down the beach, where bright green moss grew thick on black rocks and gnarled, bleached driftwood lay piled artistically by nature's hand. Warm from the sun, they'd run back into the sea to cool off, then strolled back, talking about everything and nothing.

Fun. David Lamb was fun. Not uproarious, thigh-slapping, joke-telling fun. Time with him was quiet pleasure, gentle frolicking, playful merriment. They'd shared a sense of companionship she'd not known with a male before. With the possible exception of Aaron before he'd somehow changed.

She'd felt shy at first, but even in the skimpy bathing suit, she was soon at ease. That, too, surprised her.

Through the open window, she could hear a gentle rainfall, adding a cozy touch to the atmosphere. She smiled at her host. "You're very fortunate to live and work in a place like this."

"It wasn't luck. I looked long and hard to find this house, then changed much about it until it was just the way I wanted it. I hope to live here a long time, maybe share it with someone special, raise children one day."

He was moving too fast for her again. "What if that someone special wanted some input on the kind of house she wanted to live in and where?"

David considered that for a brief moment. "Then we'd talk about it."

They'd talk about it. But David Lamb didn't seem like a man who compromised easily. Like Jared. Gussie rose, taking their plates to the sink, her eyes again drawn to the window. The summer air was so sweet, with not a trace of bus fumes or pollution. The only sound came from the sea and an occasional bird or two squabbling in the trees. She could picture herself living in a place like this, near the sea she loved so much. But not with a man who'd take away her choices. "Do you ever find it lonely here?"

Walking to her side, David shrugged. "Occasionally. I think loneliness is a state of mind. And I have a confession to make. Last night at Sid Brown's party I was lonelier than I've ever been here. I didn't see anyone I wanted to talk with, until you walked in." He saw slight color rise in her face, but she didn't lower her gaze. "Does it embarrass you to hear that?"

"You flatter me. I'm not that interesting."

"You are to me. And it's not flattery. What would be my motive in flattering you?" He saw the blush deepen and guessed her train of thought. "You think I want to get you into my bed?"

"Don't you?"

He gave her a slow smile. "Sure I do. But that's not all of it, as I told you last night. Besides, do you think I need to resort to flattery to get a woman into my bed?"

Gussie turned away, not comfortable with the way the conversation was going. "No, I don't suppose you do."

David saw her discomfort, saw the wary-rabbit look return. Time to back off, to be content with the little headway he'd made. "Tell me, what would you like to do now? Something you don't get a chance to do back home? Is there anything?"

She glanced out the window, then back at him. "Don't laugh, but I'd like to go walking on the beach in the rain. I never do that."

It was one of his favorite things to do. Opening the back door, he held out his hand.

* * *

Darkness had settled in by the time they reached the end of the weathered dock that stretched out over the splashing waves. The sky was filled with gray clouds, yet it was barely drizzling now, the rain forming shallow puddles on the old boards beneath their bare feet. They'd walked mostly in silence, each lost in their own thoughts; yet David still held on to her hand as they paused to look up.

"On clear nights out here, it seems like there are a million stars in the sky. Did you ever wish on a star?"

"Not in years."

"Then it's definitely time. Let's pretend they're up there. Close your eyes and make a wish." He watched as she scanned the heavens, then closed her eyes, her fingers tightening in his. In a moment, she looked at him.

"Okay. Your turn"

David shook his head as he headed them back to the house. "I'm fortunate, I guess. Most of my wishes have already come true." With the exception of a brand-new wish, one he'd had trouble putting into words. What exactly did he wish would happen with A.J.? He wasn't sure.

"Perhaps you were born under a lucky star."

He felt her shiver, and realized that the light rain had dampened her blouse. Without thinking, he put his arm around her shoulders and drew her near, thinking to share his body heat. To his surprise, she didn't pull away. "I'm not sure I believe in luck. We make our own luck."

He felt so solid, so safe. And he smelled so good, like a summer evening. She knew she was breaking her own rules about touching. But just for a little while, she'd indulge herself. "Sometimes. And sometimes circumstances have us doing things we might not have chosen, but we adjust and make a life."

What a telling remark. "Adjusting to circumstances is fine, on a temporary basis. But shouldn't a person have a goal of getting out from under, of moving on and living his life the way he really wanted to before he had to rearrange his priorities?"

He was doing it again, looking into her head. Just talking with David was dangerous. "Some are good at that, some aren't. Don't you feel that hurting and disappointing people is too high a price to pay for having your own way?"

"Maybe we don't give other people enough credit. They, too, can adjust and learn to live with our choices."

"Perhaps." It was time to change the subject. He was getting too close. They were at the big tree now as she turned for another long look at the sea. "It's so peaceful here."

She was closing the door again, but he didn't mind. He'd just keep opening it until she let him swing it wide. Following her gaze, he nodded. "Yes, I'm very content here."

"Be careful. Contentment makes you drop your guard."

"Is that such a cardinal sin?"

Gussie ducked around and headed for the house. "It is if you want to stay in control of your life."

Inside, David handed her a towel and took one himself. Rubbing his hair dry, he followed her down the hallway. "A person can only exercise so much control, A.J. If you're all alone, it's easier. But when you're not, sooner or later something happens and you lose it, despite your best intentions and no matter how hard you try to prevent it. I've seen it happen time and again, like with my friends, the Slades."

She draped the towel around her neck as she stopped in front of the guest room door and looked up at him with a frown. "What happens?"

"You fall in love, and everything changes."

"I don't intend to ever let that happen." She opened the bedroom door. "See you in the morning."

David listened to the firm closing of her door. After a moment, he strolled toward his room, whistling. He wondered if Miss Lyon knew what particular road was paved with good intentions.

It was midweek before David had a chance to stretch out and catch his breath. San Francisco had given them a cool, wet reception, few fans showing up to have books signed in an all-day downpour. Though his house was situated closer to San Mateo than Frisco, he considered himself a bay area person and had been disappointed at the turnout. Who was it who'd once said that you're often a stranger in your own town? he'd asked himself.

He'd finished two afternoon radio spots, and they'd flown on to Denver, where they'd all but given him the key to the city. The turnout and the enthusiasm had been fantastic, buoying their spirits. Arnie had wired that they'd sold out his latest release at every bookstore within the city limits. Happy but exhausted, he and A.J. had climbed aboard a jet this morning bound for Sioux City, Iowa.

Since this stop on the trip had been a last-minute addition, first class had been sold out. David stretched his long legs almost into the aisle of the cramped tourist section seat as he adjusted a sleeping A.J. more comfortably against his shoulder. Even strong coffee hadn't been able to keep her awake after the hectic schedule of the past three days. As he felt her shift restlessly, unaware she was snuggling into him, he was glad she was catching a few winks now. She was in for a few surprises today.

He'd talked with Brian on the phone last night, and though he wouldn't say what was planned, his old friend had advised him to brace himself for a day of homecoming. Brian Ewing and David had grown up in Lakeville, a small town just northwest of Sioux City that went from a winter population of about seven hundred to a touristy twelve hundred in the summer. The two men had played together as children, then played on the high-school basketball team and shared their first beer behind David's father's garage. It was Brian's elbow that had accidentally broken David's nose during a practice game the year they'd been juniors.

Though David had gone on to college in California and never moved back to Iowa to live, he and Brian had stayed in touch. Two years ago, Brian's father had turned over the family chain of supermarkets, numbering six at the time, to his only son who'd worked with him since he'd been sixteen. When Brian had read about David's cross-country tour, he'd written to ask him to stop. David hadn't been able to refuse his old friend, especially since Brian had featured his books from the beginning on a special rack in his book department. And after Brian was through with them, he had a surprise of his own for A.J.

The announcement that they were preparing for landing woke Gussie with a start. Finding herself all but sprawled in David's lap startled her even more. Straightening, she rolled her cramped shoulders. "Why didn't you shove me back into my own seat? I've obviously been crushing you."

David fastened his seat belt. "You can crush me anytime you want."

"Mmm." Gussie glanced out the window at the city spread out like a topography map. Iowa was still very much a farming state. "Are you going to let me in on what's happening today?"

"I would if I knew. I told you that my friend, Brian Ewing, has everything taken care of, or so he says. That's all I know."

"I'd feel better if I'd been able to at least speak to someone at the hotel or at a bookstore."

The day was out of her control, so naturally she was nervous. "Relax and just enjoy today, will you?"

"What's the name of the hotel where we'll be staying? I'm going to have to phone the office."

Time to be a little evasive. "It's out a ways. I'll update you on all that later." He leaned across her toward the window. "This town never changes."

"Do you find that boring?"

"No, I find it comforting. Everyone needs some constants in their lives, don't you think?"

Did she have any? Gussie asked herself. Her work the last few years, she supposed. Before that, not much. Jared was autocratic and unpredictable, and her mother had echoed her husband's every thought for as long as Gussie could remember. There was some continuity in that, but in an exasperating way.

Wanting some camouflage, Gussie put on her glasses.

"Do you really need those things?" David asked. "To see, I mean. Or are you hiding behind them?"

She gave him a long look, then turned to stare out the window. He was getting too close, frighteningly so.

Instead of answering him, Gussie watched the landing, wishing she knew what was on the agenda for the day. She hated not knowing, not being able to have a hand in what was going on. She felt the plane come to a stop and heard the anxious passengers scurry into the aisles, opening overhead bins to retrieve their belongings. She'd never been to Iowa. This should be enlightening.

David took her arm at the top of the ramp and paused, looking around. But Gussie spotted them first. "Look over there. A band!" Even as she spoke, the small cluster of musicians began playing. Behind a chain-link fence, stretched along the front of a goodly crowd, was a large blue-and-gold banner held by the smiling welcomers. In big letters, it read Welcome Home, David Lamb. She turned to see David beside her, looking a shade embarrassed.

He found a smile and aimed it at the group. His eyes swept past them to where the gate was standing open. Grinning and waving, Brian Ewing stood alongside a gleaming silver Bentley. Perhaps his friend had overdone things a bit, David thought as he started down the ramp steps, holding on to A.J.'s arm.

"You have to admit, though it's at least ten years old, this Bentley rides like a dream." David ran his fingers along the teakwood trim of the dash, then returned his hand to the steering wheel. "I suppose you're used to these old luxury cars, but this is a new one on me."

Alongside him, Gussie leaned back in the plush gray upholstery. "I've never been in a Bentley before, either. My father drives a Mercedes much like the one you rented, and my mother's got a very sedate Lincoln Town Car that she seldom uses. Living in Manhattan, I don't even own a car. So much for your thoughts about our decadent life-style."

"I feel a little decadent myself in this car," David said. "I probably should have refused Brian's offer to borrow it, but I couldn't resist. The whole day's been so unreal I thought we might as well finish it with a bang."

Unreal was the word, Gussie thought as she watched the flat landscape whiz by. From that nearly frantic welcome to the parade of cars that snaked through the main shopping district to the enthusiastic welcome at the hotel, where David was the star attraction at the luncheon, it had had a dreamlike quality. Old friends and former classmates had come forward to meet and greet him, shyly at first, then more confidently as they realized he was happy to see them. A local television station had captured it all on film, there'd been radio spots and a spirited autographing session that Gussie had thought would never end.

Throughout it all, the hometown boy had been a crowd pleaser, even touring two of Brian's supermarkets, the one he'd worked in as a bag boy in his teens and the one more recently opened. He'd kept her by his side everywhere, introducing her to so many people she'd finally given up trying to keep them all straight, his hand always on her elbow or at her back or nestled in hers. It had been an experience like no other.

Instead of feeling worn out by it all, Gussie felt warmed by what she'd witnessed. David Lamb had left Iowa at eighteen, sixteen years ago, visiting only occasionally, yet he hadn't been forgotten. It took a special kind of person to generate such warmth after such a long absence. The day had again subtly altered how she viewed him, her perception of the kind of man he was. Be careful, she warned herself. That line of thinking could only lead to problems.

"Are you too warm? I could turn on the air-conditioning."

"No, I love the country air. Let's leave the windows open." She watched him fiddle with the radio dials. "All right, are you going to tell me where we're headed? I think I've had all the surprises I can handle for one day."

A twangy country tune hit the airwaves. He turned it down low and glanced at her profile. She had her hair up again, her slim frame wrapped in a pale linen suit. He wanted her out of that getup, and into something comfortable and casual as soon as possible. "Okay, we're on our way to my parents' home." He saw her mouth drop open as she turned to him.

"Oh, David, I don't know. You should have left me at a hotel while you visit with them." She'd wondered why they hadn't put in an appearance all day, but she'd assumed they were probably off on one of their trips in the Winnebago David had mentioned. But this . . .

"I want you to meet them. Aren't you the kind of girl a fella can take home to meet the folks?"

There was a teasing edge to his voice, but she wasn't smiling. Gussie could only imagine that she'd be most uncomfortable, especially if David decided to act up. She cleared her throat, groping for the words that might change his mind. "Please, just drop me off at a hotel or motel nearby. There must be something on the highway. I'll only be in the way. I can wait for you, catch up on some calls and some paperwork and—"

"What are you afraid of, Gussie?"

He so rarely called her anything but A.J. that she was taken aback by that, as well as facing the question in his eyes. "I'm *not* afraid. It's just that I—"

"Good."

"David, I really don't think . . ."

"You really *do* think, way too much." Easing toward the right, he headed for the exit ramp. "We're almost there. Relax. You'll be fine." He stopped at the top of the hill, waiting for traffic. "Do you like blueberry pie? I'll bet my mom's got one all ready."

"I couldn't possibly eat another piece, Mrs. Lamb," Gussie said. "But it's absolutely the best blueberry pie I've ever tasted."

"Thank you, dear. And please call me 'Clara.'"

Gussie smiled at the slender woman who'd just served them an enormous dinner. They'd arrived at the white, two-story house with the green shutters and found David's mother cooking a pot roast and his father fixing her sewing machine. The homey scene and the big, country house had an Ozzie-and-Harriet flavor to it that had charmed her immediately.

And so had his parents. His mother, so different from David. Small and dark, only her blue eyes reminded her of him. His father, however, was how she imagined David would look in another twenty-five years—still tall, trim, his heavy blond hair whitening at his temples and a ready smile on his face.

Clara Lamb turned to her son. "A small second piece, David?"

"You twisted my arm, Mom." He glanced toward his father. "I see you sold the vacant lot next door. Who bought it?"

"Don't think you know them. Family by the name of Wolf." Robert Lamb chuckled. "Can't help but comment on it. The Wolfs are moving next door to the Lambs. And here we've got a Lyon at the table. That's a good one."

The comparison between lions and lambs had not escaped David, either. He cut into his pie, his eyes on Gussie. "Pretty hard for this Lamb to survive with a Lyon tracking him."

Gussie set down her coffee cup. "You manage quite well, I think."

Watching the two of them thoughtfully, his father fingered his pipe. "Don't tell me, Gussie, that my son's really a wolf in sheep's clothing?"

"Enough with your little name jokes, Robert," Clara chimed in, saving Gussie from an answer. "You know, I'm miffed at Brian for not letting us know what he'd put together for you, David. I'd love to have seen all those folks honoring you. And I'll bet Norma Jean will be put out when she finds they made a fuss over you without even calling her."

Setting down his fork, David shook his head. His mother had never accepted that there'd never been anything but friendship between him and her best friend's daughter. "I seriously doubt that, Mom. Besides, they had cameras everywhere, so maybe we'll be on the evening news." Finishing, he shoved back from the table. "Let me help you with these dishes, and then I want to take Gussie for a walk and show her around."

His mother patted his arm. "No, no. Dad and I'll take care of cleaning up. You two run along and enjoy yourselves."

Bending to place a gentle kiss on her forehead, David squeezed his mother's shoulders. "Thanks, Mom."

"Your dinner was wonderful," Gussie said as she rose. "Thank you so much."

"We enjoyed having you, dear."

Following David through the living room, she stopped at the stairs leading up to the bedrooms. "Do you mind if I change first? This isn't exactly what you wear for a walk in the country."

"I'd be thrilled if you would," he said, sliding his hand about her waist and leading her up.

Twilight in Small Town, USA, Gussie thought as they ambled down a dirt road bordered by a recently painted white-picket fence. Beyond the fence were hundreds of rows of corn, and in the distance was a barn painted bright red. On the other side of the road was a grassy area dotted with grazing cows as far as the eye could see. From somewhere, she heard a rooster crow. David had taken her hand as they walked, and now he swung her arm.

He strolled her past his old high school, the post office and a corner movie theater where he'd taken his first date. Along the way, he told her little vignettes about his old neighbors. As he headed down the path leading to the pond, he turned to her.

"Well, what do you think?" David asked. "Do you want to turn in your city-slicker clothes for some farmer duds?"

"I don't think it's for me, but that's not to say it's without appeal. There's a simplicity here, a tranquillity." She caught him watching her. "You seem to enjoy the country. Why did you leave?"

"There's no ocean in Iowa." He moved her to the side as a pickup truck rumbled past them. "That wasn't the only reason, I suppose. They say you can write anywhere, but I think you can write *better* if you're in a place where you're happy."

"Weren't you happy here?"

"Sure, during my youth." He laced his fingers with hers, walking closer alongside her. "My parents are great, especially for a visit. But they're smothering. I had a sister who died of pneumonia when I was four. After that, they really became focused on me. I love them a lot, but if I lived here, my mom would be bringing me chicken soup weekly and my dad would want me to go fishing with him on weekends. It's not the life I want anymore. Do you understand?"

She thought about the conversation they'd shared on his beach about other people adjusting to your choices. "Yes. Still, I envy your childhood." They left the road and walked across a grassy hill toward a pond just over the next hill. "It's lovely here, uncomplicated. And you had both parents at home, caring for you, being there." She tossed him a teasing look. "And let's not forget Norma Jean."

"Jealous, Gussie?" he asked.

"'Fess up. Was she your first love?"

He shook his head. "Norma Jean's just a girl I once knew when I was young and carefree. Don't you have someone like that in your past, someone your folks were always throwing you together with?''

She kept her voice even. ''No, I don't. My father wasn't around much in my growing-up years, and my mother was always too involved with him to notice my social development.'' Not an easy admission. Gussie wondered why she'd made it.

''I guess you can't blame your father for being away so much when you were young. He was trying to build a business.'' Yet he knew she did, as any child would.

''*Blame* isn't the word. Resent maybe. Too much time alone is bad for children.''

They arrived at the pond, rimmed with tall oak trees on the far side. She gazed out to its blue depths. ''Oh, look. Two swans. Aren't they wonderful?'' Gussie moved closer to the edge. ''They're so regal, so independent.''

He might have known that's why she thought they were great. ''Yes, they are. I understand that swans are very loyal, very faithful and often choose mates for life.''

''Sounds like they're smarter than humans.'' She looked around and breathed in deeply. ''It's lovely here. Thanks for showing it to me.''

''I used to come here a lot when I was a kid. I'd feed the swans and plot how I'd one day write a best-seller and the literary world would fall at my feet.'' He laughed at himself. ''Everybody needs a place where they can be alone, to think things through.''

''Yes. I have this ranch in Cold Springs, New York, a small town about a two-hour drive north of Manhattan. I bought this old cottage on several acres and renovated it. That's where I keep my horse, Bridget. I hired a retired farmer to take care of her when I'm not there, which is most of the time. That's where I head when I need to get away.''

''Have your folks been there?''

She sighed. "Jared would think it's a silly waste of money, and my mother wouldn't appreciate anything rural. She's very citified."

Dropping onto the grass, David pulled her down to join him. "Where was your mother all those years your father traveled?"

"With him, mostly. Then, when Aaron hit his teens, my father began taking him along and my mother was left at home. If she resented that, she never let on."

"Is that where you developed this marvelous ability to hide your feelings?" He said it gently, but the question held a punch.

Hugging her knees, she turned to look at him. The same moon that had been barely visible beneath the rain clouds several nights ago in California now shone down on them brightly, playing across his strong features. She twined her hands tightly together to keep from reaching to touch his face. If only he knew how many feelings churned inside her, wanting to break free, most centering around him. But it was so much safer to keep them to herself.

"There was one someone I used to discuss my feelings with very freely," she confessed.

Could it be that they were finally getting somewhere? David kept his face carefully blank. "And who was that?"

"I called him 'Mr. Owl,' and I have no idea where I got the name. He was an imaginary friend I made up, my constant companion from the time I was quite young, four or five, until much later. He had brown tufts of hair, as I recall, horn-rimmed glasses and wise answers to all my questions. Aaron used to make fun of me about Mr. Owl. My father grew angry and told me to stop talking to myself, and my mother ignored my lengthy conversations with a playmate she couldn't see." She laughed at the memory. "I must have been a very odd child."

David leaned back on his elbows, seeing less humor than sadness. "And what tales did you confide in Mr. Owl?"

Gussie picked up a blade of grass and fingered it. "Anything and everything. He didn't criticize, was never disappointed in me and seldom left my side. I didn't need the others as long as I had Mr. Owl." She lay back alongside him, searching his eyes. "Is your writer's mind busily analyzing my youthful weirdness?"

"How long did you keep Mr. Owl as a companion?"

She sighed. "Longer than most kids who invent imaginary pals, I would imagine."

"And then you gave him up, having learned not to need anyone, not even Mr. Owl."

Gussie thought of that long year of rebellion when she'd been eighteen, years after she'd stopped believing in Mr. Owl. She'd desperately needed someone, but her father had been too angry, her brother too self-involved and generally unavailable, and her mother had been too busy trying to pass them all off as a normal family. There hadn't been anyone, so she'd pretended that it didn't matter. "I thought I had learned that, but I was still playacting, as I had as a child." Only she'd broken some grown-up rules and had had to pay the price.

David leaned toward her, looking down on her face, so pale in the moonlight, her dark hair spread out on the fragrant grass. Her eyes were troubled, yet shuttered, closing him off again. There was a core of fragility about her beneath the strength, an innocence despite the experiences that had shaped her past. Or maybe because of them. He raised his hand to frame her face, wishing he knew the words that would allow her to trust him.

His head was silhouetted by the light of the moon, his face in gentle shadow. Gussie had never seen such tenderness, such concern, as he ran trembling fingertips along her cheek, under her jawline, then up on the other side to her temple. She'd never been touched like this, of that she was certain. If she had, she'd have remembered. His hands were so gentle on her face, learning her as if by Braille.

He traced her eyebrows, then trailed one thumb across her suddenly parted lips. She felt his warm breath fan her cheeks and knew she should stop him now, if she were going to. But oh, how she wanted it to go on, this lazy exploration, this slow assault on her senses, this gentle foray into the world of sensation.

Never had she been romanced, courted, coaxed along as David seemed determined to do. Her senses were suddenly, achingly alive, making her aware of every small thing. The summer grass still warm from the day, bristly against her back. The evening breeze rustling the leaves of the tree overhead. The fragrance of wildflowers drifting from some nearby field. The spotty moonlight haloing David's head as he bent to her. The wild thumping of her heart, pounding in anticipation, in need, in fear.

She hovered somewhere between dread and desire, and still he just barely touched her with fingertips that shook. His eyes were smoky and waiting. He'd promised he wouldn't press, and he was as good as his word. But Gussie found her own convictions to remain unaffected crumbling by the wayside as her body would not lie still.

She was a woman who'd spent ten years toughening her reactions, removing herself from all possible temptations, denying her needs. She'd been strong, single-minded, unswerving. In one bright, moonlit moment, she knew she was about to lose an important battle, if not the entire war.

With a soft moan, she reached to circle his neck and pull his lips down to meet hers.

David had watched her struggle, not daring to hope she'd reach for him. And now that she had, he used every ounce of control he could muster to go slowly this time, to not frighten her again, to let her set the pace. He moved his mouth across hers, feather soft at first, then more firmly taking possession until he felt her open to him. Her tongue sought to tangle with his, and he gloried in her response as he slid his arms around her.

Each time he kissed her, he lost ground. She was just a fraction sweeter, a tiny bit more intoxicating, a shade less easy to forget. She was drugging his senses, clouding his mind, changing his plans. He who had thought he had plenty of time for thoughts of forever, for feelings of permanence, for designs for the future was suddenly moving in a brand new direction. As her small hands clutched the shirt at his back, he knew he was a man going down for the count. Once the thought would have scared him half to death. Now he felt a sureness of purpose that had previously only entered his life with regard to his work.

Her mouth molded to his so perfectly, as if made to fit its shape. Her straining body was as eager as his, seeking contact, as if it knew what lay in wait for their joining. He wanted to free them of all barriers, to move to the next plateau, to take her right there on the grassy banks where he'd wandered as a boy. There was nothing, no one, not a single woman he'd ever wanted more. Yet he held back, then pulled away.

In the growing darkness, he saw that her eyes were dreamy, still drifting. They cleared gradually. Again he touched her mouth softly with his, instinct leading the way. No, he would not grapple on the ground with this special woman, this breakable lady who'd been hurt before. Not if he wanted to gain her trust along with the loving.

"I care about you, Augusta Jane Lyon," he said, his voice husky. "Not just your body, gorgeous though it is. Not just your fine mind, sharp though it is. You, what's inside. One day you'll believe that.''

Feeling her eyes fill, Gussie pulled him to her and buried her face in his neck. "I want to," she whispered. "I really want to."

"I know," David answered. "I know."

Chapter Seven

Chicago was a whirlwind. Never had he spent so many long hours smiling, signing, talking, eating rubber chicken and smiling some more, David thought at the end of the second day. But very soon now, it would all be over. They were flying back to New York tomorrow.

He sat at the dinner table, watching the room empty out and half listening to Arnie Walker rattle on about the success of the tour while taking generous, though undeserved credit for said success. Warm, tired and moving toward irritable, David hoped the obnoxious little man would run out of steam before *he* ran out of temper.

"It's like you were a front-runner, you know," Arnie went on, blowing blue cigar smoke into the lingering smoky atmosphere. "With your tour generating so much interest, to say nothing of selling a pile of books, I'm sure the main office will give the nod to more promotional events like this. Hey, man, I been telling them for years, publicity's the name of the game and the man to show 'em how it's done is yours truly.''

David drained the last of his watery scotch and made a face. "Then you don't think Gussie Lyon's contributions along the way had much to do with how well things went?"

Arnie waved a spread hand in a maybe gesture. "She's okay, you know. A little green around the edges when it comes to publicity, but I'd say for her first time out, she did awright."

"I'll be sure to tell her you said so. I know it'll make her day." He didn't know why he bothered with sarcasm around Arnie. It all flew right over his head. "Where is Gussie, by the way?" She'd excused herself during the last of the speeches, and he hadn't seen her since.

She was avoiding him again, most likely. She'd kept very busy the past few days and had used every opportunity to scoot out of the room, or sit at another table, or move out of reach whenever he'd come near. He'd expected as much after the moments of intimacy by the pond, the unexpected vulnerability she'd shown him. How long, he wondered, would she keep this up?

"I just dropped off some papers in her room. She's up there on the phone with some writer who left his manuscript with her back in Dallas, I think." Arnie squashed his cigarette in the ashtray. "She read it, and she sounds real enthused. I don't know why she bothers with these guys who're always coming up to her. We got a transom, you know. Let 'em mail it in. One of our paid readers will get to it sooner or later."

So she'd done it, as she'd promised. He'd thought she would. "Maybe it's because she knows how important it is to a writer to get his work read by someone who can make a difference. Maybe because some editors enjoy finding new talent and developing it. Or maybe she's just a genuinely nice person.''

Arnie considered all that but didn't look convinced. "People should stick to their own jobs, you know. Makes life easier." He stole a look at his watch. "Well, I gotta run. Got a hot date, if you know what I mean." He stood and thrust out his hand. "See you back in New York."

David shook Arnie's outstretched hand, hoping their future meetings would be few and far between. "Right." With a last glance around the room, he shoved his hands into his pockets and headed for the elevators.

"I'm so happy you're pleased," Gussie said into the phone, a smile on her lips. Jared's call had both surprised and delighted her. She'd often wondered if her father seldom gave out compliments so that when he did they'd mean more, or if he simply found it hard to express gratitude to anyone. "I'm not wild to do it again anytime soon, and I am anxious to get home, but I do feel the tour has gone well."

"*Very* well, from what I hear," Jared Lyon said. "Didn't I tell you that you'd enjoy getting out from behind that desk?"

Gussie could picture her father's smug expression as he sat in his Sutton Place town house, his fingers toying with a cigar. "I'm not certain the word *enjoy* is appropriate, but I got through it with a minimum of disasters."

"And David. How did you find David Lamb to be?"

Gussie took her time answering as she began removing the pins from her hair with one hand. It had been a long day. She heard the quiet puffing, indicating Jared had lighted his forbidden cigar. She also heard the ill-concealed impatience as he waited for her reply. "David's a natural with the press, never openly loses his temper or lets himself be goaded into a dumb answer. He has a way with the readers, both men and women. He's tireless, endlessly cheerful, witty and intelligent and usually cooperative. In short, the kind of writer Lyon Publishing should be proud to promote.''

"Good, good." A short pause. "Now that's David Lamb, the writer. What do you think of him as a man?"

Her hand stopped in midair. Why would he care? she fleetingly wondered. "I'm not sure I know what you mean."

She heard Jared blew out a whoosh of smoke. "Sure you do. Do you think he's made of the right stuff? Is he someone worth investing in as a person? Do you trust him?"

This was undoubtedly the strangest conversation she'd had with her father in recent memory. To complicate things, there was a loud, insistent knock at her door. "Just a minute," she said into the mouthpiece.

Opening the door, she saw David standing there. She fought an unreasonable urge to shut it again. "I'm on the phone," she told him.

Nodding, he walked in and handed her a single red rose. "For you." He strolled past her to the chair by the window. "I'll wait."

Gussie wasn't sure that was a good idea. She'd been given a nice room, fairly large, but it had no sitting area except for the lone chair. A huge, sprawling queen-size bed dominated the room. There was an implied intimate atmosphere when a man and a woman were alone together in a bedroom, the only light coming from a small bedside lamp. However, short of leaving the door open, she was stuck. Taking a deep breath, she went back to pick up the phone.

"Could we talk about this when I get in tomorrow?" she asked Jared as she stood with her back to David, inhaling the sweet scent of the flower. She didn't know why she tried for a modicum of privacy. The man was so astute he'd probably figure out their conversation after hearing only her side of it.

"Can't you just give me a *yes* or *no* answer, Gus?"

"Well, ah, it's not that easy...." She was unused to stammering and somewhat embarrassed that she found herself doing so.

"All right, then, we'll talk tomorrow. Damned if I know why you're so reticent tonight. Tell me just one thing. Do you like the man?"

Gussie found herself gritting her teeth. "Why do you want to know?"

Jared's temper had obviously reached its limits. "Dammit, Gus..."

"All right. Yes, I do. Satisfied?"

"Not nearly. See you in the morning." He hung up.

With a shaky hand, Gussie replaced the receiver. Something was brewing in that complex mind of her father's, and she would love to know what. She meant to find out. Turning, she gave David an absent smile. "Was there something you wanted?"

A loaded question, David thought as he looked her over. She'd slipped off her shoes and jacket and had almost all her hair down. Standing in stocking feet, wearing a striped silk dress, she looked young and accessible, her mind still on the telephone conversation, her expression unprotected. He stood, removed his suit coat and walked to her.

"I thought maybe we could have a nightcap. Sort of toast the end of the tour." Even though the thought of it ending had had him depressed all day. Her warm scent drifted to him as she placed the rose on the nightstand and struggled to remove a final stubborn pin from the back of her hair.

"Oh, thanks, David, but I'm really beat. I...what are you doing?"

"Helping you free your hair." His awkward fingers found the pin and pulled it out. Slowly he turned her to face him, then shoved his hands into the thickness of her hair, watching it untangle and fall to her shoulders. The pads of his fingers gently massaged her scalp, the movement tilting her head back. She'd managed to swallow her protest, yet her eyes watched him even while they darkened with that quick awareness he'd come to recognize. "Was that Jared on the phone?" He continued his sensual ministrations, his fingers trailing to the tips of her hair, then reaching up to begin again.

"Yes." Her voice was breathy, and she cleared her throat, thinking she was probably more tired than she'd thought. His touch was both soothing and arousing. She'd let him continue for a bit longer.

"Is anything wrong?" His voice was low, calming.

"Not really. It was a strange conversation. He's pleased with the tour, but he wanted to know..." David stepped closer, his breath warm on her cheeks, and Gussie lost her train of thought. Without the added height that shoes gave her, she felt slightly defenseless against the size of him. He placed a kiss in her hair, then bent to place his lips on her forehead. Her hands moved to his chest, intending to keep him at bay, and instantly felt the heat through the soft material of his shirt. If she'd rejected the idea of a nightcap as dangerous, she knew this was infinitely more so. Yet her treacherous body was already softening at his nearness, her pulse already pounding.

David took his mouth on a slow journey of her face, taking his time, letting the feeling build. "You're so lovely, Gussie," he murmured as he paused by her ear, "so very lovely." She was a woman born to be romanced, yet, except for the moment by the pond, he'd always approached her like a desert survivor reaching for that first gulp of water. Not this time. He felt her shiver, felt her knees buckle slightly, but he steadied her. "What was it Jared wanted to know?"

Gussie groped through the cobwebs of her mind, trying to cling to the conversation. "He wanted to know if I liked you. Not as a writer, but as a man. So odd. He's never asked me that before and I...oh!" His wet tongue slipped into her ear and her hands clutched at his shirt sleeves as an incredible shudder ran through her. How could he reduce her to this...this madness, so quickly, so effortlessly? She felt as weak as a kitten as his hands moved around her, molding her to him while his mouth pressed a soft kiss to her closed eyelids.

"And what did you tell him?" David asked, keeping her distracted with the conversation, hoping her needs would override her resistance. Tonight, he'd decided. He had to break through her barriers tonight, to find out what had hurt her and to get her past it. If he didn't, once they were back in New York, she'd become the cool professional again and he might not have another chance.

Her hands were on his shoulders now as she rose to her tiptoes, straining to get closer. "I told him I did like you," she whispered.

David touched the zipper tab at her nape, then trailed his hands down her slim sides. Too soon to tug on that zipper. If he rushed her now, it would be like a splash of cold water. His lips moved to her throat, tasting the heady female flavor of her skin. "You smell almost as good as you taste, Gussie," he whispered. "So lovely."

But her hazy mind wouldn't let it be. "Why do you suppose my father cares whether I like you or not?" she asked as her restless hands roamed his back.

"I don't know." His mouth was at the corner of her lips. "I do know I've never wanted a woman the way I want you."

Something clicked into place, a warning sound. Gussie pulled back, her eyes clearing as she forced him to meet her gaze. "He wanted to know if I trust you, if I like you." The picture was forming now. "My father spent some time with you in California before the tour was set up, didn't he?"

David took a deep breath, letting his body adjust to still another delay. "Yes, he came out to my house, brought the new contract and had lunch with me. Why?"

"Is that when you set this all up?" She shoved back from him now, feeling the heat of humiliation. "Is that when he asked you to charm me, flatter me, to draw me out of my shell? I should have guessed. God, I'm so stupid!" She began to pace as she brushed her hair back from her face.

Placing both hands on his hips, David watched her. "What on earth are you talking about?"

"Look, the game's over. You don't have to bring me flowers, say nice things to me or force yourself to make love to me. I'll explain everything to my father, that I caught on and it didn't work. I didn't realize he felt this guilty, but he can find another way to live with his guilt. I'm just surprised he got you to play along." She whirled about and stomped toward the other end of the short room, fighting bitter tears of shame.

David had about had it. He was confused, shaken and now angry. He stopped her in mid-stride, grabbed her arms and jerked her to face him. "Are you going to tell me what the hell this is about, or do I call Jared right now?"

Her eyes were bleak and filled with pain. "You can stop pretending, really."

He shook her, just once, very hard. He couldn't remember ever feeling quite so helpless. "I'm not pretending anything. Everything I've told you since we met, every touch I've shared with you, every feeling I've displayed—including the rage I feel right now—has been as honest as I know how to be. Now explain what you mean, dammit, before I totally lose it."

Gussie frowned, suddenly puzzled. "Before you met me, my father didn't ask you to be especially nice to me, to wine me and dine me and...—" She broke off, unable to say the rest.

Stunned, he could only stare at her. "Make love to you? You can't believe that." He tightened his grip. "There's a name for men who do that sort of thing, and it's not a very nice name. Your father may not be a knight in shining armor, but I feel certain he would never set you up for such a fall."

Giving in to his anger, David pulled her up until they were a breath apart. Tears trickled down her cheeks as her eyes, filled with anguish, focused on his. "Why can't you believe me, that you're a beautiful, a very desirable woman? Don't you see how warm you are, how bright and funny and wonderful? *That's* why I want you. Dammit, Gussie, how can I convince you?"

His exasperation left him, replaced by an overwhelming need to show her, to make her see, the only way he knew how. His mouth covered hers, his arms encircled her, pulling her up tight against him. He had no patience left. Passion fueled by anger and desperation ruled him as his tongue plunged into her mouth, waiting for the answering response. At last, with a heartbreaking moan, she grasped him to her. Deepening the kiss, he acted to blot out her thoughts, to replace them with feelings. Already his own were spiraling out of control as her special tastes exploded on his tongue and her small, firm breasts pressed against him.

She'd never wanted to believe anything so much in her life, Gussie thought. But dared she? From the beginning, this man had overwhelmed her, and now he was rocketing her out of control. She was afraid, so afraid. Even as she felt herself sliding down the unfamiliar tunnel of desire, she feared what she would find. Life had taught her that one night of passion could lead to endless days of regret. She had changed since that one devastating night, but the facts hadn't. Still, she clung, answering his kiss, wanting, wanting.

Time seemed to be standing still. The zipper was moving down, her dress falling to the floor and his fingers skimming to the front of her body. Through the soft lace of her bra, she could feel his hands cover her breasts. How had they grown so full, so eager for his touch? When had she given her hands permission to ease his shirt from him, to lose themselves in the golden hair of his chest?

He cast aside the wisp of lace and shifted her toward the light. Gussie's hands tightened into fists at her side as she allowed the intimacy. Dear Lord, she would get through this somehow. But his eyes as they raised from her breasts to meet her gaze were filled with pleasure, with desire. She felt more tears rush to blur her vision. Could he really think she was . . .

"Beautiful. You are *so* beautiful." In slow motion, he bent to place a gentle kiss on each swollen peak, then gathered her to him. "How could you ever have thought otherwise? How could you have believed Jared or anyone would have to talk me into wanting you? From that first day, I've wanted you. *You* made me want you, Gussie. You and no one else."

David heard the sob that escaped from her, and his heart turned over. What, who, had made this lovely woman so unsure, so fearful of loving? "Don't be afraid, Gussie. Not with me." He held her, just held her, gently pressing her breasts against his chest, basking in the pleasure of her closeness, wondering what she was feeling.

"I'm trying not to be," she whispered close to his ear. "It's just that intimacy makes you so vulnerable and I . . ."

"You hate being vulnerable so you turn from intimacy."

She knew he was right, but that was only part of it. Her face buried in his neck, it was easier to talk than look at him. "I am afraid, afraid of how much I want you. I'm not good at this...this incredible wanting. I've never had to deal with it before. I can't seem to stop wanting you, even though I know I shouldn't."

"Why shouldn't you? You must know I care about you. Physical expression of that caring is the next natural step. And I think you feel the same. Why shouldn't you?"

"It's no good." She shook her head, moving out of his arms. "Passion and I don't mix well." She went to the closet for her robe, shrugged into it, then wiped the traces of her tears from her cheeks. Feeling very tired, she walked to the bed and sat down. She had to explain. She owed him that much.

David sat down next to her. He saw her visibly control herself, her eyes watching her hand fuss with the folds of her robe. He moved toward her, took her hand in his and waited.

"Something happened to me a long time ago. I was eighteen, a bright kid who'd graduated from high school a year early. I didn't think I'd feel comfortable attending a large university, so I convinced my father to let me go to a small upstate college. It was my first time away from home and my family. I met this boy, another superstar, from a wealthy out-of-state family. He played basketball, like you, only he didn't break his nose. He was tall and incredibly handsome. When he showed an interest in me, I was flattered out of my mind."

He could picture her, young and uncertain. He squeezed her hand and waited for her to continue.

"I was anxious to taste life after the sheltered existence I'd been leading, and he seemed eager to guide me. I'd dated a few boys before, but to me this was a man, twenty-one and experienced. It took him only until spring break to convince me to go off with him to a motel room he'd rented. Afterward, at home, I spent those two weeks dreaming about him. But when I returned to school, he didn't come around anymore. Finally I couldn't stand it, so I sought him out. He told me he'd been busy with basketball and his classes. I went back to the dorm, convinced I hadn't pleased him as a lover, that I'd been inadequate somehow.''

Gussie kept her gaze on their laced fingers. David couldn't know how difficult this recital was. She'd never told anyone *all* of it, not her parents, not even Molly. But she was determined to give him the unvarnished facts. Maybe then he'd realize why things would never work out for the two of them.

"The following month, I realized I was pregnant. For several weeks, my pride kept me from telling him. But I swallowed it, more afraid of my father than what the boy would say. When I told him, he took it well. He nodded and said we'd handle it, to give him a few days and he'd talk with his folks.'' She shook her head. "I was so naive. The next thing I knew, he'd been whisked out of school by his parents. One of his friends told me he was taking his exams by mail, then going on an extended trip to Europe with his father.''

"You spent one night with him, only one night?'' His voice was strong, supportive, yet incredulous.

"Inconceivable, isn't it? Not even a full night, just a couple of hours. He'd made love to me—if you could call it that—once, only once. Every young girl thinks it can't happen to her.'' Gussie took a deep, steadying breath. "I finished the last two weeks of the term in a daze and then went home to face my father. I'll never forget the disappointment on his face. Never. He was already having trouble with Aaron's rebellion, and now his daughter was in trouble.''

"What did he do?''

"After he hit the roof, you mean? He demanded to know the boy's name so he could go after him. I refused to tell him. It was the first time I'd ever defied Jared. He was furious with me.''

"What did your mother do through all this?''

"My mother supports my father's decisions, always has, always will. I believe she stopped thinking for herself the day she said 'I do.' Jared lined up a doctor who'd do an abortion on me and keep it hush-hush.''

His lips drawn in a thin line, David felt fury, at the boy, at her father, at all that she'd had to go through.

Gussie raised her head. "I defied him again and refused to have an abortion. I told him I would quit school, get a job and raise my child. I thought he'd throw me out, but he just clammed up and left me alone.''

Something wasn't adding up. "Where is the child now? Did you decide to give the baby up for adoption?''

Her shoulders slumped, and her eyes filled. "No. I miscarried in my third month. I stayed home the rest of the summer, then I went back to college in the fall. There wasn't a whole lot of life in me, though. I was filled with shame, and with grief, and then guilt. My father only spoke to me about it once after that, two years ago, when he had his heart attack. I think he thought he might die, so he talked openly about his feelings, which he so seldom does. He told me he'd never quite gotten over the guilt over how he behaved when I needed help. He deeply regretted it. I told him I forgave him.''

"And that's why you thought Jared had lined me up to be nice to you, to ease his guilty conscience?''

"Yes. I think he feels responsible for my not dating much. He blames himself that there's no one special in my life."

David touched her cheek and turned her face toward his. "But have you forgiven yourself? Your only mistake, Gussie, was picking the wrong man to trust. You were too inexperienced to know how to handle such a smooth operator."

"You'll never know how hard it was to accept that he didn't want me. Not *me*. He only wanted sex. I didn't know what to expect, and he didn't know how to give."

"And still you protected him. Why?"

"It wasn't a matter of protection. What would have been the point of going after him, forcing him to marry me? Can you imagine anything worse than being chained to someone who didn't want you in the first place and then grew to hate you? I learned several important lessons. But every day I wish the whole thing had never happened."

He heard her voice break and slipped his arm about her, pulling her close. "You've spent too many years carrying this around, Gussie. Let it go. Lay the past to rest. Let yourself care again."

Her cheek lay against his chest. She could hear his strong heartbeat. It would be so easy to lean on his strength, to take from him, if only for the short time it would last. He offered comfort and passion. But passion was the velvet trap. Hadn't she learned that?

"Ten years have gone by since then, and I've had few problems because I put my emotions on the back burner and held myself in tight control. Then you came along, stirring me up, and I haven't had a peaceful night since."

David looked into her eyes. "Ten years. You haven't been with any other man in ten years?"

"Don't look as if I'm to be pitied. It was my decision."

"It's not pity you hear, it's surprise. You're so lovely, with so much to give that I can't imagine you shutting yourself off like this. I know you've been badly hurt. You trusted one man, opened to him, and he left you. Now hear this. I won't hurt you, and I won't leave you. Please, let yourself believe me."

"Why should I?"

"Because I care, and it's not just sex. But sex is a part of it."

She sat up at that, her chin jutting forward. "Sex is a joke, David, a moment's madness, a fleeting pleasure with too high a price."

"No, you're wrong. I'm not talking about adolescent sexual experimentation here. I'm talking about two people who care deeply for each other making love, and that can be beautiful. Madness, maybe, but beautiful. And it doesn't have to result in a child until we're both ready for that. I would always protect you."

Gussie quietly disengaged herself from him and, belting her robe more tightly about her, walked to the window. Night had fallen over downtown Chicago. From ten floors up, she could see the lights of the city in reds and greens and glaring white, beckoning and blinking. Tomorrow night she'd be standing at her own window, looking down on the streets of Manhattan. Two and a half weeks ago she'd left that haven that she'd created for herself. A lifetime ago.

He said he cared for her, that he wanted her and would protect her. She'd had no sweet words from her first lover to coax her to his bed, only a burning curiosity and an awakening woman's body to lead her. But David would give her words and tenderness and the passion she'd missed out on the first time around. It was hers for the taking, waiting a dozen feet away. But what price would she pay this time?

Gussie ran a shaky hand through her hair. She'd taken enough psychology courses to know that perhaps more than the teenage inquisitiveness that had led her to give herself to that faceless boy ten years ago had been the reaching out for the hope of love. Love. She hadn't had huge doses of it from anyone, ever. She'd never spoken of such things with Aaron. Her mother cared, she supposed, but if she ever said the words, only Jared had heard them. And Jared himself was a man of few words, rarely expressing emotion. So there it was.

Was she now, so many years later, still searching for love? Probably. In her youthful ignorance, she'd given herself to the first boy who'd glanced at her, trying to make him love her. Would she spend the rest of her life doing dumb things to get some man to love her? The very thought made her cringe. No, she would not do that. She would not fall in love with David.

Gussie turned to see him still sitting on the bed as she'd left him, calmly watching her. If love was out of the way, she could concentrate on caring for a good friend. She did believe he wouldn't knowingly hurt her, though she was just as certain that he would one day walk away. She didn't have what it took to hold a man's interest forever, but that was all right. She had a great deal else going for her. And tonight, she had David Lamb.

She went to him slowly, untying the belt of her robe as she walked. "I'm through running from this. I, too, have wanted you since the first day I saw you." She reached up and placed her hands on his shoulders and felt the robe slip open. "Please show me, David. Show me what loving can be like between a man and a woman."

It was what he'd wanted, yet David found himself hesitating. She looked so fragile in the dim light of the lamp, fragile and delicate, entrusting herself to him. The beauty of her was spread before him, and he felt his hands tremble. She was handing him a gift, and he wondered if he could find the patience, the tenderness, that she deserved.

His eyes hadn't moved from hers, and in them she saw a flicker of doubt. Oddly, it buoyed her own shaky conviction at her uncharacteristic behavior. She would have hated overconfidence or arrogance on his part. She saw the change then, saw his face tighten with desire as he dropped his gaze to her bare breasts.

The touch of his mouth on her yearning flesh aroused her intensely, and she plunged her hands into his hair, pressing him to her. Then his lips settled on one rosy peak, and as he drew in, she felt an answering sensation deep inside. Her knees quivered with the strain of standing, so he eased her down onto the mattress, following alongside her.

Inevitable. The word skimmed into her consciousness. Their coming together had been inevitable since that first hot, hungry look they'd shared in her office.

Moving with the care and the slowness she'd known he would give her, he lay above her and rubbed his chest against her bare skin. The unbearable pleasure sang through her blood like fine wine, warming her. Needing further contact, she touched the tip of her tongue to his lips, lightly at first, then more boldly. By unspoken mutual agreement, they were learning each other in this first dance of love.

Gussie felt the kiss through every pore as she arched involuntarily, unable to lie still. But David seemed in no hurry, his tongue exploring her mouth at a leisurely pace. Only his labored breathing gave hint to the fire that raced through him.

Keenly aware, she felt the smooth texture of the spread at her back, the buckle of his belt as he leaned into her, the brush of his restless leg as he shifted over her. Needs throbbed inside her, passion set free by the trust she'd placed in him. Her hands on the damp skin of his back massaged the hard ridge of muscles, exploring restively as she inhaled the musky scent of him.

David hung on to his control by a thin thread. With her innocence, with her honesty, she excited him as no woman ever had. At last exposed to him. When her hands moved to his belt, he eased away from her reach, knowing he couldn't give up that last barrier just yet. He kissed the pulse at her throat while his hands slowly stripped off the rest of her clothes. Then she was bare beneath his seeking hands, and he was pleased to see that she was too caught up in passion to be embarrassed. Another hurdle they'd overcome.

But soon touching wasn't enough for either of them as hands and lips crossed more boundaries. Gussie didn't recognize the woman she'd become as she reached up to bring his mouth back to hers. Patience fled as the urge to know more, to feel everything, surged through her. She heard his gentle words without knowing what he said, only knowing they were for her and her alone. This man wanted her, Gussie Lyon, not just a faceless woman for a quick release. He knew who she was, and now knew every secret she had, and he still wanted her. Her heart felt close to bursting, and she could deny him nothing.

The heady tantalizing scent of Gussie teased at David's senses as he buried his face in the satin of her throat. His hand drifted down. The pounding in his head seemed to echo through the room as her eyes, dark and smoky, stayed on his. His mouth nibbled on her lower lip as his fingers slipped inside her. He heard the gasp she couldn't control, felt the reflexive movement, the tightening at this intimate invasion.

"Shhh, it's all right, Gussie," David murmured, and slowly she relaxed and opened to him. He touched deep inside then and her eyes widened, but he saw no fear, only the sweet desire he'd watched steadily growing. It was time to eliminate the last barrier, and he was grateful. He didn't know how much longer he had.

Quickly he removed the rest of his clothes and reached in his wallet for a foil package.

Gussie eased herself more comfortably onto the bed and she watched him. "Pretty sure of yourself, weren't you?" she couldn't resist asking.

"I bought this only days ago, hoping." He lay down beside her, saw her mouth tremble and kissed her, deeply as only a lover can. She answered with her lips, her soft moan, her fluid body stretching toward his. His own was hot, screaming for release, muscles tight as he tried to keep a handle on his pacing. On a sigh of pleasure, he rolled onto his back, pulling her with him.

He was letting her lead, and Gussie grew a little wild with the freedom to touch him as freely as he'd been learning her. Now there was nothing between him and her greedy hands. Suddenly sure, they raced over his smooth skin, his lean flesh, his taut muscles. When at last she closed a hand over him, she heard his earthy groan, felt the shudder he couldn't prevent. Her mouth on his drew in the rich, male taste, while her skin hummed with awareness wherever his hands glided. The more she tasted, touched, felt, the more she wanted.

And then he was shifting her, arching closer, knowing the waiting had come to an end. She lay before him, her skin damp and glistening, her face expectant as her chest heaved with her breathing.

"Now, Gussie?" he asked softly, giving her the last option.

"Yes, David," she whispered, her arms reaching for him. "Yes, now."

He entered her slowly, watching her face as he filled her. Her beautiful face, rosy and heated, her eyes bright on his.

He felt her legs twine around him as he lowered to her, wanting to kiss her parted lips but preferring to watch her in her passion. With ironclad control, he tempered his movements, sliding slowly, deeply, seeing her start the climb. Her head moved restlessly. Her eyes closed for an instant, then opened again.

"Oh, David," she whispered softly. "David."

He moved faster and surer now, his joy at her pleasure making his restraint possible. A blush settled over her features as she arched into him, accepting, climbing with him.

This was flying high, this was soaring out of control, this was beyond what Gussie had dreamed possible. No man could make her ache with wanting, destroy all her inhibitions, and feel such beauty in the discovery. No man could make her feel so much. No man except David.

She could no longer keep her eyes open as her fingers dug into the hard flesh of his back. For the first time, she gave in to the glory of becoming a woman. And she went willingly, racing with him, over the edge, sliding, sliding, with his strong, sure arms holding her.

Stunned, Gussie lay in a tangle of arms and legs, damp flesh and thumping hearts. She was a woman who dealt in words and now tried to find some to describe what had happened to her. Certainly she'd never experienced anything quite like it. What she'd had ten years ago couldn't even qualify as a practice session. David's unsteady breath fanned over her skin, and she wondered if he could possibly have felt as much as she.

Slowly he raised himself on an elbow and saw she was once again herself, unsure how to react, moving toward embarrassment. He touched her face lightly along her jaw with the faintest of caresses. "Do you still feel that you're an inadequate lover, or do you think perhaps that boy ten years ago might have been?''

She smiled then, a lazy curving of her lips. ''Thank you for showing me that I'm not as inept as I'd thought I was.''

''Hardly that.'' He kissed her lingeringly. ''And you don't need to thank me. Making love is a shared experience, or it's a lousy experience. I'm just glad it was as good for you.''

Good? What a meager word to describe what she'd felt. What she was still feeling. Oh, there was much to think about, much to sort out. Despite what David had said earlier, this wasn't the solution, but rather more of the problem. But she wasn't going to dwell on that now. There would be enough time for deep pondering later.

David slipped his head up onto the pillow and gathered her to him. Would she gradually cool and send him packing to his room? Or had he really made some headway? he wondered.

Gussie lay with her cheek on his chest, her hand over his heart. Comfortable. Imagine, she was actually comfortable lying naked in a man's arms. How far she'd come, in a couple of short weeks. But she mustn't make too much of it. David had awakened her sensuality, and she'd given her body to him, but she still owned her heart. As long as she kept a firm grip on that, he couldn't control her. But as long as she had him here with her, she might as well enjoy him.

Playfully she ran her fingers along the solid lines of his chest. ''What are you thinking?''

David tightened his hold on her. ''I was thinking that you're everything I knew you would be and that I love making love with you. And I was thinking of doing it again.''

She turned her head to look at him. ''Funny, I was thinking along those same lines. Show me more, David. Show me everything.''

Anticipation heating his blood, he pulled her up to meet his kiss.

In the morning, David awoke to find her closet empty and Gussie Lyon gone.

Chapter Eight

Yes, Larry, it does seem to be edited with a bit of a heavy hand," Gussie said into the phone as she paged through her copy of the author's manuscript. "I think we were short-staffed the week this was done, so we farmed it out to a free-lancer." She listened to more complaints, frowning as she read some of the copy editor's comments penciled in the margins.

Larry Brice was prolific, imaginative and a good fiction writer. He was also a whiner who complained at every opportunity about his advances, his book covers and his editing. Currently he was assigned to Connie Egan, a bright young associate editor whom Gussie had personally trained. Listening to the man drone on, she wondered how Connie managed to keep her patience with him.

"You really think they've changed the mood of your story?"

Setting aside the manuscript, Gussie rubbed her forehead. Another headache shaping up, the third day in a row. It was not a habit she was happy to be acquiring. "Well, since you feel that strongly, how would it be if I have Connie go over the whole book herself and call you?" This was going to thrill Connie no end, especially on a Friday.

"Yes, I know you hate to go over her head and call me, and I don't like to make a habit of rescheduling an edit, Larry." Spotting Molly peeking in the door, she signaled her to come in. "I'll make an exception this time and ask Connie to be sure that particular copy editor doesn't touch your work again." Gussie rolled her eyes to the ceiling and nodded as Molly mouthed the caller's name questioningly. Everyone at Lyon was aware of Larry's constant complaints, which was one reason he rarely lasted more than a year with an editor before being passed on.

"By the way, how's the new book coming, Larry?" She pulled out her top drawer and searched about, finally finding her antacids. Popping two in her mouth, she listened to him rave about how well his next manuscript was shaping up. She certainly hoped so. His last one, according to Connie, hadn't lived up to the expectations of the proposal they'd gone to contract on.

Gussie watched Molly settle herself in the chair across from her. Her assistant looked fresh and rested. She knew that by comparison, she probably looked like the Wicked Witch of the West this afternoon. Food didn't seem to appeal to her lately; she wasn't sleeping very well; and these incessant headaches would soon leave permanent frown marks on her forehead. So much for her happy homecoming.

"Yes, fine. Send a fresh copy to Connie, and I'll tell her it's on the way. Nice talking with you, Larry." Gratefully she hung up. "I really needed him insisting on airing his gripes for half an hour today." Swallowing the mint, she scanned the mess on her desk. "Where are the Foley contracts, Molly? I guess we'd better get to them."

"Doug Foley's agent has them. There's something he wants inserted."

"Not again. What a nitpicker!" Absently she rubbed the back of her neck. "Do we have any aspirin around here?"

"A sour stomach *and* a headache," Molly commented as she stood. "You're in great shape. I'll get you a couple. Want a cup of coffee, too?"

"No, thanks. Just ice water." Maybe if she cut down on the caffeine she'd feel better. Lining up a stack of mail that needed answering, she began to read the top letter. As she finished, she jotted down her reply on a legal pad for Molly to type later, then moved on to the next.

"Here you are," Molly said, returning to hand her the aspirin bottle and ice water. She closed the door, then stood regarding her employer and friend. "Why are you doing this to yourself, Gussie?"

Gussie choked down the bitter pills with a grimace. "Doing what?" She knew perfectly well what Molly meant. Their working relationship alone would never allow the question. Their friendship all but demanded she ask, and Gussie had been expecting the inquisition.

"Staying till seven, eight at night, hauling more work home, ruining your health. You've got deep circles under your eyes, you're short-tempered and impatient. There's more, but I think you get my drift."

Reaching for the remnants of her sense of humor, Gussie looked up. "Don't hold back, Molly. Tell me how you feel."

Molly crossed her arms over her chest somewhat defensively. "I'm only saying these things because I care about you."

Another one who claimed to care about her, but at least she knew Molly's feelings were genuine. She just wasn't sure how to answer her. Gussie removed her glasses and leaned back in her chair with a sigh. "I'll be all right. It was a long, tiring tour, and I have a great deal of paperwork here to catch up on, that's all. It's taking a lot out of me." More than I can tell you. It probably would help to pour some of what she felt out to Molly, but she couldn't quite bring herself to do that. Not yet.

Molly pulled the chair closer and sat on the edge, a worried look on her face. "Gussie, we're friends, aren't we? Not just two women who work together?"

She had few close friends, but Molly through the years certainly qualified. "I like to think so."

"Then maybe you'd like to talk about what's bothering you. Because I've known you a long time, and something definitely is. I haven't seen you like this since Jared had his heart attack."

Jared. She'd already talked with him the day she'd taken the early flight from Chicago to New York. She'd gone directly to his office. He'd been waiting. She'd stormed in and watched his face carefully as she'd accused him of trying to meddle in her personal life.

Maybe David hadn't been aware of what her father had had in mind with his cross-country tour for two, but she'd finally seen through his little scheme. Get her involved with a strong, take-charge man like himself, and he'd kill two birds with one stone. His daughter would have someone to take care of her if anything happened to him, and Jared's guilt would also be alleviated. Perhaps he hadn't gone so far as to suggest David take her to bed, but . . .

He'd been evasive at her accusations, then uncharacteristically at a loss for a logical explanation beyond the fact that he'd only acted in her best interest. She'd been hoping she'd imagined everything, but he'd all but admitted it. Not to be outdone, he became angry himself, and at that she'd left his office. He hadn't spoken to her since.

Even her mother, usually silent, had gotten into the act, dropping in unannounced this morning, taking Jared's side as usual. They only wanted what was best for her, Dolores had said. One day Jared would retire. Would running the company alone be enough for Gussie, especially as she got older? She needed a home of her own, children, a good man...

She'd lost her temper hearing that. Why couldn't they both trust her to know her own mind? And to find her own man, if she wanted one. Looking as if she didn't understand her daughter, Dolores had left. Gussie had eaten a whole roll of antacids since, and she still felt the burning.

She tried to find the right words for Molly. "I wish you wouldn't worry about me so much." Everyone was concerned about her lately, telling her what she should do. Frankly, she was getting a little tired of it.

"Gussie, I'm older than you by nearly ten years, and I've been through a great deal, as you well know. I think I know what you're feeling. Sometimes it helps to talk and..."

The intercom buzzed, and Gussie was relieved at the interruption. She pushed the button. "Yes?"

"He's on the phone again, Gussie. David Lamb. Shall I put him through?" The receptionist sounded as if she'd just gone a round or two with him.

"No, Cheryl. Tell him I'm still in a meeting and can't be disturbed."

"He's awfully insistent."

"So am I."

Cheryl gave a long-suffering sigh. "All right, but he sounds mad enough to chew up the wires all the way from California to New York."

"He'll get over it. Thanks." Slowly she released the button.

Molly cleared her throat. "Three days, and you're still not taking his calls? He must have really done a number on you."

Done a number on her. Had he? Or had she done one on herself? Gussie swiveled in her chair to gaze out at the late-afternoon sky. The night she'd spent in David's arms had been without exception the happiest night of her life. With him as her willing instructor, she'd discovered a side of herself she'd never thought to see and emotions she'd never believed she'd feel. She'd felt like a desirable woman, beautiful in every way, able to give and receive pleasure without shame or fear. She'd felt whole, cherished, complete.

But as the gray dawn had replaced the night sky outside the window, she'd realized she had to leave. She was close, so very close, to doing any sappy thing he would ask of her. Give up her job, move to the West Coast, change for him. Anything, just so he would always love her. She would totally lose control, lose herself and all she'd fought so hard to be. She'd become like her mother, a fragile echo of the man she loved, her voice scarcely heard, somewhat pitiful. And she would hate herself.

So she'd carefully extricated herself from his arms, quietly dressed and quickly packed, then had stood looking down at him. Even as she prepared to leave him, she wanted him. But she knew that as bright, funny and easygoing as he was, David Lamb was a man who had to have his way, to be in charge, of the things he did and the ones he loved. And as he'd told her in his boyhood home, other people would simply adjust, as his parents had, to his decisions. She would wither and die in that atmosphere. If leaving him was difficult, staying would have been impossible.

Now she had to get through the next few days until he forgot her and moved on to someone else. Then she'd have to learn to live with her decision. She'd learned to live with tough decisions before. She turned back to face her assistant. She didn't want to hurt Molly, but she needed more time.

"I don't know if I'm ready to talk about this yet, Molly. As you've figured out, David and I became close during the past couple of weeks. He's very charming, very easy to like, and I . . . I lost control for a while there. But I came to my senses. He's not for me, and I'm not the kind of woman he should have. So we agreed to part. End of story."

"Is that so?" Molly sounded unconvinced. "A man who phones you morning, noon and night for three days running and gets more agitated with each call you refuse doesn't sound like someone who's agreed to part to me. I just want you to know, if and when you need an ear, I'm here, and it'll never go farther. I hope you won't take what I said the wrong way, Gussie, but I'd hate to see you hurt again."

Gussie was moved and reached out her hand. This caring business was emotionally draining. "Thanks for your friendship, Molly. I was hoping you'd understand."

Molly grasped her fingers warmly. "I'm trying. But why anyone would let a gorgeous man like David Lamb get away is more than I can fathom. Now why don't you . . ."

A quick knock came at the door, and it opened as Connie stuck her head in. "Hey, guess what?" she asked, walking in and going over to the credenza on the far side of the room. "Your superstar writer's on Channel 2, Gussie, a taped interview on CBS from last week." She snapped on the small television set and adjusted the picture. "There he is. Lord, but that man's handsome."

Molly had already walked over, and Gussie felt she'd look odd if she didn't join them. Rising, she strolled nearer, her hands crammed into her jacket pockets. There he was, all right, wearing jeans, a blue shirt and a tweed jacket, comfortably chatting with talk-show host Evan Maxwell, who wore an impeccably tailored suit, a crisp white shirt and a silk tie. She remembered she'd asked David to dress up for the interview, but he'd just smiled at her and told her he wasn't trying to impress anyone with his clothes, just with his books. And didn't he manage to outshine Evan by a mile.

"Were you there when they filmed this, Gussie?" Connie asked, her eyes still on the set.

"Backstage, yes." Why was her voice suddenly husky and her palms damp? Because he looked so damn good, and she was remembering, remembering.

"I'm surprised he's not wearing that awful tie he wore in here that first day," Molly commented. "He looks like a man who might slip that ratty thing on for national TV just for the fun of it."

"He's color-blind, you know," Gussie said softly. "He'd put the most outlandish clothes together, like a walking rainbow." She heard the two women chuckle, but she didn't join in. Probably because she suddenly felt more like crying.

One of the secretaries stopped in the doorway. "It's five o'clock, ladies, and I'm leaving. See you all Monday."

Gussie heard the goodbyes but didn't trust her voice just then. Turning, she went back to her desk, pulled out her briefcase and began stuffing files and envelopes inside. She had to get away, to be off alone, before she embarrassed herself.

Molly walked over, her shrewd eyes studying Gussie. "Are you all right?"

She continued cramming the case. "Yes, fine. Just tired." She zipped the case closed, grabbed the handles and reached for her shoulder bag. "Molly, I probably shouldn't right now, but I'm going up to my ranch for a few days. I need . . . some time away. Can you handle things?''

"Don't I always?" She moved to give Gussie a quick hug. "Do I tell anyone you're in Cold Springs?"

Jared wouldn't ask because he was still angry with her. David would give up after being repeatedly rebuffed by her office and finding only her answering machine on at her home. "I'd rather you didn't. Besides, as you know, I purposely didn't have a phone put in up there. I'll rent a car, and if I don't drive back Monday morning, I'll go into town and call you. If anything urgent comes up, send me a wire through Silas, as usual.''

Molly nodded. "You rest. Time has a way of easing things. We both know that, don't we?"

Gussie shoved in her chair. "We ought to.''

"Well, that handsome devil,'' Connie said as a commercial flashed on the screen. "Do you know what he just told Evan Maxwell? That there was only one thing he and Beau Kendall had in common.''

"What's that?" Molly asked.

"That like Beau, when he met the woman of his dreams, he'd move heaven and earth to make her his.'' She clicked off the set and smiled dreamily. "There's one guy who can park his shoes under my bed anytime.''

Move heaven and earth, would he? Gussie pondered. What else, chain her to the bedpost until she agreed to his ways? Was that what he meant, or was she reading too much into a simple statement? "Connie, you'll probably be hearing from Larry Brice next week.'' She went on to explain her conversation with Connie's author.

"Terrific. Thanks for the warning." She went to the door. "Have a good weekend.''

Molly slipped her arm around Gussie's waist as they followed. "Have a good run on Bridget. That always makes you feel better."

"I will. And you have a good time with the man of the hour, whoever he may be."

"Still Elliot, and I will. Good night."

Squaring her shoulders, Gussie headed for the bank of elevators. Some hours in the sun, riding like the wind on Bridget's back, feeling free. Yes, that's what she needed. Then, perhaps when she returned, she could concentrate on her work.

David was having trouble concentrating on his work. He kicked at the sand as he walked along the beach behind his house. Trouble concentrating, trouble enjoying himself, trouble sleeping. And trouble was spelled *G-U-S-S-I-E*.

Hands shoved deep into the pockets of his white dungarees, he squinted up at a bright noonday sun. He'd run the gamut of emotions the morning he'd awakened in Chicago and found Gussie gone. Surprise, disappointment, hurt, anger.

He'd thought they'd shared something very special. Not thought, knew. He *knew* they had. He couldn't be mistaken about such a thing. Despite her one encounter ten years ago, Gussie Lyon had been all but virginal. Innocent, inexperienced, untouched by love. He'd shown her the way, and she had opened to him like a new flower reaching for the sun. She'd reveled in her newfound sensuality, and they'd spent a wondrous night. Why, then, had she slipped out like a thief in the night before he'd awakened?

Stopping to watch a low-flying gull, he breathed in the clean, salty air. A thief, for she'd stolen his heart, his peace of mind, his concentration. He'd been hurt and much too angry to phone her or go after her. After all, he had his pride. He had questions, a lot of questions, but he'd be damned if he'd let her know. No self-respecting man went on wanting a woman who could so easily walk away from him. So he'd come home to lick his wounds, to get back to work, to get over her. Only it wasn't working.

He'd phoned her then, to talk about his new book, he'd told himself. Molly had been polite, but firm. Gussie Lyon was in a meeting, or out to lunch with an author, or gone for the day. Molly had offered her assistance on the manuscript, but he could hear in her voice that even she doubted if that was what his call was all about. He'd politely and firmly thanked her.

Five days, and several unfruitful phone calls later, David was still fuming and ranting and raving. He'd tried drowning his disappointment by consuming an extraordinary amount of wine one evening all alone on his moonlit patio. The next day he'd worked till the wee hours, then thrown most of it out the following morning. He'd swum and run along the beach until he could scarcely move, yet sleep hadn't come. And neither had the answers to his questions.

Head bent, David headed for his house. Ending a relationship had always been easy for him. Usually he and the woman mutually agreed that what had once been exciting no longer was, and it was time they both moved on. But not this time. Not with Gussie. Even though the two of them agreed on practically nothing, the thought of not seeing her again had his palms damp and his heart racing.

Entering his sunny kitchen, he noticed that even that cheerful atmosphere didn't brighten his mood. Something had to be done. Only what? What would Beau do? he asked himself as he poured a cup of coffee. Beau would go after Mandy, talk with her, and only if she told him in so many words that she didn't care, didn't want him in her life, only then would he walk away permanently. As Beau's creator,

David would probably have him thinking that pride was a lonely bedfellow, something only arrogant men boasted of.

Finding the coffee bitter, he dumped the rest into the sink. Maybe he had been prideful and a touch arrogant. He'd never had to pursue a woman before and had told himself he wasn't about to start now. Only this was different, special. Because Gussie had become so special to him.

Enough! He'd go, hear it from her own lips, and settle things one way or the other. Picking up the phone, he dialed his travel agent. There was some comfort in having reached a decision.

The receptionist for Lyon Publishing sat behind a large desk facing a bank of elevators. As David approached her, he wondered if she'd been given his name by Gussie with an explanation that if he called or showed up, she was not in. He put on his most charming smile and stopped in front of her. Her nameplate read Cheryl.

"Good morning. I'm here to see Augusta Lyon," he said, making his voice sound impersonal and businesslike. "The name's David Lamb." He thought he saw a flicker of recognition in her eyes at the mention of his name before she lowered them to check her appointment sheet.

"I'm sorry, Mr. Lamb, but I don't see your name on here. Did you have an appointment?"

He recognized the voice of the woman on the phone who'd been making Gussie's excuses for her. "No. I just got into town, and I need to consult with her." He held up a large manila envelope. "It's about my new manuscript."

"Ms. Lyon isn't in. Would you like me to ring her assistant, Molly Judd?"

So she was still playing hide-and-seek. Workaholic that she was, she was here, all right. Would she hide in the rest-room once she was informed that he was in the building? he

wondered. Maybe he could convince Molly to tell him. A
he remembered, she'd been quite friendly when they'd met
He gave the receptionist an agreeable smile. "Yes, woul
you, please?"

David tried not to pace while he waited. Waiting was no
something he did well, or often. Since meeting Gussie, he'
done far more than he preferred.

"Mr. Lamb," Cheryl said, "Molly said to go right or
back to her office. Down that hallway, turn left, and it's th
second door from the end."

"Thank you, Cheryl." He was mildly surprised tha
Molly hadn't claimed to be too busy, also. Her door wa
open, and as he paused in front of it, she looked up from he
desk and smiled.

"Good to see you again, Mr. Lamb," Molly said, stand
ing and reaching out her hand.

He gave her a firm handshake. "You, too, Molly, and cal
me 'David,' won't you?"

"Have a seat, David." Molly, too, sat, then folded he
hands atop a manuscript she'd been working on. "I'm sorry
Gussie isn't here. Is there anything I can help you with?"

Obviously a hardworking woman, David surmised
glancing about. Books, manuscripts and papers wer
stacked everywhere, on shelves, the wide windowsill and
even the floor. Framed book covers and a few pictures dot
ted the wall behind her desk. A lone rubber-tree plant oc
cupied a corner and a huge stuffed koala bear leaned agains
another. Yet there seemed some organization to the chaos
and a warmth that undoubtedly reflected its occupant. Da
vid tried to look relaxed as he returned Molly's smile.

"It's too late for breakfast, too early for lunch and too
ridiculous that she'd be in another all-day meeting. Wher
is she, Molly?" He watched her calm blue eyes reassess him

"I imagine, if she wanted you to know, she'd have told you herself."

Good. She wasn't going to pretend she didn't know what he was talking about. He crossed his legs and leaned back. Molly was in her mid-to-late thirties, he would guess. She seemed smart, loyal and protective. A confidante? Probably. He'd try a long shot. "Do I look like the kind of man who'd push myself on a woman?" Her lips twitched a little at that one.

"You don't look as though you'd need to, no."

"How long have you known Gussie?"

"Ten years, six working with her and four before that."

They had to be close. What would it take to get this woman to open to him? "All I want to do is talk with her."

Molly picked up a pen and toyed with it. "You were together for nearly three weeks," she pointed out.

Not nearly long enough, he wanted to scream at her. He shifted in his chair. "We were working. Interviews, autographings, tapings, traveling. I want to talk with her alone, away from the pressures of work."

"When she returns, I'll tell her that."

He was having more than a little trouble keeping his temper in check. "And when is she returning?"

"I can't really say."

David shot out of the chair, unable to sit still. Marching to the window, he leaned against the frame. He'd always admired loyalty, but today he was finding it highly annoying. "I won't hurt her, you know." Hearing only silence, he turned back to see a skeptical look on her face. "Do you think I would?"

"I don't know you, David."

"Molly, I care about her." Though Gussie had dismissed his feelings breezily, perhaps Molly wouldn't.

"Have you told her that?"

"Yes." He returned to drape himself on the chair. "She didn't believe me. I need to convince her."

Molly came around the desk and leaned against the edge, studying him for long moments. "Gussie prides herself on always being in control. Someone who cares can frighten a person who fears a loss of control. Since you came into her life, I see her uncertain, confused, doubting herself."

"Good. That's a start. At least she's admitting to some feelings."

"For what it's worth, David, I think Gussie needs someone. Whether that someone is you, I can't tell."

"How can I convince her that I care if I can't find her?"

"I'm sorry. I can't divulge a confidence. I value Gussie's friendship too much. She's been as miserable since her return as you look. She had to get away for a few days, to be alone and do some thinking. We all need to regroup once in a while." She walked back to her chair.

So she really wasn't in the building. Why couldn't she have been here? Why did she go away now and...what? She'd needed to be alone, to think and regroup? David sat up taller in the chair. Of course, why hadn't he remembered that sooner. That had to be it!

Getting a grip on himself, he stood, making an effort to keep his expression blank. He didn't want Molly to realize he'd guessed Gussie's probable location, or she just might call and warn her. "I'm sorry to have taken up so much of your time."

Molly shook his outstretched hand. "No problem."

"By the way," David said as he handed her the manila envelope, "here's part of my new book. It isn't finished yet, of course. I'm a little concerned about the opening. Maybe you'd like to take a look at it."

"Thank you. I will."

"I'll be in touch." He went out the door, and stood just outside it.

He heard Molly sigh as she riffled through the pages of his manuscript. Every sheet was blank except the first one, which contained one sentence: It was a dark and stormy night. He listened as Molly laughed out loud. Then he headed for the elevator.

Once back on the ground floor, David hurried over to the information desk. The young man behind it looked up as David stopped in front of him.

"I need to get to Cold Spring in upstate New York as quickly as possible. Do you know where I can rent a car?"

Bridget was a palomino, a two-year-old beauty whose colors ranged from pale cream about her face to a rich gold near her tail. Gussie had fallen in love with her gentleness, her independence and her white mane at first sight. As the late-afternoon sun hung low in the sky, she hefted the saddle onto Bridget's back and murmured sweet talk into her twitching ears.

"Let's go race the sun, old girl, just you and me and the hot summer wind." Grasping the saddle horn, she swung up in one graceful movement. She let her eyes roam over the long stretch of green grass as she took the reins.

She'd ridden every morning and afternoon for the three days she'd been at her ranch, and found that each time she enjoyed it more. The kinks were out of her muscles and the cobwebs out of her brain. Almost.

She'd walked through the wooded area to the north of her acreage, waded in the cool water of the little creek, read a great deal, slept late and spent much time thinking. Silas, the retired farmer who lived two miles away, had come daily as usual, to see to Bridget, to chop wood for her fireplace and just to chat. Her sanctuary. This place had been her

sanctuary for years now, a place to retreat to when the outside world overwhelmed her. And this was one of those
times.

This morning when she'd stopped at the small grocery
store at the crossroads and called Molly, she'd almost decided to head back to the city tomorrow. But hearing that
things were under control, with no new crises on the hori-
zon, she'd decided a few more days wouldn't matter. And
no, no one had been looking for her, Molly had said. Not
Jared and not David. Well, good. Wasn't that what she'd
wanted?

With a kick of her heels, Gussie sent the palomino toward their usual run. Bridget wanted the release of speed
after the confines of the barn, and Gussie didn't blame her.
She let the horse have her head, let the warm air beat about
her face and toss her hair about.

This was freedom and pleasure and the thrill of a powerful strength beneath her. And it was a unique shared trust,
she in the horse's instincts and Bridget in her skill as a rider.
She felt at home here, confident, unafraid. After the past
week, it was a joy to feel that way again. Laughing into the
wind, she let the horse pound up the dusty turf.

David parked the gold Mustang in the graveled driveway
and turned off the engine with a sigh. He'd rented the
powerful little car because he'd been in a hurry, and it had
served him well. Rolling his shoulders, stiff from the tense
drive, he got out and looked around.

The house looked like a fieldstone hut, not too large, with
a sturdy slate roof and leaded-glass windows. Old but recently refurbished, as Gussie had told him. He cocked his
head at the fireplace chimney, where small puffs of smoke
drifted toward a graying sky. Someone was here, all right,

he thought as he pulled on his sweater. It was much cooler this far north, but, then, he'd been expecting that.

Walking to the front door, he used the heavy brass knocker and stepped back. He'd rehearsed a dozen openings and discarded each, deciding finally to go with his instincts when Gussie opened the door. Only she wasn't answering. He knocked again, harder.

Impatiently David peered in through one of the window panes. Yes, a fire going, though nearly out. A cup sitting on the low coffee table in front of the fireplace and a planter overflowing with flowers. African violets. He smiled.

Going around the side, he checked the garage and found a red Toyota inside, a rental sticker on the bumper. Definitely on the right track. Circling around back, he spotted the barn some distance from the house and headed for it. Had she gone for a walk or was she riding her horse? He stepped around a sawed-off stump and stopped, listening. Horse's hooves hit hard-packed dirt, some distance away yet. He walked to the weathered wooden fence, stuck his foot on the lower rung and leaned on the top to wait.

When she came into sight, he realized she was too engrossed to notice him. As she neared, he saw the skillful movements of her hands and knees that slowed the palomino. She turned her just before the edge of the grass line. She handled the horse with style, with control, with a certain flare—as he'd known she would. He'd never seen her look so appealing, hair wild from the wind, casual blouse worn with blue jeans. Prancing in place, the horse wasn't ready to end the run, but Gussie talked lightly to her, soothingly, until she quieted and moved to a cooling walk. It was then that she looked up and saw him.

He watched emotions play across her face as horse and rider came to a halt. At the corner fence line, she dismounted, tied the reins to the post and stroked the palomino's thick neck for long moments as she stared at David. With a final touch, she left and slowly came toward him. He walked to the open gate and waited.

Gussie was a hundred yards from him when he saw her break into a run, arms outflung, aiming right for him. His heart soaring, he ran to meet her. At the instant she touched him, he grabbed her into a bear hug, swung her around and buried his face in her hair.

"Thank God you've come," Gussie whispered into his ear.

Without a word, David lifted her into his arms and made for the door leading into her house.

Chapter Nine

Inside, the house was cool, sheltered by the overhanging trees. David was hot, his skin already damp, his clothes sticky obstacles he could hardly wait to be free of. He marched through the kitchen and down the hallway as if he knew the way to her bedroom, as if he'd been there before. Maybe he had, in his dreams.

When he'd picked her up by the barn, she'd clasped her arms around his neck and clung to him, her head resting on his shoulder. But David knew the submissive posture was temporary, for he felt her heart pounding against his, felt the breathy release of air from her lungs against his throat. They were both coiled with need, heightened by their days spent apart. The time for slow loving was past.

He pushed open the door to her room and strode to her bed. The slatted blinds let in only shadowy light, enough to see the excitement on her face as he lowered Gussie to the mattress and lay down beside her. He pulled off her boots and slipped off his own shoes and sweater. The bed was un-made. The intimate fragrance of her on the pastel sheets still lingered from the night before. He found the scent irresist-ible. He touched his mouth to hers and inhaled.

Under Gussie's fingertips, the pulse in his throat throbbed, matching the wild cadence of her heart. She felt a need to touch, to soothe, to love. She knew this man's body better than she knew his mind, yet she sent her hands on a journey to know him better. She thought she heard a whippoorwill call to its mate outside the window. Then she thought only of his mouth, hard and firm yet infinitely gentle, pressing to hers, deepening the kiss. Heat spread within her, racing helter-skelter, rising from her toes to flush her cheeks. Her fingers tightened, clenching the material of his shirt. His hands were in her hair, on her face, then mov-ing to the opening of her blouse.

Her eyes were smoky as he gave a quick yank and sent the last button flying across the room. He saw she was stunned as always at the spiraling need clawing at her within mo-ments of his touch. He felt it, too, and saw the arousal that had him trembling with answering desire.

"No one's ever kissed me the way you do," she mur-mured, raising her hips so he could tug off her jeans. "No one's ever set me on fire like this. How do you do it?" His whispering breath on her stomach was more potent than a hard fist in getting her attention. He flung her bra aside, and she closed her eyes as his warm mouth moved to taste what he'd uncovered.

For the first time in her life, Gussie didn't want to be in control, but rather to follow his knowing lead. Suddenly he, too, was naked, and she had no recollection of when he'd shed his clothes. Steeped in pleasure, she could only feel. Her one thought was that she wanted this feeling to go on forever. With the slightest urging, she would walk on hot coals for him, if only he wouldn't stop. "How?" she asked again as her world tilted and swayed.

"Method-acting classes," he said as he shifted to draw on the rosy readiness of her other breast. David's whole body ached with such overwhelming need for this woman that he thought it just might shatter. How was it possible to want so badly, to be consumed so thoroughly, so that the very essence of her hummed in his brain like a symphony out of control?

"And how do you bring me to my knees by just entering a room? How do you drug my senses from thousands of miles away? How?"

Now she was moaning softly, her hips arching to meet his seeking hand. He returned his lips to hers, needing to sample more. Desire was a white-hot flash that stripped him of all patience, passion a red flame that made him a little crazy. He could feel the hammer beat of her heart as his mouth moved lower to taste more of her, to make her his in a way she'd never known.

David felt her nails scrape the flesh of his back, heard her cry out his name as she shuddered to the first delirious peak. Her breathing was ragged, her eyes filled with the shock of an impossible elation that rippled through her still. As she floated in the aftermath, he moved back up to kiss her, then entered her with a wildness that stunned him.

But not Gussie. She shifted to accommodate him more fully, then urged him closer with hands suddenly sure, suddenly knowing. She felt his pulse pound and sighed as she tightened around him. He was pounding for her, throbbing almost out of control for her, aching with need for her. Not for *a* woman, but for *this* woman. He'd come three thousand miles after her, his cravings as desperate as hers, his loneliness as obvious as hers. No one else ever had. If she didn't have everything, at least she had this, a passion few women had known. It would have to be enough.

She began to move with him then, slowly at first, then more frantically. His mouth descended to hers, fusing them together. The blood was roaring in her ears as his breath trembled against her damp skin and the fire threatened to consume her. At last, she let the explosion take her.

Waking to find a man quietly watching her was something Gussie had never experienced. Awareness came back slowly, of where she was and what she'd been doing right before she'd drifted off. Making love. She'd been making love, and then her sated body, exhausted from a week of wakeful nights, had dragged her into a deep sleep. How long she'd slept, she had no idea. She knew only that evening shadows were filtering in through the high windows and David's stomach was growling.

With a laugh, she brushed back her hair. "Still hungry, I hear. I thought men smoked afterward, not yearned for food." She made as if to rise, but with a lazy movement, he pulled her back down to him.

"I don't smoke, so I wouldn't know. But hunger is a relative term. One man's appetite is another man's gluttony." He tightened his hold on her. "With you, I find myself suddenly ravenous." He touched his mouth to hers in a long, lingering kiss.

"This *could* get to be habit-forming."

"Not all habits are bad for you."

Gussie eased onto her own pillow, wishing the top sheet was within reach. This was still difficult for her, chatting with a man while lying naked in bed. It was one thing when passion was clouding her mind, and quite another when her thoughts were sharp and clear. "The trouble is that you don't know if it's a good habit or a bad one until it's too late and you're already hooked."

David rolled to his side and propped his head so he could see her face. "Tell me, as a professional worrier, doesn't it get awfully tiring fretting over every little thing, examining every emotion and feeling? Don't you ever want to just go with it, see what will happen?"

"Obviously I do, or I wouldn't be here with you."

"But I'm the one who came after you. Why did you walk out on me, Gussie?"

"Because you're a weakness in me."

"How flattering. Like a tendency to catch colds or an inclination to drink too much."

"Sort of." She laid a hand on his arm to take the sting from her words. "You make me forget myself, forget my goals, forget everything, give in. I've seen what weaknesses can do to people—my mother, for instance."

David played with a lock of her hair, intent on letting her talk. Maybe, if he listened long and hard, he'd find the key to this complicated puzzle named Gussie. "I would think it would take a strong woman to live with Jared Lyon all these years."

"I suppose it depends on what you mean by 'strong.' My mother didn't give up a potentially dazzling career, nor have I ever heard her say she wanted anything other than to be Jared's wife. But she gave him something infinitely more important." She looked at him, narrowing her eyes intently. "She gave up her opinions, her thoughts, even her desires. She lives the way he wants to, dresses to please him—I doubt if she even remembers what her favorite color is, but his is blue, and, therefore, that's the dominant color of her wardrobe. She eats what he likes best, vacations at the places he loves and reads his favorite authors. My God!"

The picture was becoming clear. "And so her weakness is that she loves your father too much and therefore loses herself in the process?"

"Well, doesn't she?"

"I don't know, Gussie." He lay back, bending his arms and placing his head in his hands on the pillow. "It's not a weakness if she genuinely wants to do all that."

"She's so busy doing what he wants that she no longer remembers what she wants. If that's love, they can keep my share."

"But do you think she's happy in the life she leads?"

"For a puppet who's letting someone else pull the strings, I guess she is."

Abruptly he turned and leaned over her. "We're not talking about your parents' situation here really, are we? We're talking about you and me. You think if you let yourself love me that I'll want to be in charge of you, of your thoughts, your work, your very life, to change what you want and make it into what I want. Am I right?"

"You already are changing me. Why do you think I'm here at my ranch? Because I couldn't work efficiently. Because you filled my thoughts, my waking moments, my sleepless nights. I don't have the experience to cope with you, or my feelings about you. I didn't give you permission to do this to me, and I don't like it one bit."

"Neither do I." He saw her arch a brow in surprise. "Why do you think *I'm* here? Because *I* couldn't work, couldn't think of anything or anyone but you. I didn't intend for this to happen, either." He watched that sink in.

"Well, then." Gussie took a deep breath. "So what do we do now?"

"We fix it." David rolled from her, sat up on the edge of the bed and reached for his underwear. He'd taken a great many psych courses in college, figuring he'd need them to develop strong characters in his writing. More than once, he'd had to reach for some scrap of acquired knowledge to motivate the people in his books accurately. But this was real life, not a book. Yet the same principles applied.

Many times, though he'd planned that a character would behave a certain way, he'd had to alter his plan to conform with that character's emerging personality as the book progressed. He'd thought he had a handle on Gussie, thought that by offering her the love she'd never had, she'd come willingly to him. His take-charge-of-the-situation attitude had always worked in the past. But not this time. He had no choice but to try an about-face to see if that would work. He tugged on his jeans.

"What are you doing?" Gussie asked.

"Getting dressed. Leaving."

"Leaving? Why? Is that how you intend to fix us, by running away?"

Shirt in his hand, he turned to her. "Look, Gussie, we're two intelligent people who happen to be attracted to each other, but we can handle that. We want the same things from life. You want to be in control of your own life, to be independent, to one day run Lyon Publishing your way. I want to be in charge of my life. I didn't move away from the well-meaning but suffocating environment of my youth to where I could be alone in my house by the sea to give it all up for an iffy relationship. So we'll clench our teeth, get over this passion we seem to feel for each other and go on with our lives. We've overcome tough problems before and will again. You were right. It's best this way."

He shrugged into his shirt, watching her from under lowered lashes. He hoped he hadn't overplayed his hand.

Slowly Gussie slipped off the bed and went to the closet. She grabbed an oversize shirt and put it on, buttoning it slowly. An iffy relationship. Yes, she supposed that's what they had. "I'm glad you're being reasonable about this. I mean, I love the way you make love with me, but . . ."

"But there's more to life than lovemaking, right?"

"Yes, right." She shoved back her hair with a hand that wasn't all too steady. Why was she uncomfortable with his attitude when it was exactly what she'd wanted? Wasn't it?

David sat down and picked up a shoe. "I suppose we'll have to have some contact. After all, you're my editor. But we can do most of our work by mail or phone."

He was really serious. She felt a little hurt that he was willing to impersonalize their relationship so quickly. The thought of not seeing him again *ever* was not sitting too well with her. She'd once quit smoking, and she'd had to do it in degrees, not cold turkey.

"Well, we needn't get drastic about this whole thing." She switched on the bedside lamp. "I mean, you don't have to rush off right away. It's a long drive back to New York. We can have something to eat, and you can go back tomorrow morning." She walked over to him as he sat holding one shoe in his hand. "I do care about you, David, and we...we interact well together. I'd like us to stay friends."

Interact well together? With effort, David kept his face straight. "I'd like that, too." He stood, brushed a silky strand of hair from her cheek and smiled into her confused eyes. "We can be anything you like. Coworkers, friends, even lovers. We just won't let our emotions get involved. That's where the rub comes in. Am I right?"

"Yes."

He took a step closer, ran a fingertip along her jawline and saw a small muscle twitch involuntarily. "You've recently discovered you're a very sensuous woman. There's no need to end that part of our relationship. That is, if you want to continue. I love making love with you, too. I know I can keep a handle on my emotions if you can."

"Certainly I can."

His hand moved to the back of her neck, and he saw her fight a shiver. "You're sure?"

"Absolutely." Gussie wished her voice didn't sound so unsteady. He was being extremely reasonable and very practical. There was no reason for her to feel anything but relief.

Leaning down to her, David touched his lips to the tender spot at her temple and watched her eyes drift closed. "Do you want to stay lovers, with no strings attached?" He felt her arms slowly creep around him, then her hands clutched his shoulders as he let his lower body come into intimate contact with hers. Caressing her hair with one hand, he pressed her closer to him with the other. "Do you, Gussie?"

Too late. All her fine warnings to herself, her wonderful resolutions, her amazing self-discipline were all too late. He was in her blood, in her very pores, in her heart. Sure, she would strike a bargain with him, because she couldn't refuse, not now, not just yet. And maybe, from somewhere, she'd find the courage to keep her end of it.

She drew her head back and got lost in the deep blue of his eyes. "You writer types all talk too much, did you know that?" she asked. As a sigh trembled through her body, Gussie reached up to bring his mouth down to hers.

She'd never seen a man bake cookies before. Tongue caught between his teeth and eyes narrowed against the oven's heat, David crouched to peer inside, checking on his cookies. Gussie leaned on the kitchen counter, enjoying the sight. A most unusual man, she decided, not for the first time.

They'd made love after their little talk, then shared a shower and made love again under the cooling spray. Gussie had never thought herself insatiable in any sense of the word, yet when it came to David Lamb, she definitely was. Studying him now in his sweater and well-fitted jeans, a lazy smile on his face, she wanted him. Who would have believed it?

She'd pulled on a pair of sweatpants and a long shirt, shoving up the sleeves as she'd marched into the kitchen to fix dinner—such as it was. She hadn't been expecting company. But David had made the hot dogs and potato chips seem like a feast, insisting on eating by candlelight with the radio playing softly in the background. The bottle of Bordeaux they'd found in the cupboard had lent a festive air. But his sweet tooth craved cookies, he'd told her, so she told him where the ingredients were kept and he went to work while she watched.

Watching David was no hardship. He was tan and lean, with smooth skin over hard muscles and that unruly hair she loved to run her fingers through. Now that they'd made a pact of sorts, she could relax and enjoy him without worrying that he'd misinterpret her long looks or she his.

Thank goodness they'd gotten that potential emotional messiness out of the way. Friendship she could understand. Lust, also, it would seem. Working well together, sharing fun such as this evening. But loving deeply meant adjustments, changes, transformations. They were neither of them willing to go that route, so they'd come up with the perfect solution. Caring without commitment. It would take a little getting used to, of course, but Gussie knew she could do it.

"First batch is ready for the taste test," David said as he held out a fragrant peanut butter cookie.

She took a cautious bite, rolled it around on her tongue and sighed. "Perfect. Did your mother teach you to bake these scrumptious things?"

David crunched on a tasty mouthful. "Nope. A woman I knew, a couple of years ago. A redhead with incredible green eyes. She used to ask me up to her place, and always she'd bake these. She used to say she loved the smell of cookies baking almost as much as eating them." He reached for another.

Gussie picked up her wineglass and strolled into the living room by the fire. It was stupid to be jealous, she chided herself. Years ago he'd said. Probably the redhead was history. Chances were baking cookies wasn't *all* they'd done. She took a sip, letting the wine warm her. It was none of her business. Not then, not now. Friends, that's all they were. She plopped on the couch and stared into the flames.

"I brought over a few more, in case you want another." David placed a dish of cookies on the low table in front of the fire.

"No, thanks, I think I've had quite enough."

He sat down, frowning. "Is anything the matter?"

"No, not a thing." She set down her glass just as a loud pounding sounded at the front door. Glancing at the clock, she saw it was nearly nine. She rose and went to peer out the window.

"Expecting someone?" David asked.

"No, it's my caretaker, Silas. He's the only one who knows I'm here, other than Molly." She swung open the door. "Hello, Silas. Come in. What brings you out so late?"

Silas stepped in, his silver hair windblown from the late evening breezes. "Got this here telegram delivered to my house a short time ago. Thought it might be important, so I brought it on over."

"How nice of you. Thank you." Gussie found her hands trembling. What if Jared had had another heart attack...no! She remembered her manners. "Would you like to stay and have some cookies? I have a friend visiting and..."

"No thanks, Gussie. I got to get back. The missus doesn't like being alone at night. But I thank you." Stepping back onto the porch, the old man waved to her. "I'll be over to-morrow to see to Bridget."

"Thanks again." Quickly she closed the door and ripped open the telegram.

David had seen her go white and guessed her fear. He moved to her, his eyes full of concern. "Anything wrong?"

She laughed in relief. "No, just Molly. I don't have a phone here, but I've told her to send a wire through Silas if something urgent comes up. Evidently she thinks this woman requesting an exclusive interview with you is important enough to warrant scaring me half to death."

"You thought it was Jared?"

She shrugged, trying to look unconcerned. "After a heart attack, you can't help but always be waiting for the other shoe to drop." She reread the telegram. "This television program is highly rated and would be wonderful exposure." She studied his face. "Does Molly know you're here?"

"I don't think so, though I did go to see her this morning, trying to find you."

"And she told you where I was?" She hadn't given a moment's thought to how he'd found her.

"No, your secret's safe with that woman. She did tell me that you had to get away, to do some quiet thinking. And you'd mentioned your ranch up in Cold Spring. The man at the grocery store in town knew where you lived when I described you."

"Thinking of competing with Beau Kendall, are you?"

"Maybe. So who wants the interview?"

"Andrea Wong. She's new to the East Coast, but well thought of, I hear. She's evidently heard how well the tour went and wants in on the momentum. They say she's tough, but she's got a tremendous following. It's a guest spot, a fifteen-minute segment on Friday night, nationally telecast from Boston. I don't think it would be wise to turn it down because . . . why are you smiling like that?"

"I went to college with Andrea. We even worked together one summer on a small San Francisco paper that folded the following year. I'd love to see her again. She's beautiful and bright, but she goes for the jugular. Let's do it." He pulled her into a casual embrace. "Besides, Boston's one of my favorite towns. Do you like lobster?"

Beautiful and bright, and he'd love to see her again. Terrific. "I don't think you need me for this one, David."

"Ah, ah. Where I go, you go, remember? Part of my contract." He nuzzled her ear, then the sensitive spot just under it. "We can walk in the Common, stroll around Faneuil Hall and make love on some creaky dock overlooking Boston Harbor for variety. What do you say?"

She pushed back from him. "*If* I decide to go with you, and that's still a big if, we can't go strolling around the city like two teenage lovers. It would be a business trip, and we'd have to conduct ourselves like professionals."

David sighed deeply. "You know, Miss Lyon, sometimes you can be a real pain in the rear with your tightly wound hair, your Victorian notions and your clipboard always at hand. Times like that, I want to shake you until all your hairpins drop out and you lose your notes and your cool."

Slipping his arms around her and pressing her soft curves to his lanky frame, he smiled down into her eyes. "On the other hand, I love to be with Gussie when she forgets who she is, when she's hot and churning under my hands, when her eyes go all cloudy and her mouth begins to quiver when

I kiss it like this." He brushed his lips across hers, whisper soft, and heard her pull in a sharp breath. His desire for her was evident now, throbbing between them, and he felt her begin to move, straining to get closer.

His eyes bore into hers. "So who's the real Augusta Jane Lyon, the proper lady or the fiery lover?"

Gussie could hardly stand, could hardly breathe. While her eyelids grew heavy, she slid her hands between them and closed her fingers around his fullness, watching his control slip a degree. Did he think only one could play this game? "You figure it out," she whispered.

Andrea Wong was gorgeous, a stunning Eurasian beauty who also had more than her share of brains, wit and charm. Gussie hated her on sight. She stood watching the taped interview on her office VCR and searched her pocket for an antacid. Finding a lone survivor, she bit down on it viciously.

She should have gone with him. That way she could have . . . could have what? Hovered over him, kept glued to his side, made sure he didn't succumb to the plentiful charms of Andrea? Ridiculous! And what if he did? She had no strings on him, at her insistence. So be it.

Gussie shut off the machine and wished she could shut off her jumbled thoughts as easily. Sitting down in her chair, she leaned back and closed her eyes. Nothing seemed to please her anymore. She hadn't wanted to hear words of commitment and forever from David, so he'd stopped giving them to her. She had wanted to maintain a casual, friendly relationship with him, and she couldn't fault him on maintaining that. She hadn't wanted to go to Boston with him so he'd accepted her answer and had gone on alone. Alone if you didn't count his old and dear friend, Andrea. Andrea who'd overnighted a tape to her office immediately for private viewing. Sweet. Considerate.

She hadn't wanted to feel this damnable jealousy, but there it was, hot and furious and all too frequent. Why, she asked herself, should she be jealous when she'd been the one who had wanted no part of deep feelings? Had she expected him to be her friend, her lover and a good little boy who wasn't susceptible to other women, as well? How very reasonable she'd become. Thoughts about having her cake and eating it, too, sprang into her mind. Yes, indeed, very reasonable.

And, like a dutiful author, David had called his editor and told her yesterday that he'd finished the taping, had a little shopping to do and would see her tonight. He had a few days before he had to get back to California. He'd told her to have the wine chilled and to have very little on. She'd told him to go soak his head.

She had half a notion to visit a friend and leave a note on her apartment door that something had come up. Of course, sleuth that he was, he'd probably ferret her out. She had half a notion to tell him she had a pounding headache and couldn't see him. That wasn't far from the truth, for since knowing David Lamb, she'd had more than her share of headaches. She had half a notion to leave early, stop at the grocer's and prepare the best dinner he'd ever eaten, chill the damn wine and be waiting in her filmiest negligee. Oh, God! This ambivalence was going to drive her crazy.

Arriving at a decision, she crammed several files into her briefcase, grabbed her handbag and headed for the door. She'd tell Molly she planned to finish her work from home. Yes, that sounded good. Lots of editors did that. Putting on a practiced smile, she left her office.

Something definitely was going on. The security guard in the lobby of her building flagged her down and told her to wait by his desk while he went to get the manager. Gussie shifted her briefcase, trying not to drop the heavy grocery bag she held in the other hand. What now?

The bustling little man with the lopsided toupee rushed out to greet her. Alex Fry claimed to be French, but even his accent was questionable. "So sorry to delay you, Miss Lyon, but I needed to explain."

"Yes, Mr. Fry, what is it?" Patience was not on the agenda this evening.

"I took the liberty of using my key to put everything in your apartment. I hope you don't mind, but we had no place else to put them."

Riddles yet. "What did you put in my apartment, Mr. Fry?"

"The flowers, ma'am. So fragile. But you see, storage for us is a problem and . . ."

"Let me get this straight. Someone sent me a bouquet of flowers, and you had them put in my apartment. Is that it?"

"Not a bouquet. Plants. White, purple, pink. So lovely."

They had done that before in her absence. Why was he so concerned this time? "Did you go up yourself and . . ."

"Oh, yes, madam. I was there the whole time the florist took them in. And I personally locked up." He gave her a toothy grin. "It is all right?"

Her bundles were too heavy to continue this nonsense. "Yes, fine. Thank you." Gussie shot him a parting smile and dashed for the elevator. The man made mountains out of molehills. At her apartment, she struggled to find her keys, then unlocked the door and shoved it open. Wearily she went in, thinking to get the groceries in first. She turned to go toward the kitchen, then stopped.

They were everywhere. Pink, white and shades of purple from light to deep. African violets in all manner of pots and dishes and baskets. One on each table, the mantel, the bookcases, the room divider. Perhaps Mr. Fry had a point. Stunned, Gussie made for the kitchen.

More. On the windowsills, the counter, the table. The dope, Gussie thought, fighting a silly smile. The big, overgrown dope. By the time she got to the bedroom and saw still more, she was grinning like an idiot, yet there were tears in her eyes, too. Just a few. No romancing, he'd promised. No, of course not. How did one fight this? Gussie wondered.

Later, showered and changed, with dinner preparations at the ready and the wine chilling, she walked around her apartment and touched each delicate plant, gently, lovingly. There were enough to open a greenhouse. He definitely knew how to mellow her. Furious and jealous by turns this afternoon, now here she was by evening, sighing like a schoolgirl.

When the doorbell rang, she tightened the belt of her gold silk jumpsuit, put on a friendly but dispassionate expression and went to answer it.

Her firm resolve lasted no more than ten seconds. David rushed in, shoved the door shut and reached for her. He twirled her around once, then bent to give her a long, open mouthed kiss that had her head whirling and her mind emptying. Caught up in it, she could only cling and let her senses spin until he set her down and lifted his head.

"Did you get my flowers?"

"I believe I did. But I counted, and you're one short. There's only forty-nine."

"Easy enough to remedy." He retrieved the box he'd left by the door, opened it and turned to her with one perfect white rose. "Number fifty."

Overcome, she buried her nose in the soft petals. Again tears threatened, but she pushed them back. "David, I thought we weren't going to do this . . . this romancing."

"Why not? We're friends, right? And lovers? Romance definitely is called for. That's a flower you're holding, lady, not a wedding ring. No commitments. Just beautiful flowers for a beautiful woman." He pressed a soft kiss to her forehead. "I missed you, A.J."

Melting. She was melting. She didn't have the strength to hold out against this, nor did she know of anyone who could. "But David, this isn't necessary. I . . ."

He frowned down at her. "Necessary? It wouldn't be fun if it were necessary. Pleasure, Gus. It gives me pleasure to please you. Say thank you, David."

"I'm *always* saying thank you, David."

"All right, tomorrow you send me flowers, and I'll thank you. Deal?"

Gussie shook her head. "I'm not making any more deals with you. They only get me in deeper." She dropped her eyes to the rose. "The wine is chilling, and I do have a special dinner nearly ready."

He looked surprised. "I thought you didn't cook."

"I don't, not often. I wanted to tonight."

He moved close, placing his hands loosely on her arms. "What do you want to do first—have a glass of wine, hear about my trip or show me your bedroom?"

Gussie felt the heat rise in her face. To hell with Andrea Wong. David was here and he was hers. To hell with wine and dinner, too. She took his hand and pulled him along the hallway. "I decorated it myself." He followed her into the room.

He never took his eyes from her. "I'm sure your room's lovely, but right now, I want to look at you, to touch you, to hold you." He lowered his head to kiss her, his arms pulling her against him so she could feel his heart beat. Two days apart, and he'd missed her so damn much. That kind of thing had never happened to him before with any other woman, and he wasn't quite sure how to handle his feelings. Was she really just stringing him along? Was she ever going to admit to her feelings, or was this the way it was going to be between them?

Gussie was becoming light-headed from the reality of kisses she'd spent two nights dreaming of. She nibbled at his lower lip, her hands roaming over him as she felt his fingers fumble with the silk belt at her waist.

"How do I get you out of this?" David asked.

Laughing, she stepped back to help him, when the phone rang. A smile still on her lips, she reached to pick up the bedside extension. "Hello?"

David watched the color drain from her face, then saw her sit down on the edge of the bed.

"No! My God, no!" Gussie closed her eyes. "Yes, all right. I'll be right there." In a daze, she replaced the receiver and turned bleak eyes to David. "That was my mother. Jared's had another heart attack."

Chapter Ten

He looked smaller somehow, and frail. She'd never seen her father look frail, not even after the first heart attack. Jared Lyon lay very still while an assortment of needles taped to him sent life-sustaining fluids into his body and tubes in his nose supplied oxygen. Behind him, machines that blinked little green lights and gave out subdued bleeps monitored his vital signs. Gussie stood studying the maze of modern medical technology and prayed all of it would somehow bring her father back.

Only five minutes, the nurse with the quiet rubber-soled shoes had told her as she'd allowed her into the intensive care unit. Not far from Jared's bed, the nurse kept watch inside a glassed-in office. All six beds were occupied, so she had her hands full monitoring the patients, each separated by a cloth partition, each fighting for life. Dry-eyed, Gussie pulled up a chair alongside her father's bed and sank into it.

Reaching through the bars of the aluminum guard rail, she laid her hand on his. His skin was dry and cool, his fingers not responding to her gentle squeeze. Fighting tears, Gussie looked at his face, always so ruddy and tan, now nearly as pale as the sheets. She'd been through this nightmare before, with the first attack. Why was it that he seemed further withdrawn from them this time, as if he hadn't the strength to fight his way back a second time? Or was it her own guilt making her feel that way since their last few conversations had not been friendly?

The day after she'd returned from her ranch, she'd gone to her office and found a summons to stop in to see Jared. Not a request, more a demand. Ordinarily she'd have bristled at the commanding tone of his note, but she'd been feeling mellow from the wondrous hours spent in David's arms. So she'd gone to his office with an open mind and a smile.

The old war horse had held a firm line, wanting to discuss a change in print run on a certain book that he hadn't authorized, a reprint of an old best-seller by one of her authors that was scheduled for release next month. He also wanted to know why she had left without telling him where she was going and why. Holding firm herself, but never losing her smile, she'd answered all his business questions calmly. They'd seen eye to eye until he'd started in on her personal life again.

She had lost her smile then, and a good deal of patience. Where was David Lamb? he'd wanted to know. Why hadn't he come to see Jared? Why wouldn't Gussie discuss David with her father, and just what was her relationship with David, anyhow? He had a right to know, he'd told her as he'd lit his cigar.

Gussie had stood then, pointed out the report on his desk that she'd sent detailing the tour with David Lamb. If he had any further questions after reading it, she'd answer. As to their relationship, it was none of his business. With a nod, she'd left his office, but not before she'd noticed the surprise on his face. Jared Lyon was not used to people refusing him, or standing up to him, not even his daughter. She so seldom had. It had felt good to beat the Lyon at his own game.

Now, looking down at him as vulnerable as she'd ever seen him, the memory didn't feel good. Had her adamant stand contributed to this attack? she asked herself. "People with the very best intentions will try to manipulate you," David had told her in discussing his own parents. "Other people can adjust and learn to live with our choices," he'd said. "But at what price?" she'd countered.

Gussie stood and squeezed her father's unresponsive hand again. "Is that it, Dad?" she asked in a hushed whisper. "Is that why you're here, because you can't adjust to my living my own life, because you can't respect my choices since that one big mistake years ago?" She leaned down to kiss his hand. "Get well, please. We need to hash this out, to settle things between us. We're long overdue. Don't die, please. Mother needs you more than the air she breathes. And I need you, too."

She caught the signal from the nurse as she laid Jared's hand down. Walking toward the doors, she dabbed at her eyes quickly as she made her way to the ICU waiting room.

Gussie stood in the doorway, giving herself a moment to compose herself. Dolores Lyon stood looking out the window at the night sky, lost in her thoughts. She was dressed beautifully, as always, every hair in place, her back ramrod straight. She was dignified even in her pain—an amazing woman, Gussie thought, if not a warm one. She had to admire her strength of purpose, if not her strength as an individual. She was there for Jared, always at his side, never wavering. It was hard for Gussie to comprehend such utter devotion.

Clearing her throat, she stepped into the room. "Mother, are you all right?" They'd hugged briefly when Gussie had first arrived. Her mother had never been one for touching.

Dolores turned, her blue eyes filled with concern, but dry. "Yes, of course. How is he?"

Gussie sat down on the small couch. "The same as you found him, I'm sure. What does the doctor say?"

Choosing the chair at the right angle to her daughter, Dolores sat down. She looked amazingly calm, Gussie noticed. The shredded tissue she held in one hand was the only sign of nerves to be seen. Well-bred men and women didn't show emotion in public, Gussie had often heard her mother say. The truth was, she'd seldom seen Dolores show emotion in private, either. Perhaps she only gave in to tears in the solitude of her bathroom with the door locked. Or perhaps she'd given up giving in to the futility of tears.

"Dr. Gellis said it was too early to tell how much damage this attack has caused. They're running some tests. If they find arterial blockage, they may have to do bypass surgery." Dolores took in a deep breath. "Your young man's gone to get us some coffee, though I told him not to bother."

Her young man. When, Gussie wondered, was her mother going to step into the eighties? She still spoke like a turn-of-the-century matron. She rubbed the back of her neck where tension had her muscles pulled taut. "He's not my young man, Mother, despite what Dad may have told you."

"Your father told me very little about him, but I do know he has the utmost respect for David Lamb, both as a writer and as a man."

"Do you find that reason enough to shove me into his arms?"

"Your father's an excellent judge of character, Augusta. You might allow yourself to learn a little something from him."

"Oh, I've learned a great deal from him, Mother."

"I'm glad to hear that. Jared told me that David is the first man he's met in years who is as strong as he himself is. Perhaps that's why he wanted you two to meet."

How could she tell this woman, who thought her father walked on water, that David being so like Jared was more a minus than a plus in her eyes? "Well, we *have* met, so let's leave it alone, shall we?" This wasn't the time or place to discuss relationships. Annoyed, she searched through her bag for the tin of aspirin she'd begun to carry with her. If she didn't get out from under all this tension soon, she'd be hauling around a whole pharmacy in her purse. Her mind traveled back to the pale man who lay fighting for his life at the end of the hall. "When can I talk with Dr. Gellis? Is he still here?"

"He's gone home but left word that he's to be called if there's any change in Jared's condition. You can probably catch him in the morning." She glanced to the doorway. "Oh, David, how very kind of you."

David came in carrying a small tray with three coffees. "I persuaded this woman in the cafeteria to make a fresh pot and to let me borrow these cups. That stuff in the machines is awful and I hate disposable cups."

"How thoughtful," Dolores told him as she took a cup.

Gussie wasn't surprised he'd charmed the waitress into fresh coffee. She was surprised the woman hadn't tossed in a chicken dinner, as well. Finding the aspirin, Gussie shook two into her hand and reached for her coffee. Swallowing, she made a face. Her stomach rolled in protest and she pressed a hand to her midsection. The antiseptic smells, the aspirin on an empty stomach and the strong coffee made a bad combination.

"How's Jared doing?" David asked as he sat next to Gussie. She was popping aspirin again, but he supposed under the circumstances it was to be expected. What he hadn't expected was to see her looking more irritated than upset. Had she had words with her mother?

"His condition is listed as critical, according to the nurse." Gussie got up and began to pace. She hated hospitals, hated having to speak in hushed tones, hated the waiting most of all. "Guarded, but critical, whatever that means."

David followed her, caught her at the window. He touched her hair lightly, then trailed his fingers down her cheek. "It means that they're doing everything possible and that he's got a fighting chance. We all know what a fighter Jared Lyon is."

She took a moment to absorb his comfort, to take solace from his solid presence. Back at the apartment, she'd argued that he needn't come with her, that she could handle going alone, but he'd insisted. She'd changed her mind. "I'm glad you're here." Her voice was barely a whisper, for his ears only. Seeing her mother's watchful interest, she moved from him.

"Mother, why don't you go home, get some rest," she suggested, walking to her side. "I'll stay and . . ."

"No, dear. I'm staying."

"But they'll only let one of us in for five minutes each hour."

Dolores looked up, her eyes suspiciously bright for the first time since Gussie had arrived. "I *want* those five minutes."

To love like that, Gussie thought in a moment of insight. Could she ever love like that? Her eyes rose and locked with David's over her mother's head. Perhaps she already did.

"You go home, dear," Dolores said. "I know you'll need to check in with the office in the morning, before you return. I'll call you if anything develops."

Gussie leaned down to give her mother a quick hug and found her arms tightening. When had her slim frame become this fragile? she wondered as she felt the outline of shoulder blades through her thin dress. Had she been too busy, too preoccupied to notice? She placed a light kiss on Dolores's cheek, then straightened. She turned to pick up her handbag and to hide a quick rush of emotion.

"Call me if you need anything," she told her mother.

"I shall."

"Mrs. Lyon, I'll see you tomorrow," David said as he clasped her hands warmly.

"Thank you."

David slipped his arm around Gussie's waist and guided her through the door. He was aware that her mother had been watching him carefully and wondered what conclusions she'd drawn. She'd asked a few seemingly innocuous questions while Gussie had been in with Jared. Dolores Lyon was sharper than he'd been expecting. Even in the midst of her concern for her husband, she'd probed a bit on behalf of her daughter.

Gussie was silent during the elevator ride, and he let her dwell on her own thoughts. He wished things were different, that he wouldn't have to play this game with Gussie. Being pals wasn't exactly what he'd had in mind.

But Jared's heart attack may have changed things. Now perhaps his poor health would cause him to step down. That would put Gussie in charge. Would work consume her then, effectively shoving David out of the picture except for an occasional visit? He couldn't second-guess that one. He'd just have to be patient.

Cabs were lined up outside the hospital, so David had no trouble hailing one. He didn't say much to her until they were back in her apartment.

"I know you've got a lot on your mind," he said as he followed her into the bedroom. It was nearly one in the morning, and they were both tired. "Maybe it'd be best if I check in at a hotel."

Gussie stepped out of her shoes and started to unbutton her jumpsuit. She didn't know quite how to tell him of her feelings; she only knew it had to be said. He was some distance from her as she raised her eyes. "Don't go, please. I need you tonight."

David was absolutely certain that that was the first time Gussie Lyon had ever admitted to needing anyone. It wasn't everything, but it was a step in the right direction. He nodded, then watched her go into the bathroom. In moments, he heard the shower running. Sighing, he started to undress for the second time that night.

He was lying on the bed, wearing only his briefs and browsing through a magazine, when she came back into the room. She didn't look at him, just went to her dresser and started brushing her hair. She needed space tonight, and he was willing to give it to her. She had complex feelings about her father to sort out. If she wanted to talk about them, he'd listen; but if she didn't, he wouldn't push.

"I'm sorry about dinner," she said almost absently. "I'll make it up to you."

He set aside the magazine. "That's not necessary. Are you hungry?"

"No, but I think I'll make a pot of tea. Want some?"

He shoved off the bed. "I'll make it. You relax."

Gussie didn't have the energy to protest, so she watched him pad barefoot toward the kitchen. She pulled the brush through her hair, letting the strands dry. Odd to have a man in this place where none had been before him. Odd but very nice. Too nice. She could get used to having him around. And soon she'd rely more and more on him. That wouldn't be nice, or practical.

She flung down the brush and went to the window. A million stars filled the night sky. "Please don't die, Dad," she whispered into the quiet. "I thought I was ready to run the show, but I'm not. Maybe I never will be. Maybe I never wanted it in the first place. Maybe I was fulfilling your dream and not mine."

Angrily she swiped at a lone tear trailing down her cheek. And she wasn't ready to lose him, either. God knows they hadn't been close. If only it wasn't too late, maybe they could be. Maybe this second heart attack would accomplish what the first hadn't—frighten them both enough to talk to each other, *really* talk. Maybe even big, strong, invincible Jared Lyon would have come face to face with his own mortality. Maybe they could be honest at long last.

Wearily she sat down on the bed, then stretched out. The past few days had taken a heavy toll—struggling with her feelings for David and then rushing to her father's bedside. She didn't want to think anymore, or even to feel. It would be rude to fall asleep before David had time to fix the tea she'd requested. She'd just close her eyes, she decided. Just for a minute.

David took his time. It felt good to be puttering around her kitchen, searching out cups, slicing a lemon. He had no idea how she took her tea. There were so many things he didn't know about her. Yet. He meant to discover them all.

He set the things on a tray, then hunted through her cupboards for a bud vase. He found one and placed in it the rose she'd left on the table in the foyer. Walking toward the bedroom, he found himself anticipating her smile when she spotted the flower. He'd come to look forward to that smile, to look for ways of bringing it about. He wanted to remove the sadness, the worry and confusion he saw on her face tonight, if only for a little while.

At the doorway he paused. She lay like a child, curled into herself, her head resting on her outstretched arm. He set the tray down and moved to the bed. She wore only a short satin robe, her hair dark against the spread. In the pale light from the bedside lamp, her skin looked almost translucent with smudges of fatigue under her eyes. He'd watched her sleep before in the aftermath of passion and during a couple of catnaps on the plane between tour stops. But he'd never seen her like this—completely unguarded, vulnerable, unprotected.

She was a tough lady in a tough business, and could hold her own with the best of them. She fought the good fight with her demons from the past and was winning, though she hadn't seen that yet. She was passion and poetry in bed, a student who'd all but surpassed the teacher. She brought out in him emotions he hadn't known he had: tenderness, compassion, the sudden need to protect.

Unable to resist touching her, he brushed her hair back, losing his fingers in the silky texture. He moved not with the impatience of building passion but with the patience of affection, of love. He willed her to waken, his heart suddenly filled with feelings.

Gussie stirred, slowly opening sleepy eyes. She was too tired or too relaxed to put up the shields she usually hid behind. He saw the soft welcome, the quick pleasure as she rolled onto her back.

"I didn't mean to fall asleep."

"It's all right." He leaned over her, propping one arm on the other side, dipping his head to nuzzle her cheek. It had been hours since he'd shaved, but she didn't seem to mind as she reached a hand to touch the stubble on his face. Tenderness moved through him like an ache, making him aware of a need to cherish this fragile woman.

He lowered his mouth to hers and kissed her softly, with no greed and no haste but with a silent urge to savor. She responded slowly, her lips returning the light pressure, exploring this new phase with him. He'd taught her so much, yet she was ready to learn more. He thought he might weep with the beauty of her trust. If only she could let herself trust him out of bed, as well.

"You are so lovely," he whispered. In her darkening eyes, he saw her dismiss that thought, and it angered him. "Don't brush my words away."

She frowned, fighting the haziness. "I don't need the flattery of words."

Yes, you do, more than most. "Maybe I need to say them." He slid a hand to the knot of her belt and undid her robe.

"What I need is for you to make love with me, so I won't have to think, just feel."

The warm scent from her bath enticed him. "I *am* making love with you." His fingers moved aside the robe and touched bare skin, lightly, gently, skimming over the satiny surface.

"Faster then. I need you to make the outside world go away, so that there's just you and me and this quiet room."

"Not speed, not today, Augusta Jane." He touched his lips to the corner of one eye, then the other. "We need to go slowly, to discover, to appreciate each separate pleasure." His mouth moved with infinite patience to circle her face, planting tiny moist kisses, finally stopping at her lips for a long, lingering taste. "You just lie still and enjoy. I'll do all the work."

She couldn't have moved if she'd wanted to, so languid were her limbs, so lax were her hands. She let the pleasure of his touch move through her like the finest wine. Gradually the tension she'd lived with for days slipped away, and Gussie felt the beginnings of surrender. She heard herself sigh his name, and, for the first time ever, she truly turned over her mind as well as her body into the care of another.

He felt the compliance and gathered her to him, cradling her in his arms. His mouth settled on hers, wanting to kiss away the fears that plagued her, the nightmares that haunted her. He used only gentleness as he deepened the kiss, only sensitivity as his tongue touched hers, only patience as she began to respond. He didn't want just the acquiescence of her body but the involvement of her emotions, the very thing she fought to withhold from him. He wanted to touch more than her skin; he wanted to reach her soul.

When he raised himself from her to remove his clothes, Gussie opened her eyes to watch. It was a sight she never tired of, the slow exposure of his exciting body. And still he didn't hurry, though this time she would have urged him to. Letting him set the pace, she waited, then shifted when he slid her robe from her.

Gussie saw his eyes wander over her, slowly, so very slowly. The blue seemed to darken as he gazed at her breasts, down over her trembling stomach, the length of her legs, all the way to her toes. And when he returned to meet her gaze, she saw admiration there, appreciation and an intensity that sent her heart soaring. Perhaps, if he could feel so much, she really *was* beautiful. Perhaps, if he wanted her this much, she really *was* lovely. Perhaps if he cared enough to let her see, love really *was* possible.

David was drugged with the sight of her lying quietly, letting him devour her beauty. Her scent wrapped around him as he bent to taste the slight indentation in her belly. He caressed the inside of her elbows with his tongue, then moved to linger at the pulse behind her knees. He'd told her to lie still, but she no longer could as he led another assault up her body. She moaned softly.

How could he have known that to watch this woman come alive under his hands and mouth would be more fascinating than rushing to his own fulfillment? How could he have known how arousing it could be to let her take over and trail her lips down the hard length of him?

Nothing before could have prepared Gussie for this invasion of her senses. She'd known that lovemaking would release passion and satisfy desire. But she'd not know that making love with David could comfort, could erase pain, could make her whole again. She'd entrusted him with her body before and this time had handed over her troubled mind. And he'd not let her down. But even his control had its limits.

She felt him shift her onto her back, then slip inside her as easily as if he belonged with her. She was beginning to think he did as he found the rhythm and began to move. As if made to cradle him, her hips kept time with his. Softly he whispered her name as he kissed her ear, his breath warm on her throat.

Gussie climbed the roller coaster with him, higher, and higher still. Then she was whirling, free-falling in a clear blue sky, her hands and heart joined with his.

There were cobwebs everywhere. Even in the dim light, Gussie could see them. Cautiously she moved forward, afraid to touch the tunnellike walls on either side where the filmy webs stretched and beckoned to her in a chilling wind that licked at her face. She had to get out of there, she knew, but there seemed no end to the tunnel.

She kept on going, needing to find the light. Then she heard the moaning, an awful keening sound, bouncing off the tin walls. Just ahead was a figure, a woman in a dark dress. She strained to see her. As she neared, Gussie saw that the woman was her mother and the terrible noises were coming from her.

"What's wrong, Mother?" she asked, but Dolores only swayed back and forth, chanting and weaving, her eyes tightly closed. Her pale face was streaked with mascara, a sight Gussie had never seen before. How could that be? Her mother prided herself on her appearance. Perhaps the woman only looked like her mother.

She turned to gaze down the corridor and saw a tall man with blond hair, his hand stretched toward her. Gussie ran toward him, reaching out to him. David. David would save her. But the faster she ran, the farther away he seemed. She screamed his name, but he just kept floating out of reach.

"Too late." She heard the words and looked around. Jared in his hospital gown was standing beside her. "We're both too late," he said. "I'm so sorry." But when she reached out to touch him, he was no longer there. Behind her, the woman who looked like Dolores moaned louder. Gussie turned back to David, saw him smile and wave to her.

"Wait for me," she called to him. She began running again, running and reaching out, faster and faster.

"Wait, please wait," Gussie muttered, her head thrashing on the pillow. "Don't leave me."

"I won't," David said, and pulled her to him, smoothing the hair from her face. "It's all right, Gussie. It was a bad dream. You're all right." Her restlessness had awakened him. Her cries had him reaching for her.

She came awake with a start, disoriented for a long moment, still picturing the long, black tunnel. She turned dazed eyes to David and sat up. Taking a deep breath, she shook her head, trying to dislodge the picture in her mind.

Next to her, David eased himself into a sitting position, touching her arm. "Do you remember the dream?"

She closed her eyes and let her head drop back. "Yes, all too vividly."

"Do you want to tell me about it? It might help."

She wasn't one to dream, certainly not like this. Before she could ponder the wisdom of it, she began to describe it to him. As she got to the end, she looked at him. "And you were there, at the end of the tunnel, holding out your hand and smiling. But I couldn't reach you. And the woman kept on sobbing."

David wiped the tears from her face with his fingers. "It's all right. I'm here. Everything's going to be okay."

She hadn't realized she was crying. She usually didn't put much credence in dreams, but this one had been so real, so frightening. She saw again the bleak face of her father saying he was sorry. Jared Lyon never apologized. What did it all mean?

David gathered her to him and settled them back against the pillows. But she broke free and scooted off the bed.

"I need to call the hospital. I have this awful feeling..."

He waited while she used the bedside phone. He felt a wave of relief when he heard Gussie ask again if the nurse on duty was certain her father's condition hadn't changed. Hang in there, Jared, he silently prayed. For your sake as well as for your daughter's. He watched Gussie hang up the phone and sit down on the edge of the bed. It was several moments before he realized she was silently weeping, her shoulders shaking.

Quickly he moved around and took her in his arms. He held her loosely against his chest, letting her cry it out of her system. He'd been wondering when it would happen. No one could lock as much inside as Gussie Lyon did without breaking sooner or later. He was just glad he was here when she did.

It took quite a while for the tears to subside, leaving her snuffling and hiccuping and embarrassed. In control again, she pulled back and reached for a tissue.

She handed him several, as well. "I...I'm sorry. I got you all wet."

"I'll dry."

"I don't know what came over me." Gussie mopped her face and threw away the tissues. "I'm really sorry."

"Don't be. I'm not." He slid an arm around her. "Give in, Gussie, just this once. Let me comfort you. Let the guard rails down."

"I don't know if I can, David." Slipping under the sheet, she lay down and turned on her side, away from him. God, how she hated someone to witness her loss of control. "I never do that. I just..."

David lay down behind her, close up against her. "You should do it more often. It's human and quite acceptable. I'm glad I was here for you."

"Do you enjoy holding sobbing women?"

He turned her in one swift movement and put his face very near hers. "I enjoy holding you—smiling, sobbing, sick, well, whatever. No restrictions. Don't you know that by now?"

"I don't want you to see me this way. Talk about shattering what few illusions you may have left about me."

"I don't base my feelings on illusions. I base them on reality, and that's what we had here. Your father's critical, and you had a nightmare about him and a very natural re-action afterward. There's no need to be ashamed of that."

Gussie thought again of her dream. "My mother's makeup was streaked in my dream. She must have turned her back when Jared showed up. She'd never let herself be seen that way."

"That's a shame. We all have a few imperfections we hide from the world, but not from the one who loves us the most. We expect that person to love us, warts and all." He touched a fingertip to the end of her nose. "I love you, warts and all."

She was silent, perhaps speechless. But her eyes were alive, boring into his, trying to ascertain if he meant it, trying to deal with her feelings. David watched and waited.

Gussie shook her head. "Don't love me, David."

"Too late."

"I'll probably hurt you."

"I'll risk it."

She drew in a deep breath. "Why are you doing this to me?"

He shrugged. "I don't know. Just thought it up for kicks. Tell the lady you love her and make her cry. Think it'll catch on?"

Gussie narrowed her eyes at him. "This isn't funny."

"I'm not laughing."

"It doesn't mean much when you have a long list of lov-ers you've said it to over the years and . . ."

"I've never said those three little words to any other woman, with the possible exception of my mother when I was around four. Maybe five. You can check that out with her, if you like."

Her eyes were skeptical. "No one? Not anyone?"

"No one."

"I'm the very first?"

He felt the warmth spread as he noticed the hope in her eyes. "Yes," he said softly. "And you're the very last, too." While she pondered that, he touched his mouth to hers.

Chapter Eleven

He's giving the nurses a hard time this morning." Dolores Lyon chuckled. "Dr. Gellis thinks that's definitely a good sign."

Gussie leaned back in her desk chair and let out a breath she didn't know she'd been holding. A good sign. She'd cling to that. She collected her thoughts and shifted the phone to her other hand. "So he's awake and talking? What's the prognosis? Will he need surgery? Is Dr. Gellis still there, because I can come right over?"

"Slow down, dear, please. He's awake, groggy and quite cranky. We won't know if he'll need surgery until sometime later today. Dr. Gellis just took him down to another floor for more tests. He told me to go home because Jared won't be back for another hour and then he'd need rest."

"That's a good idea, Mother. You must be exhausted."

"I managed to doze off a few times, but I will go home to shower and freshen up."

Gussie mentally ran down the list of things she had to do today. "I think I'll get some work done here and then go to the hospital in a couple of hours, so you needn't rush back. You'd better catch a nap. You won't be any good to Dad if you collapse."

"All right, dear, then I'll see you later."

Gussie paused a moment, then decided to ask. "Mother, there isn't anything you're not telling me, is there?"

"Why on earth would I hide anything from you, Augusta? Honestly." Dolores sounded irritated.

"Thanks for calling." Thoughtfully she hung up the phone. She'd checked with the hospital, speaking directly to the ICU nurse, several times since awakening early this morning. Each time they'd told her that Jared was holding his own, still in guarded-critical condition but in no imminent danger. So she'd come to the office to try to make a dent in the work on her desk before the rest of the staff arrived. She'd phoned Molly and had her come in earlier than usual, explaining about Jared's heart attack and asking her to confer with his secretary to see if there was anything he had scheduled that couldn't be postponed.

It was almost nine now, and she heard the opening and closing of doors and the phones already ringing. Lyon Publishing was getting ready to face another day.

"Hey, lady, thought you could use this." Molly bustled in carrying a mug of fresh coffee.

"Bless you." Gussie took a bracing swallow.

Sitting down, Molly referred to her notes. "I've met with Jared's secretary, and we went over his appointments. She's calling a couple to cancel, handling the minor ones herself and here's two she thought you might want to look into. One's an award luncheon and the other's a meeting with this hotshot agent who gets his nose out of joint easily and often."

"Fine, I'll take care of those." She reached to hand her a stack of files. "I've finished these. There are notations on each as to their disposition."

"I'll get right to them. I've posted a notice on the board about Jared's condition and said we'd be updating as the day went on. You want to go over your calendar and see how much I can handle for you?"

"Mmm, that would be great." Gussie searched through the papers on her desk for her daily schedule. Before she found it, the phone rang.

"You want me to have them hold your calls?" Molly asked.

"No, that's all right. Hello?"

"I don't like waking up and finding you gone."

Gussie's hand stopped in mid-motion. His voice was husky with sleep, deep and intimate. She leaned back in her chair and swiveled it to the side. "It couldn't be helped." She'd left close to six, restless and unable to sleep. He'd been lying on his stomach, the sheet tangled about his feet. She'd stood staring down at him for a few long minutes, then hurried out of the apartment before she changed her mind and awakened him the way she longed to, slowly, thoroughly.

"The sheets smell like you. Maybe that's why I had so much trouble leaving your bed."

Gussie felt the heat rise in her face and wondered what Molly must think. She cleared her throat and sat up taller, trying for a businesslike approach. "I've got a lot to do here, and then I'll be going to the hospital. I don't know when I'll get back."

"It's okay. I'll manage to amuse myself."

She heard a sound, like the slamming of a door. "What was that?"

"The cupboard door. Do you know there's nothing in this kitchen except last night's dead dinner, some instant coffee and a jar of peanuts?"

"Yes, well, I told you I wasn't much of a cook." She glanced over and saw Molly browsing through one of the files, but knew she couldn't help but hear every word. "Listen, I've got to go."

"I've checked with the hospital, and I'm glad Jared's coming around. I talked with your mother for a few minutes. I think she likes me."

"Don't let it go to your head. She's drawn to bossy men who like to have their own way." She took a sip of coffee.

"She asked me if I'd moved in with you."

Oh, Lord! "What . . . what did you tell her?"

David laughed. He loved to tilt the proper Miss Lyon's world. "I told her not yet, but I was working on it. She wished me luck. I think I'll need luck to win you over, Augusta Jane?"

"Yes, lots of it. I've really got to get back to work."

"Don't get too busy to forget what I said last night."

"You said a lot of things."

"That I love you."

She nearly dropped the coffee cup. "David, I . . ."

"See you later, Gussie."

Swiveling back to her desk, she set down the cup. Absently she searched for the schedule, but stopped when she saw that her hands were shaking. Clasping them together, she slowly raised her eyes and found Molly watching her.

"Are you all right?"

"Yes, of course. I just have a lot on my mind. My father's heart attack, the extra work, and . . ." *And a man who is making me question all that I am.*

Molly glanced behind her to make sure the door was closed. "It's David Lamb, isn't it?" Gussie didn't move. "You're in love with him." It wasn't a question.

"I'm that transparent?"

"You're never transparent. I just pick away until I find out. From what I overheard, David feels the same. What's the problem? The Lyon doesn't approve?"

Gussie let out a huff of air. "On the contrary. I think Jared purposely threw us together to see how well we'd mix. He likes playing God."

"So who cares how and why you met? If you love each other, what difference does that make?"

"I have my reasons. David's strong, forceful, a take-charge sort of man."

"You'd rather he was weak, wishy-washy?"

"He's so much like my father."

"There's a lot to admire about your father, Gussie."

"You haven't lived with him."

"No, but I've lived with weak and wishy-washy, if you'll recall. I'll take strong anytime, if I could find him."

Gussie drained her cup. "Oh, I don't know, Molly. David makes me *feel* so much. If I admit I love him, he'll have me right under his thumb. He'll have me changing my clothes—he's already told me I dress too conservatively. He says that I hide behind my glasses, and he hates the way I wear my hair. He'll want me to work less, maybe give it up altogether. Next thing you know, I'll be cooking his favorite foods, moving to California, living as he chooses. Just like my mother. There won't be anything of *me* left."

Molly shook her head. "I don't think there's a danger of that. You're very much your own person. Your mother never was. She married very young, and she chose to be your father's helpmate. It takes a strong woman to handle a strong man, despite how the marriage may look to others."

"You know, at first I thought he was easygoing, just a romantic character with his mismatched clothes, his lighthearted approach to work, the way he kept bringing me flowers. But he's very intense, and he *cares* so much. It's frightening."

Molly crossed her legs and nodded. "Sure you'd be frightened. You've kept yourself away from men and relationships for ten years, Gussie. And you *do* hide behind those prim little suits, your glasses, your workload. Along comes a guy who makes you question all that. A man who sends you flowers, whose telephone calls make you forget about work, one who makes you feel like a desirable woman, and it scares you. But don't turn away from him too quickly. Do you know what I'd give to have a man love me that intensely, to care that much? My right arm, maybe my left, too."

"I don't know, Molly. This living on the edge of excitement all the time, it's . . ."

"It's scary. And wonderful. With a man like that, you feel alive, and glad you are. Don't you?"

Gussie thought a long minute before answering. "But strong men want to rule you, to change you."

Molly's sigh sounded a bit exasperated. "I believe that if a strong woman changes, it's because she saw the need for it and changed herself. If it happens to coincide with what he had in mind, what does it matter?"

"You're really good at playing devil's advocate, Molly. With all these answers, how is it you've never gotten involved for more than a few weeks after you divorced John?"

Rising, Molly picked up her papers. "Maybe it's because I've never found a strong man who cared enough about me to risk committing again. In the long run, Gussie, it's still a gamble, but one I'd be willing to take for the right guy." She turned to leave. "If there's nothing else right now, I'll get started on these files."

Gussie sat staring at the door Molly closed behind her. A gamble, she thought. "I'll probably hurt you," she'd told David. "I'll risk it," he'd answered. But was *she* willing to risk getting hurt again?

With a glance at her watch, Gussie picked up the next file. She'd work another hour, then go to the hospital. Maybe Jared would be awake and they could talk. Maybe she could at least get that settled today.

His color was better. Gussie gripped her father's hand and saw his eyes slowly open. She leaned toward him as he tried to focus on her. "It's about time you woke up."

"Gus." He took a shaky breath. "Damn medication. Makes me so drowsy."

"It's all right. You need the rest."

He waved a hand. "Tubes everywhere. I hate it all. Takes . . . takes away a man's dignity."

She swallowed a lump in her throat. "Not yours, Dad. You just hate taking orders from a doctor."

"Damn right." He blinked, fighting heavy eyelids. "I want to talk to you, but . . . so sleepy."

"They won't let me stay much longer anyway. You rest, and I'll be in later. We'll talk then." She brushed her lips across his unshaven cheek, then stood leaning on the bed-rail for several moments as he drifted off, the drugs taking him away. With a sigh, Gussie left the ICU and returned to join her mother in the waiting room.

"He's better, don't you think?" Dolores asked as Gussie sat next to her.

Across the room on a two-seater couch, a man lay curled up in sleep, snoring lightly with his mouth open. Gussie nodded to reassure her mother, though she wasn't thoroughly convinced herself. "He's got more color, but he's fuzzy from the medicine. They tell me Dr. Gellis is in surgery, so I can't talk with him right now. What did he tell you?"

"He suspects a blockage in one of the main arteries leading to the heart. If the tests bear that out, he'll do bypass surgery tomorrow or the next day. If he doesn't, the next attack could be fatal." Dolores's eyes were clear, but her hands were once again shredding tissues.

Gussie put her own hand over her mother's. "He's your whole world, isn't he?"

"Yes. Yes, he is. He has been from the first." Dolores looked down, blinking. "You've never understood that, have you?"

Gussie sank back into the seat, wondering if her mother could handle the truth about how she felt. "Not really."

"Women today, your generation of women, are stronger, I suspect. And they have more choices." She raised her eyes to look out the window, seeing another time. "When I was young, proper young ladies either married or taught school. I hated school. But I loved your father, and all I really wanted to do was to make him happy. There's a real magnetism in strength, to men who know their own minds." She turned back to Gussie. "I know you think Jared dominates me, but the fact is, there have been times, quite a few, when he's leaned on me."

"I'm sure you're right. Especially when Aaron died."

"He took that hard. He had such high hopes for that boy, but Aaron chose to live his life irresponsibly, tempting fate."

"And then I disappointed him shortly after. Even though I was second choice, I think he . . ."

Dolores pulled back in surprise. "Second choice? Augusta, where *do* you get your ideas? You were the apple of

Jared's eye, always. Aaron knew that and was quite jealous. He didn't give either of us the attention he gave you.''

"Oh, come now, Mother, you know he'd rather Aaron was still around to run the company.''

"You're quite wrong. Jared's told me a number of times that you've twice the business head that Aaron had. He blames himself, of course, for telling Aaron that he'd never make it in the business world, that he hadn't the self-discipline to apply himself, though he had the brains. Jared feels that if he'd have been tougher on Aaron, less apt to excuse his absences and his laziness, that he'd have straightened out. I don't agree. When your father did point out his mistakes, he simply quit and became a playboy.'' She shook her head sadly. "I loved my son, but he had many weaknesses.''

Gussie leaned forward. "I didn't realize. I thought Aaron quit because Dad was too demanding. That's what he'd led me to believe.''

"No, not demanding enough. That's why he's so tough on you, though we both know you're nothing like Aaron. You've got enough strength for ten people.''

Gussie all but groaned aloud. "Oh, Mother, I don't at all. And if Dad feels this way, why hasn't he ever told me? He questions my judgment at every turn, especially about people, ever since... since that incident in college. I know I disappointed you both terribly, but...''

"You're not still whipping that dead horse, are you? You were so young, and we'd kept you too sheltered. You made one mistake. It could hardly be a mark against you forever. Of course, Jared was furious that you wouldn't tell us the boy's name. He wanted badly to get hold of him. But disappointed in you? No, not that. I believe he's been carrying around a bundle of guilt about how he treated the whole matter. And lately, we've both become worried that you loved that boy so much that you can't forget him and that's why you haven't found a new love.''

Gussie waved a hand in dismissal. ''Hogwash, Mother. I can't even clearly remember what he looked like. And how could I love someone who'd run away and leave me to face the music alone?''

''Well, I'm relieved to hear that. But, of course, we didn't know that.''

''Why didn't you come right out and ask me?''

Dolores folded and refolded the pleats in her skirt, her eyes downcast. ''I didn't want to pry. Talking about personal things has just never been my way. I find it very difficult. I should have. I see that now. But when Jared came back from that West Coast trip and told me about his meeting with David Lamb, about how strong, how sure of himself, how attractive and talented he was, we both felt that perhaps, if you met someone like that, you'd forget that boy and learn to care for someone new.''

''It didn't occur to either of you that I might like to pick out a man to care for myself?''

''Now, Augusta, don't go getting on your high horse. We meant no harm. We only saw to it that the two of you met and spent some time together. The rest was up to you.'' She cocked her head at her daughter. ''Was I wrong in what I noticed last night, that you seem attracted to him?''

Giving in to a smile, Gussie shook her head at her mother. ''Don't play games with me, dear lady. I know you've already asked David if he's moved in with me.''

Dolores blushed becomingly. ''Well, I know that that sort of thing goes on these days. You're certainly old enough to...to...''

Gussie laughed out loud. ''You're priceless, Mother. To satisfy your curiosity, no, I haven't invited him to live with me, but yes, I'm very attracted to him. However, it's not that simple. There are problems."

"Since we're speaking frankly, can you tell me what they are?"

"I'm not sure I can live with a man so strong that he's easily capable of taking over my life. I did that once, and I didn't really become my own person until I'd moved out of his house."

"That was different. Women today don't cater to a man, nor do the men expect it. There's more of a fifty-fifty sharing in a marriage. Perhaps, if I had it to do over, I'd aim for that. But perhaps not. In any case, I don't think David Lamb has any intention of taking over your life. At lunch, he told me that since meeting you, he hasn't been able to think of anyone else, to work or do much else because he's so gaga over you." Dolores chuckled. "His words, not mine."

Gussie found that her mouth had dropped open. "At lunch? You went to lunch with David?"

"Why, yes. He came here shortly after I'd run home to change. He even spent a few minutes with your father. The nurse wasn't going to let him in, but somehow..."

"Somehow he talked her into it. Yes, I'm quite familiar with the effect he has on women."

"The man's a real charmer. So he asked me if I'd had lunch, and I told him I'd been in too much of a hurry. We just went down to the cafeteria. The food's not very good."

"I'm surprised he didn't have Romanoff's run over a catered lunch. You see what I mean, Mother? He takes over. He simply can't resist being in charge."

"I find that rather appealing. The woman who'd made the fresh coffee for him last night came over three times to refill our cups. She certainly wasn't coming by to see me."

"I don't deny his appeal. But..."

"But, dear. He may smile and charm those women. It's *you* he wants. I should think that would be enough."

"Was it enough for you, Mother? To sit at home and wait for the charming rascal to return?"

"Yes, Augusta, it was. And I'd do it again."

"But I'm not you, Mother." Gussie stood and checked her watch. "I've got to get back to the office. I'll call in later."

Dolores reached for her hand as she looked up at her daughter. "I'm glad we talked, dear."

"So am I."

"Augusta, just one more thing. What kind of man *would* be right for you?"

"A man who gives me choices and respects my decisions, not one who makes up my mind for me." She squeezed her mother's hand and hurried from the room.

Perhaps she had been better without these in-depth conversations. Wearing They were very wearing.

By nine o'clock, Gussie was certain that this day would never end. She'd stayed in her office working until long after everyone had left, hurried over to the hospital, spent five minutes holding her father's hand and watching him sleep and another fifteen talking with her mother. Now, walking down the hall toward her apartment, she thought she'd like nothing better than a hot soak in the tub and about eight hours of oblivion in her bed, in that order. The moment she opened the door, she doubted if she'd get either.

Soft music from the stereo drifted throughout the apartment, and enticing smells drew her to the kitchen. She stopped in the doorway and leaned against the frame.

He was wearing an apron over blue jeans and a look of concentration as he basted something in a shiny new roasting pan she didn't recognize. And humming. He was humming along with the music. The table was set with a pale blue cloth, wineglasses in place, and a bouquet of daisies in the center. A large wooden salad bowl with greens peeking out was on the kitchen counter and thick bread sticks waited in a basket. He'd completely taken over. She didn't know whether to laugh or cry.

"Find everything you need?" Gussie asked, too tired to hide the hint of sarcasm.

Looking up, David smiled. "Not by a long shot," he said as he covered the roasting pan. "I couldn't even find a decent pan in this sorry excuse of a kitchen. So I went out and got a few things." She looked tired and a little unsteady on her feet. "Glad you're finally here. I was beginning to think we'd have to throw away another dinner, but your mother said you'd just left."

Setting her purse and briefcase on a chair, she walked to the stove. "You and my mother have become great pals, I hear. Lunching together, chatting on the phone." She tipped the lid of the roaster. "What's for dinner?"

"Coq au vin. It's a French dish, chicken and—"

"I *know* what coq au vin is, thank you." She leaned in for a smell. Wonderful. She wished she felt more hungry and less irritable. "Where did you learn to cook French food?" She turned and caught his look. "Don't tell me, let me guess. There was this woman who used to cook these magnificent French dishes, and you used to go to her apartment, researching a book, no doubt. And while you were there, she taught you her favorite recipes. Among other things." Gussie moved around him, picked up her things and headed for her bedroom.

Frowning, David removed the apron, flung it aside and followed. "I know you've had a hard day. Molly said . . ."

She whirled in mid-stride, causing him to nearly collide with her. "You talked with Molly, too? Have you been tracking me all day? Did you check with the doorman on my comings and goings? The cafeteria to make sure I ate all my lunch?''

"Not quite." What the hell had gotten into her?

"No. Some of the time you were out shopping for pans and bowls and enough food to last a month." She was working up a fine head of steam and not even certain why. Turning, she went into the bedroom, threw her things onto a chair and reached for her robe. Turning, she stopped in her tracks.

The bed had been stripped and remade. She moved closer. Pale blue satin sheets. "Well, you did say you liked satin, didn't you? It's too bad you didn't stop to ask if I did."

David stepped into the room. Something wasn't right here. He'd thought to surprise her, to please her, to comfort her at the end of a long, weary day. And all he'd managed to do was irritate the hell out of her. "Evidently, I've upset you..."

She gave a short, mirthless laugh. "How very astute of you to notice."

He'd had enough. Moving to her, he turned her to face him. "All right, dammit, talk to me. What's the matter?"

"Nothing. Everything. I don't know. David, let me go."

"Not until you tell me what I've done, why you're angry."

"I'm not angry." Pulling free, she opened the nightstand drawer and rummaged about. Her stomach was on fire, had been all afternoon. Too much coffee and too little food. She found the antacids and tossed one in her mouth. "I'm sorry if I'm not reacting the way you expected. I know you've gone to a lot of trouble..."

"Forget that. What's eating at you?"

"This, this whole thing." She waved her arm, indicating the room, the apartment, all of it. "You overwhelm me,

David. While some of it's exciting, much of it's frightening. You take away my choices. You decide I need to eat, so you fill my kitchen with food and even fix it for me. You don't send me one flower, you send me fifty. You think my bed needs changing, so you buy new sheets. Your decisions, all of them.''

She touched her hair, feeling helpless, then pointed to her closet. "Did you buy me a whole new wardrobe, too, since I know you dislike my choices? What else, David? When do I get asked how *I* feel about something?''

"You're overreacting, Gussie.''

"No, I'm not.'' She was pacing now, fighting back the frustration. "For nearly twenty years, I lived with a father who ran my life for me. The moment I stepped away from him on my own, the first decision I made turned out all wrong. So I decided I was incapable of thinking for myself. For a while. Then I went to work, got my own place, and *had* to make independent decisions every day. And you know what? They were right more than they were wrong. I decided I'd never let myself be ruled by a man, woman or child who thinks they know what's best for me again. And then you came along.''

Stopping, Gussie blinked back the tears and looked up at him. For years there'd been misconceptions between her and her parents because they hadn't dared air their differences. She had to let him know how she felt. She'd never really thought they had a future together, but she owed him the reasons why.

"I'm sorry if I've hurt you.'' She wanted desperately to touch him, but knew if she did, she'd crumble. "I do care about you, David, but I won't give up what I am for you. I can't let you dominate me, not even for love.''

"Are you finished?'' His voice was cool, unemotional. But inside, he was churning. No woman had ever been able to rile him the way this one could. Not looking at him, she nodded. "Then it's my turn."

He ran a hand through his hair, wondering how to reach her. "This isn't about dinners or flowers or even clothes. This is about fear, Gussie Jane."

She sighed, turning from him. "I'm too tired to argue with you."

"Oh, no. You're not running away this time." He pulled her to him and saw a small twitch under her left eye. Good. He wanted her nerves alive and jumpy. "I'm getting too close, that's what this is about. You grew up in a household where to speak of your feelings was unheard of. If you denied you had any, then no one could hurt you. And it worked for a long time."

"You don't know what you're talking about. I just told you how I felt."

"Did you? Maybe you don't see the whole picture. I see a woman who's learned to guard her feelings so carefully because if she lets them burst free, she's afraid of what might happen. And then I came along and shook up your world, didn't I, Gussie? I made you laugh, and I made you cry, but I made you feel. Now, when I look at you, I see a soft, vulnerable woman trying desperately still to be a cynic, to protect herself. I see changes—sensitivity, warmth, empathy. And I see love."

It wasn't love, Gussie reminded herself, not in the sense of the emotions. It was physical love he felt for her and she for him—fleeting, temporary. "We don't think alike on this."

"We think alike more than you know. I don't want to dominate you, I want to love you. I don't care what you eat or when you eat. I don't give a damn about your clothes…" Growing angry now, he started undressing her, shoving the jacket from her, then unbuttoning the blouse.

"David, no . . ." Halfheartedly, she tried to stop him, but she was no match for him in his frenzy.

"Truth of the matter is, I like you best *without* clothes." He had her nearly stripped now, his hands moving fast, fueled by his fury. She stopped struggling as his fingers shoved into her hair, scattering pins everywhere. "And you can wear your hair in a pigtail, a ponytail or shave your head bald, for all I care."

He was struggling out of his jeans. "It's *you* I care about, Gussie."

Impatience ruled him as he closed his mouth over hers. He'd never wanted any woman this much, never needed any woman this fiercely, never loved anyone this deeply. Words didn't seem to work with Gussie, so he'd show her. It was the only way left to him. He sensed her uncertainty, her hesitation, then she breathed a sigh into his mouth and grasped him to her. She aroused something primitive in him, and he let it have free rein. He felt her heartbeat pound against his, and knew she felt it, too. When he tasted the first hint of surrender from her, he felt a surge of victory. This wasn't merely hunger, or a throbbing desire. It was possession, pure and simple.

Passion ruled her. Gussie moaned as he rolled on the bed, dragging her with him. Passion roared through her blood and pounded at her pulse as she drew him to her, unable to get close enough. She'd known he could do this to her, known the moment he'd touched her that she was lost. But he wanted more, always more. She would give him this, and she would take the pleasure he offered. But somehow she'd cling to her resolve not to let him have all of her. Because if she did, he'd own her.

The sharp male scent of him had her breathing deeply as she rained kisses on his face while her hands ran along the hard, taut muscles. His mouth tormented, his hips teased, his fingers thrilled as they raced over every inch of her. She moved to taste the heat of his skin while his bold hands took her breath away.

Legs tangled together. David rolled her to her back and lifted his head to look at her. He found he needed more than the touch of her flesh, more than the kisses that drugged him. He needed the words. "Tell me what you feel, what you want."

Gussie's breathing was ragged and uneven as she stared into his eyes. He was overwhelming her with sensations, yet she was afraid to say it. She could offer him her loving, but she held back offering him her love, afraid she would lose herself in the giving. "I feel so much," she whispered. "And I want you."

It wasn't enough, but maybe it was all she had to give. "Tell me again."

"I want you, David." She took a deep breath as she saw him poised above her. "I want you, I want you." Wildly he plunged into her. She cried out his name as her body arched up and she raced to an uncontrollable climax. Stunned, she reached for him as the waves shook her, reached because she needed to hold him close.

David saw a lone tear slide from the corner of her eye and disappear into her hair and felt a wave of sadness. He began to move then, feeling her grab on to him, though she'd barely recovered. Her eyes were open now, a little glazed, as she rose with him. And then they were flying, streaking, hurtling, and David held her to his heart.

She'd lost, Gussie thought as she lay still, wrapped in his arms on the satin sheets. Lost, but she mustn't let him know. She'd tried to hold on to her heart, but quietly it had slipped away and become his. She'd known it when she'd walked in the door tonight, perhaps even last night, maybe days ago,

She held him gently as his breathing slowed and wondered what she'd do.

Reluctantly David shifted from her. He saw something in her eyes, something different, just before she looked away and sat up. Had he imagined it? He touched her arm. "I want to ask you something."

Feeling defenseless, she reached for the robe she'd dropped. "Ask away."

"I want us to live together." He saw the quick surprise, the furrowing of her brow. "Let's try it, see if it works out. I can write anywhere, Gussie. California, New York. We can split our time between both coasts. You seemed to like my house on the beach, the peace and quiet. You can delegate a lot of your work here, use the phone, the mails. My place, your place or somewhere in between. Your choice."

Her eyes were clouding now as she shrugged off his hand and stood to put on her robe. He waited while the silence stretched out.

Living together. Of all the questions she'd thought he might ask, that hadn't entered her mind. So that's what loving meant to him. Not a commitment, not marriage, not the forever dream. Just his place or hers, her choice. Let's try it, see if it works out, like choosing a new restaurant, a new car. Perhaps it was good she found out now, though it hurt. She hadn't guessed it would hurt so much. "David, I don't know. I've lived alone for six years now. I'm not comfortable with sharing my space, and, as you saw tonight, I'm not fond of letting others do for me."

He hadn't mentioned emotions, knowing how she ran from those discussions. He'd thought to give her time, and her space, hoping she'd find the arrangement worked well, that he wasn't trying to dominate her, and then he'd take her to the next step. Only she wasn't having any. David stood and grabbed his jeans. He was through trying to compromise. "All right then, that's that." He pulled on his clothes.

She watched him, clinging to a small morsel of pride and pushing back the tears. Hadn't she known it would end like this? Love. Boomeranging back again to slap her in the face, still the joke she'd known it was all along.

It was amazing how quickly he could pack when he was driven by anger and hurt. Dressed, his bag in his hand, he turned to her. "I'll have the manuscript to you on schedule."

"Thank you." She wished she could have kept her voice from trembling. She did manage to keep her eyes steady as he stared at her for a long moment. Then he turned on his heel and walked down the hall.

Gussie stood rooted to the spot. She heard the door close and let out a deep breath. For years, she'd managed to avoid intimacy because she'd chosen to. With David, she'd chosen to open herself to him, an adult decision. And we always have to pay for the consequences of our decisions, don't we? she silently asked the empty room.

Slowly she walked over and lay down on the satin sheets. Alone, she finally gave in to the tears that had been aching to fall.

Chapter Twelve

She heard a ringing, an incessant ringing that seemed to be coming from a distance. Gussie bunched the pillow beneath her head and rearranged herself. Still it went on. Opening her eyes, she saw only dark shadows and a pale light behind the curtains of her bedroom window. The ringing again. Sitting up with a start, she stretched to reach the phone. "Hello?"

Heart pounding, she listened to the hushed voice of her mother. Complications during the night. The bypass surgery scheduled to take place in two hours. If she wanted to talk with her father before they took him up, she'd have to hurry on over. The bedside clock read almost five. "I'm on my way, Mother. Are you all right?"

She listened as her mother calmly reassured her. How had she ever thought the woman weak? Gussie hung up and lunged for the bathroom.

At five-forty, she was rushing down the hospital corridor toward the waiting room. Breathless, she arrived to find her mother quietly standing by the window.

Hearing her, Dolores turned. "He's waiting for you. I've already talked with him."

"Is he—"

"A little groggy, but quite coherent."

Nodding, Gussie moved to the ICU room and entered. The round-faced nurse recognized her as she looked up and waved her in. She walked to the bed and saw her father open his eyes.

"Sorry to disturb your sleep, Lady Jane," Jared Lyon said, his voice a little weak but still firm.

Lady Jane. Gussie leaned over the guard rail, took his hand in hers and smiled at the pet name. "No, you're not, you old war horse. You love disrupting us all, having us at your beck and call."

Jared smiled. "Yeah, I kind of do."

The bantering. She'd forgotten the bantering they'd shared when she'd first come to work at Lyon Publishing. She hadn't realized she'd missed that easy camaraderie these past few years as she'd become more and more determined to stand alone. "Are you in any pain?"

"No, they gave me a shot of some sort." He eased a little higher on the pillows, with her help. "I want to talk to you about a couple of things."

"After your surgery. Save your strength."

"Can't. Long overdue as it is. I've had a lot of time to think, trussed up in this bed. Time to review my life a bit, to add up the pluses and the minuses, to face the regrets."

She squeezed his hand. "I think I know what you're going to say, and it isn't necessary."

Jared shook his dark head. "Yes, it is. Maybe if I'd have spoken up sooner, things would have been a little smoother

for all of us. When the heart threatens to quit, it makes a
man think, long and hard. I've already talked with your
mother, and she understands. That woman's a rock, you
know, Gus. Doesn't look it, but she is.''

"I'm beginning to see that."

"She always understood me, and that couldn't have been
easy. I've had a few mild flirtations, Gus, but I never
cheated on your mother. I think you should know that. I
have trouble putting personal feelings into words, but she
always knew how I felt without the words. Amazing
woman.''

His hand in hers was trembling, and his voice had become a bit shaky. "Please don't tire yourself, Dad.''

"Since when do you give orders to me, young lady?"

That was the feisty man she knew. She felt her vision blur
a bit. "No one gives Jared Lyon orders, right?"

"That's right." He took in a deep breath, searching for
the words. "Men like me can be difficult, Gus. We're used
to having our way, of not having our authority questioned,
you know?"

Oh, she knew all right. "So I've noticed."

"We're always so damn sure we're right, for ourselves and
for our family. Sometimes, we're wrong, like I was when I
gave you such a hard time over that college boy. If I could
take that back, Gus . . .''

"I've forgiven you for that a long time ago. It's time you
let that one go."

His fingers curled around hers tightly, his dark eyes
growing more intense. "You wouldn't tell me that kid's
name, and I felt so frustrated. Then you lost the baby, and
I felt so bad for you. I always wanted what was best for you,
but sometimes I went about it wrong. I was hard on you,
because I messed up with Aaron. I never told you, and I
should have, that you have more ability than the next six of

my best people. And you come by most of it naturally." He allowed himself a chuckle.

"Taking credit, are you?"

"I didn't so much teach you as let you inherit all my good points."

"I see."

"And a few of my bad ones. Don't let yourself get so tangled in work that you let life pass you by, Gus. I wish now that I'd have spent more time, with your mother, with you and Aaron. You need that, too. You need someone special in your life, a home—not some apartment, and children. Work is good, it's wonderful. But it's not everything."

Gussie leaned back a bit so he couldn't read her eyes. "Perhaps one day."

"You're not getting any younger, you know."

"Well, thank you for reminding me." Keep it light, she thought. There was no point in arguing with him just before they wheel him into surgery. "How are you feeling?"

"A little woozy but alert enough to know you're trying to change the subject. What about David Lamb?"

She stiffened and hoped he didn't notice. He'd never been a man to beat about the bush. "What about him?"

"I know you've been upset that I kind of shoved the two of you together. But your mother tells me he's crazy about you. Are you going to marry him?"

Gussie cleared her throat. "David isn't into permanent commitments any more than I am." *He wants to make love, not be in love. He wants to live with me, not marry me.* "As mother noticed, we were attracted to each other for a while, but it's over. He's gone back to California."

He was quiet so long she wondered if the medicine they'd given him to relax him had dragged him under with his eyes open. Then suddenly he squeezed her hand hard.

"I'm damn sure you're not telling me all of it. Gussie, there's nothing more difficult than two strong people getting along together. Your mother was strong in her own way, but she gave in to me, made me *feel* stronger. You're not about to do that, though, are you? Too independent. Not about to admit you might need someone. Am I right?"

Gussie straightened, brushing back a lock of hair. "Dad, there really isn't any point in pursuing this. We've agreed to part."

"Agreed to part? Is that why I see tears in your eyes?"

"They're for you, old man. I hate to see you have to go through all this."

"For me? What for? I'm going to pull through this with flying colors. And when I do, we're going to talk again about this."

"All right, it's a date."

The nurse was standing at the foot of the bed. "Mr. Lyon, they're ready for us."

"Right away," he told her, gripping Gussie's hand. "I've never been one to say the words. Maybe that's why you can't seem to do it, either. But I love you, Lady Jane. I always have."

She was no longer trying to hide her tears as she bent down to kiss his cheek. "I love you, too, Dad."

"And if you've inherited just a fraction of my good sense, you won't wait as long as I did to admit to being human, to needing someone. You made a wrong choice once. You were eighteen, so that's understandable. But you're a grown woman now. May not get another chance. Make the right choice."

There were no words she could come up with. As the nurse began to roll the bed toward the double doors, she let go of his hand and watched them go.

"Be careful there, Missy," he said to the nurse pulling him along. "I don't take well to being pushed around."

Truer words were never spoken, Gussie thought as she dabbed at her eyes. Putting on her glasses for some small measure of protection, she went to the waiting room.

She'd never known five hours could seem so long. It was nearly noon when Dr. Gellis appeared in the doorway. Gussie jumped up, but her mother just turned to look at him, outwardly calm.

"Everything went well, ladies. That's one tough old bird." Dr. Gellis wiped his brow on the sleeve of his operating greens. "We found nothing we didn't expect. The recovery should go well, though he'll have to take it easy longer than he'd like, I suspect. They'll be wheeling him down to the ICU shortly and closely monitoring him, of course. You'll be able to see him in a couple of hours."

Gussie took a moment to close her eyes and offer her private thank-yous. She heard her mother's deep sigh of relief. "Does this mean he probably won't have another attack?"

"There're no guarantees, not with the heart. But we repaired the damage, and his other arteries look good."

"Will he be restricted further, Doctor?" Dolores asked.

"Shouldn't. We'll have him up and walking in a couple of days. He can play golf after a while. Probably have to definitely forbid those cigars he likes so well, but that's all."

"Will he be able to go back to work?"

"Oh, sure. In time." He patted her on the arm. "Work's what keeps some of us going, Dolores. Now you get some rest before I have you as a patient, as well. You, too, young lady."

"Thank you, Doctor." Gussie shook his hand. She turned to her mother. "Well, I'm glad that's over."

"You know what he told me this morning, Augusta?" Dolores Lyon wore a tender smile. "That he wished he could do it all over again, go back to the beginning, start the company, start our lives together, all brand-new. He said he'd revise some of his choices."

There was that word again. Choices. *Don't wait as long as I did, Gussie. Make the right choice.* She hadn't told Dolores about her conversation with Jared and she hadn't asked. She hadn't talked much at all, just paced and prayed. She looked at the woman who was her mother and wondered how she managed to stay so calm.

Rising, she rubbed at the knot of tension in her neck. "Well, now he'll have a second chance to mend a few fences, if he needs to."

Dolores looked up at her daughter. "We all need to, occasionally, Augusta."

Impatiently Gussie walked out into the hallway, wondering when her mother had taken up mind reading.

It had taken him longer to finish the book than he'd counted on. But he'd taken the manuscript to the post office this morning and over-nighted it to his editor. The same editor he hadn't heard a word from in four weeks. David dived into a high furling wave and let the cool ocean wash over him. With steady strokes, he swam out to sea, stretching his muscles, kicking his legs.

He was out quite a ways from the beach when he shifted onto his back to float and to rest before starting back. Four weeks and nothing. He'd been foolish to expect a note, a call, some word. Lyons didn't apologize, didn't reach out first, didn't open themselves up to possible rejection. He'd called finally, after hearing from his agent that Jared had had surgery, just to see how he was doing. Molly had given him a medical bulletin and precious little more. That staunch loyalty of hers. And he'd had too much pride even to mention Gussie's name.

And now there was the invitation.

David started back to shore, using slow, easy strokes. He'd picked up his mail while at the post office and found the formal envelope. The invitation was engraved, embossed, impersonal, sent to all Lyon Publishing authors. They were throwing a gala midsummer launching party previewing their fall lineup of new releases. A personal invitation from Jared Lyon, president. Black tie. Seven p.m. The Plaza Hotel.

No one could fault the old man for not doing things first class, David thought as his feet touched the sandy bottom. He shook the water from his hair as he walked onto the beach and flung himself down on his towel. Was the foxy old Lyon using the party as a show of strength, to tell the publishing world that, four weeks after a double bypass operation, he was back and he was still in charge? How did that sit with Gussie? he wondered. Did Gussie want to run the show? In all the weeks with her, she'd never confided her thoughts on that. Not surprising, since she hadn't confided her thoughts on a lot of things.

Leaning back, David raised his arms and rested his head on his folded hands. Why should he care who ran Lyon Publishing, as long as his books were edited to suit him? Why should he care if Augusta Jane Lyon was happy or unhappy? Why should he care about a woman who could so easily dismiss him from her life? He watched a puffy white cloud drift lazily across the clear blue sky. He didn't know why, he only knew he did care. And the plain fact was, he couldn't go on this way.

She was uncertain, vulnerable and afraid. And he loved her. She was stubborn, opinionated and pigheaded. And he loved her. She was difficult, closemouthed and untrusting.

And he loved her, plain and simple. No, nothing was simple with Gussie.

Jumping up, David shook off the sand, grabbed his towel and headed for his house. Would she read his manuscript right away? Would she see the clues he'd planted there for her eyes only? Would she realize that that's why it had taken him so long to complete this book, because he was sorting out Beau and Mandy's relationship, which just happened to parallel theirs? He slammed the kitchen door behind him. She was bright; she'd see it. But would it make a difference to her, that he'd realized he'd made a few wrong moves, but he was willing to compromise?

David looked again at the invitation on the table. No pain, no gain, he thought wryly. He would go, and he would make her see. He reached for the phone.

Gussie finished the last page of the manuscript, set the pile of papers aside and leaned back into the cushions of her couch. So, at long last, Beau and Mandy were altar bound. That would probably please most of David's female fans, though some men would be less than impressed. It wasn't the new mystery Beau had solved that had held her interest, clever and complex though it was, or even the fact that he'd proposed. It was the *how* that had jumped out at her.

The San Francisco Caper had arrived two days ago and, as usual, Molly had grabbed it to read first. When she'd brought the book to Gussie the next day, she'd made an odd statement. "Read it," Molly had said. "This one's for you."

Stubbornly Gussie had let it lie until she'd been ready to leave the office that evening. Curiosity had won out, and she'd even eaten her dinner while pouring over his words. Now she sat back and thought it through.

Mandy was an attorney, and a damn fine one, as well as a strong-willed woman. Her love for Beau was evident, but so was her involvement in her work. Early in the book, she's offered a position in a very prestigious law firm in Washington, D.C. Beau operates out of San Francisco, and, though the brunt of the book concerned itself with his latest mystery, David managed to weave in the personal dilemma they faced. Would this job decision break up their relationship, and, if not, who would win as to where they'd live? Would they marry or would they just go their separate ways, wedded to their work?

Gussie had scarcely been able to turn the pages fast enough. Finally Beau decides that he loves Mandy enough to let her go, that he respects her too much to insist she stay where his work is. He would learn to live without her. But the problem involved more than job differences and city locations. It boiled down to control, to who called the shots in the relationship, to commitments and sacrifices required in loving.

In the end, Beau realizes that compromise is part of the answer. Giving one hundred percent to a relationship is another part, while sharing the decision making fifty-fifty another part. He goes to her and, in a beautiful scene, tells Mandy that he's come to realize that he *can* live without her. But he *chooses* not to. He asks her to marry him, to work out a compromise where they can commute, share living quarters in both places, anything as long as they can be together. Because he loves her, and love, after all, is all that matters. Given that choice, Mandy accepts.

Gussie reached for the cup of tea that had grown cool as she'd finished the book. Was this one for her, as Molly had indicated? Was David trying to tell her something, or was she just so eager for him that she'd grab at any straw?

The invitations had gone out, and the party was in two days. Perhaps, if he came, she'd find out. And perhaps, if he didn't, she'd be ready to crawl on her knees to him.

Picking up the manuscript, she hugged it to her chest and closed her eyes. Love, after all, is all that matters, he'd said. Yes, David, I think so, too.

Gussie finished adjusting her father's black tie and stepped back. "You'll undoubtedly be the most dashing man at your own shindig," she told him with a smile. He'd regained a little of the weight he'd lost and no longer had a sickly pallor. On doctor's orders, he'd been walking daily in the sunshine and had developed a deep tan. Yes, Gussie decided, Jared Lyon looked very handsome in his formal evening clothes.

"*Our* shindig," he corrected as he checked his image in the mirror. They were in the foyer next to the ballroom where food and drink tables were set up and waiters were fussing with last-minute details. He turned to gaze at his daughter, and there was open admiration in his dark eyes. "May I say, Lady Jane, that I've never seen you look lovelier? The changes you've made lately in your appearance are astounding."

"Thank you, I think."

"It was always there, Gus. I never did understand why you chose to camouflage yourself."

Protection, Gussie thought. But somewhere along the line, she'd decided she didn't need it any longer. The dress was new, and unabashedly romantic. Creamy lace clung to all the right places, then flowed to a swirling fullness at her feet. Her hair hung to her shoulders in soft waves, and her brown eyes were huge in her small face. Perhaps she *had* picked up a few pointers from David.

"It doesn't matter why, as long as the changes are for the better."

"Definitely." But Jared couldn't hide his concern. "I wish you were as happy as you are beautiful."

Gussie gave him a small, practiced smile. "I *am* happy. Things are going well at the office, you're nearly back in top form, soon a great party will begin and . . ."

"Do you think he'll come?"

Gussie's smile slipped a little. Since his surgery, Jared had changed, warmed, become more the parent she'd wished he'd been years ago. It was difficult not to respond to his fatherly interest. She thought of the manuscript, the scarcely veiled message. "I don't know. You didn't call him, did you?"

"I promised you I wouldn't. He received an invitation like all the other authors." He brushed his fingertips along her cheek, just for a moment. "You're hurting still. Why wouldn't *you* call him? Is it so hard for you to concede that you might be wrong, so difficult to admit you care?"

Gussie fiddled with the lace at her wrist. "It's not just that. The only place we didn't argue was in bed." Was that the truth? They'd been contented strolling on his beach, happy feeding the swans at the pond, looking for reasons to touch, to hold hands as they'd scurried to the appointments.

Jared fingered the cigars in his pocket longingly. "That's not a bad beginning, Gus. A lot of marriages have survived if that important aspect was a joy to both. Provided there was love. Do you love him, Gus?"

Her first thought was to deny, to defend, to lie. Somehow, the words wouldn't form. "I didn't think so, at first."

"And now?"

She bit her lip, struggling to remain composed. She could hear people arriving and the musicians setting up. Blinking rapidly, Gussie gave in. "I miss him terribly, I think of him far too much, I . . ."

"Say, it, Gussie, out loud, to me, at least."

She dropped her gaze to the floor. "Yes, I love him."

Slipping an arm about her waist, Jared drew her close. "Now go find him, tell him." He saw her hands tremble as she clutched them together. "Yes, I know it's frightening. Love is the most frightening emotion we'll ever face. I'd rather go toe to toe with bankers, board of directors, CPAs, attorneys, anyone, than face an emotional problem with your mother."

Raising a brow, Gussie looked up. "But she's always been on your side. How..."

"Always? Not quite. It took me two years to convince her to marry me. Two long, frustrating, embattled years." He chuckled at the surprise on her face. "Didn't know that, did you? Things didn't always come easily to me, either, Gus. But she was worth fighting for and giving in for. Is David?"

"I think so." She took a deep breath. "But what if..."

"What if he no longer wants you?" Jared shook his head and let a smile take over his face. "That much of a fool he's not." He glanced toward the ballroom. "Now come on. I think, as host and hostess, we'd best get in there."

Gussie leaned in to her father to kiss his cheek. "Thank you, Dad."

"You're looking lovely, as always."

"Why, thank you, David," Dolores Lyon said, looking regal in pale blue. "And I must say you're tan and fit."

Tan, perhaps, David thought. Fit was up for grabs. "California sunshine, you know." He gave the room another quick glance. Odd that he hadn't been able to spot her. Turning back to her mother, he smiled. "Quite a bash."

"Yes, isn't it? I seldom attend these things anymore, but since Jared's surgery, I like to keep an eye on him, make sure he doesn't overdo."

"Good idea." He spotted Jared alongside one of the long tables laden with an assortment of elaborate hors d'oeuvres. "He doesn't look any the worse for wear." His gaze kept moving.

"Have you seen Augusta?" she asked, her eyes narrowing shrewdly.

"No, is she here?" Did he sound casual, unconcerned?

Dolores laughed. "You're almost as transparent as she is."

Turning back, he conceded the point. "I'm a writer, not an actor. How is she?"

"About like you. Anxious looking, nervous, thinner."

"I thought you said I was fit?"

"Mmm. That was the polite hostess. This is the honest woman." She touched his arm lightly. "I'm glad you came, David. She's longing for you."

"Is she? She's done a remarkable job of hiding it for four weeks."

"Oh, Augusta's very good at hiding her feelings and very poor at showing them. And even worse at speaking of them." She made a waving gesture. "My fault, I suppose. This family's shared some good times and several tragedies and . . ."

"Yes, I know."

Dolores was clearly taken aback. "I see," Dolores said with a nod. "The fact that she confided in you tells me more about the depth of her feelings than anything either of you could have told me." Her fingers tightened on his arm. "You're a writer, David, a man who deals in words. Go to her. Give her the words she needs. Then maybe she'll find some of her own."

"What makes you think she won't throw them back at me? She has before."

"Because I've watched her the past four weeks. The light has gone out of her eyes. I think you might be able to remedy that."

"You're quite a lady, Mrs. Lyon." Raising her hand to his lips, he kissed it, then went to find Gussie.

She was exhausted, and the evening was scarcely half over. She'd gone from group to group, introducing people, greeting writers she knew, meeting new ones. Guests mingled, laughed, ate, drank and danced on the polished terrazzo floor while the band played on. She'd shared a quick glass of wine with Molly, but hadn't felt like eating from the sumptuous buffet.

She'd checked on Jared periodically, spoken briefly to her mother and sent her eyes on a trip around the room every ten seconds, searching for that tall blond head that was like no other. Then suddenly he was there, by the open doors to the balcony, watching her with a sober face and those intense blue eyes. He was attractive in anything he wore. In a tuxedo he was devastating. Pushing aside a flash of panic, she walked to him.

Stunning. He'd seen many of her faces, but never had he seen her look so stunning. Or was it his own need to see her that made it so? As she approached, he held out his hand.

Hesitating only a moment, Gussie placed her hand in his. Her heart was thudding so loudly she wasn't sure she could be heard over the drumbeat. "I'm so glad you're here."

His fingers tightened on hers. "It's good to see you, A.J." His eyes locked with hers. He nodded toward the room. "You throw a hell of a party."

She'd been waiting for this moment all evening, perhaps all her life, and now her mind was empty and her mouth dry. She reached for the familiar. "I read *The San Francisco*

Caper.'' She thought she saw his eyes darken, but she couldn't be sure since he stood in half shadow.

"I think it's . . . it's your best one so far."

A noisy couple moved closer, their laughter echoing loudly. David eased her out onto the terrace. Still holding her hand, he drew her to the railing overlooking the lights of the city. "So old Beau's won you over then?"

She turned to face him. His hair ruffled in a light breeze. She fought to keep from reaching to run her fingers through it. Now or never, she told herself, heart hammering. Some risks were worth taking. "Yes, he has. He makes perfect sense."

"How's that?"

He wasn't going to make it easier for her. Gussie took a deep breath. "I know I can live without you, David. But I *choose* not to. If you still care, I'd like to try again."

"Why?" His hands at his sides ached to touch her, but she'd come this far. He decided he wanted it all.

She frowned, doubt flickering quickly across her face. "Why? Why do you think?"

"You tell me."

Gussie ground her teeth. She'd imagined a dozen scenarios. This had not been one of them. Slowly she looked at him, eyes flashing fire. "Because I love you, dammit."

David burst out laughing just before he gathered her to him. "Oh, Augusta Jane, there's no one like you." Leaning back, he smiled down at her. "How I've missed you. Missed fencing with you, laughing with you, loving with you. Don't you *ever* put me through another four weeks like this again, or I swear all five of our sons will be born with their mother's cantankerous streak and you'll never have a moment's peace."

With that he crushed her to him, taking her mouth in a fierce kiss, as he'd been dreaming of doing for weeks. But the moment he felt her avid response, he softened his mouth and loosened his hold on her. He didn't need to hold her tightly anymore. She was his.

Finally Gussie leaned back. "What did you say about five sons?"

"That's what it takes to make up a basketball team. Do you remember, I like basketball?"

"Should I be grateful you don't prefer football?"

"Yes, I think you should. All right, we'll negotiate numbers later." And he leaned down for another lingering kiss, then pulled back to look deeply into her eyes, shiny with unshed tears and a trace of relief. "You know, I liked my life just fine before I met you. Now, without you, I don't like it anymore. Your fault."

"I'll accept the blame, if you'll accept me, just the way I am. No revisions."

He ran his hands down the lace that covered her back. It felt so good holding her. "I'll sign a lifetime contract stating just that, dear editor. I love you, Gussie."

She swallowed and dared to move closer. "I was sure you didn't mean it when you only suggested we live together."

"I wanted to prove to you that I had no intention of changing you, of ruling you. I was convinced you'd run if I talked about feelings."

Gussie shook her head. "No more running. This is exactly where I want to be."

He moved his hands to frame her face. "And exactly where I want you. We'll work out the details of where we'll live and work later. Marry me, Gussie. I want a lifetime with you."

"Oh, yes." And she met his kiss hungrily.

"How long do we have to stay at this party?" He raised a brow suggestively. "We've got a little unfinished business I'd like to get to soon."

"Considering it's costing my father a small fortune for this bash, the major purpose of which was to bring two somewhat stubborn people together, I'd say we should linger a while."

Moving them toward the doorway, but keeping his arm about her, David looked surprised. "No! Jared Lyon matchmaking?"

"I believe so."

"Then I need to go shake his hand. And by the way, speaking of needs, do you believe I need you?"

She smiled at him flirtatiously. "Need is a relative term, or so I've been told."

"No, I mean *really* need." He pulled up his pant leg to reveal a bright pink sock.

Laughing, Gussie hugged him to her. "I guess you do." Sobering, she touched his check with a lover's hand. "Don't ever stop needing me."

Before they returned to the main room, he moved her back into the shadows. "Tell me again how you feel, this time without the *dammit*."

"I love you, David Lamb. I love you so much."

He held her close. "Never stop telling me."

*   *   *   *   *

COMING NEXT MONTH

#583 TAMING NATASHA—Nora Roberts
Natasha Stanislaski was a pussycat with Spence Kimball's little girl, but to
Spence himself she was as ornery as a caged tiger. Would some cautious
loving sheath her claws and free her heart from captivity?

#584 WILLING PARTNERS—Tracy Sinclair
Taking up residence in the fabled Dunsmuir mansion, wedding the
handsome Dunsmuir heir and assuming instant "motherhood" surpassed
secretary Jessica Lawrence's wildest dreams. But had Blade Dunsmuir
wooed her for money...or love?

#585 PRIVATE WAGERS—Betsy Johnson
Rugged Steven Merrick deemed JoAnna Stowe a mere bit of fluff—until
the incredibly close quarters of a grueling motorcycle trek revealed her
fortitude *and* her womanly form, severely straining *his* manly stamina!

#586 A GUILTY PASSION—Laurey Bright
Ethan Ryland condemned his stepbrother's widow for her husband's
untimely death. Still, he was reluctantly, obsessively drawn to the fragile-
looking Celeste...and he feared she shared his damnable passion.

#587 HOOPS—Patricia McLinn
Though urged to give teamwork the old college try, marble-cool professor
Carolyn Trent and casual coach C. J. Draper soon collided in a stubborn
tug-of-war between duty...and desire.

#588 SUMMER'S FREEDOM—Ruth Wind
Brawny Joel Summer had gently liberated man-shy Maggie
Henderson...body and soul. But could her love unchain him from the
dark, secret past that shadowed their sunlit days of loving?

AVAILABLE THIS MONTH:

Silhouette Special Edition®

proudly presents

Taming Natasha
by
NORA ROBERTS

In March, award-winning author Nora Roberts weaves her special brand of magic in TAMING NATASHA (SSE #583). Natasha Stanislaski was a pussycat with Spence Kimball's little girl, but to Spence himself she was as ornery as a caged tiger. Would some cautious loving sheath her claws and free her heart from captivity?

TAMING NATASHA, by Nora Roberts, has been selected to receive a special laurel—the Award of Excellence. Look for the distinctive emblem on the cover. It lets you know there's something truly special inside.

❧ SILHOUETTE®
Desire™

Award of Excellence

Double the Excellence
Twice the Spice!

February is the month of love, and this month, *two* of your favorite authors have something terrific in store for you.

CONTACT by Lass Small
Ann Forbes had been burned in the past. But her determination to remain a solitary woman was *severely* tested by persistent Clint Burrows.

MAN OF THE MONTH

A LOVING SPIRIT by Annette Broadrick
Sabrina Sheldon never dreamed she had an angel on her side when she met sexy police officer Michael Donovan. He took her under his protective wings, and together their love soared....

Those sizzling stories have merited the Award of Excellence and are available now from Silhouette Desire. Look for the distinctive emblem on the cover. It lets you know there's something truly special inside.

At long last, the books you've been waiting for by one of America's top romance authors!

DIANA PALMER

DUETS

Ten years ago Diana Palmer published her very first romances. Powerful and dramatic, these gripping tales of love are everything you have come to expect from Diana Palmer.

In March, some of these titles will be available again in **DIANA PALMER DUETS**—a special three-book collection. Each book will have two wonderful stories plus an introduction by the author. You won't want to miss them!

Book 1
SWEET ENEMY
LOVE ON TRIAL

Book 2
STORM OVER THE LAKE
TO LOVE AND CHERISH

Book 3
IF WINTER COMES
NOW AND FOREVER

 *Silhouette Books*®

DP-1